GOLD HORIZONS

HORIZONS VALLEY NOVEL
BOOK 3

KATHRYN ANDREWS

permission. The publication/use of these trademarks is not authorized, associated with, or sponsored by the trademark owners.

FBI Anti-Piracy Warning: The unauthorized reproduction or distribution of a copyrighted work is illegal. Criminal copyright infringement, including infringement without monetary gain, in investigated by the FBI and is punishable by up to five years in federal prison and a fine of $250,000.

This book is dedicated to those who are the black sheep of their family.

1

CORA

I was ten years old the first time my parents dolled me up in concert black, a ridiculous string of obnoxious gaudy pearls, and had me perform for their friends. They were known for entertaining the upper echelon of the Upper East Side of New York City with their formal cocktail parties, sought-after chefs, and high-profile entertainment, and it only took less than two years for me to realize they didn't do this because they were proud of me. They did this as their way of keeping me present while removing me at the same time.

Over the years, I've often thought about my childhood and tried to view the why of this from different vantage points. The first is that children do not attend dinner parties, so my parents gave me a role in the evening. It was a way for them to include me without me feeling left out. Even though my older brother was always present and allowed to mingle and eat the food.

Second, it's not lost on me that I was a child prodigy cellist, and what parent wouldn't want to show off their child's talent to their friends? I started music lessons with the violin initially, but the instructor felt I would be better suited for the cello based on its size and position. The act of leaning over it and wrapping my arms around it required less discipline than being forced to sit upright while loose but flexible and keeping the violin tucked under my chin, against my collarbone, and parallel with the floor.

But third, the view that whispers to the part of my soul that says, "You know this is the real reason." Even though my performances stunned anyone close enough to listen, I've never quite lived up to their strict expectations. This was their way of dealing with me without dealing with me.

Even now, at twenty-nine, I'm still only invited to their parties to perform. Never to socialize.

Unlike my brother, Winston.

The doorbell rings, and I'm again grateful that my condo does not open straight from the elevator. I know Winston was coming up because security called to announce him, but this door gives me one more barrier to collect myself before he storms in and stares at the boxes I've set in the foyer. While I didn't tell anyone in my family that I had bought a house, I'm not surprised that they know or sent Winston to attempt to put me in my place.

Winston is three years older than me but acts like it's a solid decade. We used to be close, and I would even dare say friends, but once he became a teenager, our relationship took a turn. Better for him, worse for me. I would watch him at those parties from my place in the corner, and he rarely was alone. Winston stood with our father, who kept his hand firmly planted on his shoulder, and he would tap Winston with approval every so often.

I've never gotten that tap, but I got the stern look telling me I had better behave.

It should be said here that I never misbehaved. I did everything I could to try to get the same gleaming appraisal from our parents that Winston got, but it rarely came. I honestly have no idea why I was treated the way I was.

Pausing in front of the mirror next to the door, I tuck away a few loose pieces of hair to look less like a mess, pull my shoulders back, take a deep breath, and open the door.

Winston immediately shoots me a disapproving

glare as he storms past me into the living room. It's a Saturday, and he's dressed in a three-piece suit. Come to think of it, I can't remember the last time I saw him in anything other than a suit or a tux. He wears those frequently as well. With every year that passes, he looks more and more like our father and acts like him too. He's cold, detached, and one hundred percent caught up in reputation and appearances.

Not for the first time, I can't help but wonder how did I fall so far from the family tree? Maybe this is why I never received their approval. Even though I've always done just as they asked of me, they knew deep down I was different from them.

Instantly, I deflate. I know this look. It's the one my parents are actually giving because they've sent him over to "deal with me." Regardless of the fact I'm a grown woman, they still continue to treat me like an unruly child who's the black sheep of the family. Again, I was never an unruly child—curious and clumsy describe me better—and to my knowledge, I've never done anything to outright embarrass our family.

What would it be like to have a sibling on my side? One who embraces my uniqueness, one who embraces me.

"I can't believe you're actually doing this," he says,

running his hand over the back of his neck but never through his hair because God forbid he messes it up.

"Why not?" I ask in a neutral tone, moving past him and stacking the bricks that belong strictly to my family around my heart. They shouldn't be easy to stack, but unfortunately they are. I learned a long time ago that there's no place for my emotions in our family. Having them means I've become irrational and more like the general population who are beneath us and less like the dignified lady they've raised me to be.

"Because it's North Carolina," he seethes.

Yep, not only do they know I bought a house, but they know where too. I wonder if our parents keep tabs on Winston like they do me?

My heart sinks as I take in his reaction, which makes no sense. Everyone we know has vacation homes. That's right—homes, as in more than one. Why can't I?

"Do you hear yourself right now? And what is wrong with North Carolina?"

I move past him to take down a large painting in my living room that I want to be moved to the house. I'm not sure exactly how much time I'll spend in each location, New York and North Carolina, but this painting is modern Post-Impressionism of a garden and feels like it belongs there instead of here.

It's my favorite painting and represents a dream I've always wanted.

"No one we know lives in North Carolina. It's, it's, southern." He says this like it's a dirty word or old gum stuck to the bottom of his shoe. "The Hamptons, Cape Cod, Aspen, literally anywhere else, that is where you live."

I cut him a look filled with disbelief. "You're unbelievable."

What's also unbelievable is that he's acting like this is some rash decision. I've been going to Horizons Valley with my friends for years. I love it there, and they know this. Maybe that's the problem—they don't like that I've chosen to spend more time with my friends and less with them.

"You know very well that the Rhodeses have a reputation to uphold. This reputation has always been the foundation of our grandfather's business model. It's what our parents have worked so hard to maintain, and quite frankly, it's what has funded your life." He throws his arms out and looks around my condo.

Reputation.

I've heard this my entire life, and it's fitting that it rhymes with expectation.

"Funded my life. You're joking? You do realize how much money I made last year, right?"

"Yes, thanks to those elite private lessons our parents paid for."

I want to argue with him, I do, but I just know after all these years there is no point. He is their puppet, and they can do no wrong in his eyes.

Then again, he's their prize, while I'm just the second child. That phrase, "the heir and the spare," truly fits us. The plan has always been for him to take over the family business and for me to just marry someone advantageous to the family.

"Winston, I am almost thirty years old. I make my own income, and quite frankly, I don't owe anyone anything. Just myself. You can stand here all you want and try to lecture me, shame me, whatever you think you're doing to get me to stay, but it won't work. I'm going. And after this conversation with you, I can't get out of here fast enough."

He sighs, then places his hands on his hips and frowns at me.

What also rhymes with reputation is frustration and devastation.

I understand him. I understand them all. I do. They've allowed society to mold them into this lifestyle where keeping a pretentious, better-than appearance is more important than living a fulfilling life that makes them happy. They're very successful, and they've acquired all this wealth, yet when I'm with them, I'm nauseated by the lack of genuineness. I'm sad for them and sad for myself. I want more for them and me, but it will never happen.

"Why do you always have to be such a problem?" he asks.

"How am I the problem here? I've done nothing to any of you. I stay out of your way, I purposely don't mingle with anyone from your crowd, and I have a very successful career."

He snorts. "Successful for now. You don't actually think playing your little cello is a sustainable career, do you?"

Playing my little cello.

All I can do is stare at him. Has he not followed my career at all?

I know his words shouldn't hurt—after all, what I do isn't a hobby—but they do.

Being a child prodigy, there was no question in my parents' eyes that my only worth was what I could do with the instrument. They never entertained any other ideas that I might be good at something or simply dreamed of something else.

Yes, during my adolescent years, I had the best tutors they could find, and for college, they sent me to Juilliard here in New York City, where I wasn't required to leave home. I didn't even have to audition. I was just accepted. I don't know if that was due to them pulling strings, and by that, I mean donating money, or if my name and skill level were already known. But I went like I was supposed to, and day in and day out, my soul drowned in music theory, music history, and composition classes.

Don't get me wrong, I love playing the cello, but I wanted to play what I wanted to, not what I was being forced to do.

A few blocks off campus is a local bar called Talents. Every night, it is wildly overrun with students from my school because that place offers an open mic night seven days a week. It's a place where students like myself can go and express themselves. Instead of playing Elgar's "Cello Concerto," I could play my version of songs like "Wildest Dreams" by Taylor Swift.

It was freeing.

It was also where I met Avery and Emma. Both also attended Juilliard, but Avery played the piano and Emma the violin. The three of us formed our own version of a band known as Avery, Emma, and Cora, and we started performing together. Think classical pop music. Each of us can sing, so we performed covers and occasionally one of our own pieces.

Not long after we started playing together, we were scouted and signed with the Three Little Birds recording studio. People really liked our music, and we went from hitting top played lists on Spotify to performing sold-out shows. Famous isn't something I ever thought I wanted to be, but regardless, that's what we became. We've played in venues around the world, awards shows, and even for the president.

Of course, my family was horrified that I chose the path of "a rock star" instead of my perfectly chosen path at the New York Philharmonic, but for once in my life, I didn't care. While I loved playing in the orchestra, a space my parents procured for me, playing with my friends outweighed the heavy disappointment I felt from home. I loved the sound and the vibe we created, and apparently, everyone else did too.

Everyone but them.

Nothing about this is a hobby. I've carved this career out for myself, and it isn't going anywhere.

Adding a few more bricks around my heart, I stand directly in front of him and square off my shoulders. We are the same height, and he's never liked that.

"Winston, what does it even matter?"

His lips turn down, and two lines strike between his eyes as he considers my question. He's trying to touch on a subject dear to me, hoping to get me to react, but he won't. I stopped reacting a long time ago. He just doesn't seem to remember that about me.

It's then the second reason for this impromptu visit comes out.

"I have someone I want you to meet."

If I truly found this situation funny, I would laugh, but I'm so over it that the only answer his statement warrants is me saying, "No."

Turning away from him, I pick up a blanket placed along the back of my couch and fold it. Most of the things I'm going to need for my new home I've ordered online to be delivered, but I do have a dozen medium-sized boxes or so that I've packed with personal items from here.

He lets out another sigh. "You do realize sooner or later you'll have to marry. Running off to your lake house doesn't negate the fact you have responsibilities. Why won't you meet someone I think would be a good fit for you?"

"Winston, no one you pick will ever be a good fit for me. They are a good fit for you, and I'm tired of you pushing your own agendas onto me. I will never marry if for no other reason than to spite all of you."

It's not that I don't want to get married. I might one day, but with the constant pressure from him and my family, it's just not worth it right now. In their eyes, no one will ever be good enough unless they're hand-picked, and unfortunately, I don't have the mental capacity to deal with more of their disapproving glares and subtle failure reminders.

Which is completely ridiculous.

I'm even more grateful now that this new home is in North Carolina. Discovering that they hate it there means they will never visit. Not that I really expect them to. I've been on my own for a long time.

"Forever the disappointment."

"Forever the doormat."

Turning, he shakes his head as he walks toward the door. I used to feel sorry for him, but I realized he's doing exactly what he wants, with who he wants. He thrives on maintaining the image, the fake image, whereas real people don't care. I've never understood what the allure is.

"You will be here for our parents' fall soiree," he says as he reaches the door.

I can't tell if this is a question or a statement, not that it matters.

"Have I missed one yet?"

Glancing down at the boxes, he frowns again. "I hope you at least hired someone to help you with these."

And then he's gone.

The quiet settles around me as I slowly remove the

unwanted bricks. I don't want to be closed off, but how can I not be when I'm surrounded by people like him?

No, I did not hire anyone to help me carry a few boxes. I can do it myself. He could too, but what would that say to the outsiders? Outsiders who choose to see what they want versus taking the time to discover what is real. After all, salt looks like sugar, and sometimes not all that glitters is gold.

2

CORA

Have you ever done something so outlandish, it isn't until after all the dust has settled that you take a look in the mirror and ask yourself, "What did I just do?"

That's me right now as I stand in the entryway of my new mountain home and stare at the mess before me. Well, it isn't actually a mess. All the boxes of the brand-new home goods I ordered need to be unwrapped and set up or put away. Buying things one at a time, it's easy not to realize how many things there actually are, and well, my new house is overflowing.

The first time I came to Horizons Valley with Emma and Avery, I thought the little lake town was quaint and cute to visit. Emma's parents live in Atlanta, and she grew up coming here in the summers, so when she invited Avery and me, of course we said yes to the week getaway. The second time we came, I was excited to return because we had created some amazing music in the basement of Emma's parents' house. I was also fond of the previous summer's memories of backyard barbecues, renting a boat and waterskiing on the lake, and spending our nights at a country bar called Smokey's. But the third time we came, it felt a lot like coming home.

It's fascinating to me how someone can live somewhere their whole life, but after only a few short trips somewhere else, that somewhere else changes everything. But then again, maybe it's about the people, my people, who now mostly live here and not in New York City, where we're from.

Closing the door behind me, I breathe in the smell of pine, fresh paint, and freedom. In New York, I have my own place, which I bought with my own money, but being in the city, I've always felt like I was still under my parents' thumb. Oddly enough, I feel one hundred percent free here.

Free and on the mountain that overlooks the town and the lake. Avery and Emma now live on the lake, and I see the appeal one hundred percent, but I wanted more. More land, more space, just more. More like the dream of my painting, with a garden overflowing with fruits, vegetables, and flowers. So when I saw this listing pop up, even though there's only one other person who lives up here, I knew it had to be mine.

My new house was built in the early 1900s. In the mid-1950s, it was renovated and updated. It has white siding, a brick chimney that runs from the ground up, and a large wraparound porch. It's only about twenty-five hundred square feet on the inside, and the original floor plan has the rooms squared off instead of the space being open. There's one large bedroom upstairs with a bathroom and two downstairs that share a bathroom in the hall. One room I plan on maintaining for guests, although I don't know who will be coming to visit, and the other is my office and where I plan on keeping anything related to music. Except for my favorite cello, it has its own home in the living room.

Prior to moving in, I did have contractors come and remove the wall between the kitchen and the living space. They changed out the appliances and the countertop, put an island up between the two rooms, helped me by removing old carpet and wallpaper, painted, polished, and updated the bathrooms. While it's all still a work in progress, I'm excited to finally be here and moving in.

And that's when I scan over all the boxes in the front rooms again. Ash, Avery's husband, has been stopping by once a day since I told everyone that I'd bought the house over the Fourth of July weekend to oversee the construction, be here for furniture delivery, and bring in the packages. I'm grateful to him. I'm also appreciative he left it somewhat organized, as the boxes are stacked in rows.

From my back pocket, my phone rings. Avery's calling. I make my way to my new couch, which is still covered in plastic, and smile.

"Are you here yet?" she asks as I flop down and let out a huge exhale.

"Just got here." I look at my phone and see it's a little past two. Could I have made the drive from New York to North Carolina in one go? Yep, but knowing the bed would not be made up when I arrived, I decided to break halfway and then drive in this morning. I also stopped at the grocery store to pick up a few essentials until I got more settled in.

She squeals. "I'm still in shock from when you announced this at Clay and Emma's. I can't believe you bought a home here too. I know this is something that you did for yourself, but I can't tell you how much it means to me. I'm just so happy you're here."

And this right here is one of the reasons I did. Avery and Emma have always loved me for me, not for what I can do for them. The only expectation they've ever put on me is that they want me to be happy, and the same goes for them. That's what it's supposed to feel like when you love someone like they're family.

"Well, that phrase 'Gotta keep the band together' feels fitting." I'm smiling from ear to ear, and I kick my feet up to rest them on one of the boxes in front of me. The walls are this beautiful shade of sage green, and everything smells fresh and clean.

"Can I come over and help you? Ash told me you would need his truck to haul off the garbage."

Where this house is located, you have to take all your garbage to a local dump. No one is coming up here to get it. At first, I was shocked to hear this, as I've never been to a place where the trash wasn't picked up, but I can see how that makes sense.

"Avery, you're pregnant. I don't want you lifting anything, but yes, I will take you up on the truck offer another day. I have to return the U-haul trailer tomorrow, so after the dump run on the way into town, I'm just going to break down these boxes and set the garbage out on the front porch."

My eyes glance out the window. The porch on this house is amazing, and I have visions of all the plants I plan to keep on it, but I can see the lake past it and through some trees. I have an idea of where her house is, so while I look at that spot, I pretend she's closer than she is.

"I might be pregnant, but that doesn't mean I can't help you unpack. Also, I know I don't need to tell you this, but just a reminder, don't set bags of food out on the front porch. Otherwise, you'll have nighttime visitors."

I haven't researched the types of animals I might come across here on the mountain, but thoughts of bears and bobcats wandering around my house and making themselves at home cause me to shiver.

"How about you give me a few days to settle in, and then you can come over?" It's not that I need everything to be perfect for her to see it the first time. I just want it to be a little more hospitable and less like a hazard.

"I hate that you're up there all by yourself."

Avery is the worrier when it comes to the three of us. Emma is always happy, and as for me, I like to think I'm independent and carefree. I've essentially been on my own since I was thirteen and no longer needed a nanny, and I don't let things weigh me down.

"You know I love being by myself. I'm excited to get everything settled." I again glance at the boxes, and where some might dread what's ahead of me, I feel nothing but excitement. This is like Christmas morning.

I loved the things I bought, and now I get to unwrap them.

"Well, you don't get a few days. I'll be by tomorrow with some food," she says, and I laugh.

"Okay, food sounds good. But no lifting anything when you're here. I've got this." Leaning over, I drag the closest box to me and begin pulling off the tape.

"I know you do," she says confidently.

"I also might have some Kelly's Kupcakes here for you too," I tease. I was going to run them over to her, but if she's coming tomorrow, they'll still be delicious.

"You didn't!" she squeals.

"I did."

This box is from Restoration Hardware, and I pull out the large wide-brimmed linen shade to the table lamp I bought for this room. The base is a large terra-cotta olive oil jar. It's not white or gray or green. It's kind of a mixture of all three, textured, and I love it.

"I've been craving them something fierce. Ash offered to fly us to New York just to get them, but I told him he was being crazy."

"There's a blueberry pound cake one in the box calling your name."

I get up to pull the rest of the wrapping away from the pot. This lamp isn't modern, but I didn't want this house to feel that way. I'm in the mountains. It should have a bit of a cottage feel, but at the same time, I want it to be contemporary.

She groans. "Speaking of berries, Ash said the bushes in your backyard are covered with blackberries."

"Really?"

"Yep, 'tis the season, so I'll be picking some of those tomorrow when I'm there."

"They're all yours," I tell her, knowing that something delicious will be coming my way. Avery loves to bake. It's her love language. Over the past couple of years, she's stepped up on the types of food she's making as well as the quantity. Poor Ash, while he loves everything she makes, he's had to work out more to burn off the calories.

Emma, on the other hand, has just discovered she loves to knit. She's obsessed with yarn. Bright colors, pastel colors, neutral colors, in varying textures—she loves them all.

As for me, I love plants, and the small travel U-haul attached to the back of my car is full of them. You'd think it was for the dozen boxes I brought, but nope, it was for the plants.

After Avery and I hang up and get off the phone, I spend hours unboxing and finding a home for everything. I position the rug in the front room, unwrap the living room furniture and the dining room furniture, and wash the dishes. I haul in the plants, set up my bedroom, and hang my clothes. It's after I've showered that I remember the blackberry bushes outside. Blackberries would go great with the yogurt I bought for breakfast tomorrow.

Slipping out the back of the house, I breathe in the earthy smell of the mountain and head toward the blackberry bushes that line the road and divide my property and the neighbors. I thought about going over there this afternoon to introduce myself, but I was sweaty from unpacking, and well, that feels strange. That's not something we do in New York. This tiny part of me had hoped they would come over to welcome me themselves, but they didn't.

Ash was right. These bushes are huge and covered in berries. I pick them off one by one and place them in the bowl I brought. I've never had a need to cook much, as we always had someone cook for us or we ate out, but with the number of berries out here, my mind spins with ideas of jam, cakes, and cobblers.

My mother flashes through my mind. She would be appalled by this entire scenario. She was never very domesticated, so the idea of keeping a home or cooking is just beneath her, and she let everyone around her know this.

"Oh, look at that one," I say as I reach deep into the branches to grab it.

But just as I lean over and stretch my arm to pull the berry off, the bush underneath shakes.

Four glowing eyes pop open and stare back at me. My breath catches in my throat, and my heart starts galloping to a very alarming speed. I'm frozen in fear as we continue our face-off, and then whatever it is . . . it growls.

3

BRIGGS

*S*creaming.

High pitched–fear for your life–screaming echoes across the mountain and sends me immediately into fight mode. I'm out of my chair, grabbing my rifle, which sits next to the front door, and I'm over the steps of my house, across the dirt road, and down the driveway of my closest neighbor. My only neighbor.

I had heard through the grapevine back in June that the house across the street had sold. Poor Mrs. Benson had lived there alone for the past twenty years after the passing of her husband. She was a true modern Appalachian homesteader and lived her whole life in that house, well before Horizons Valley became what it is today. She lived off the land, and even my orchard was hers at one time. I had thought that one of her kids or grandchildren would take over the house, but nope, they sold it and took the cash instead.

Now, it's almost August, and every day, it seems there have been construction or delivery trucks rambling up the mountain and tearing up the gravel road we share. Until today, I saw a small SUV with an attached trailer turn off toward the house and not leave. I don't want to be that neighbor out of the gate, but I gritted my teeth with each truck and told myself it would be the last one. Eventually, we'll have to discuss the maintenance of the road. It has to be resurfaced every year after winter, and it's our responsibility as the property owners to maintain it.

Speaking of maintain, my mind starts racing as I think about what I'm about to encounter in the yard. Is it an animal? Is a woman being attacked? I have no idea, but I'm determined to do my best to protect her.

Coming around the bend and into the neighbor's yard, I stop dead in my tracks as I take in the sight before me. A woman about my age is flailing around. Her blonde hair flies in every direction as she jerks and continues screaming, and the part that has me completely speechless is that she's damn near naked.

"What the fuck is going on!" I bellow at her.

She freezes and locks eyes with me, finding me

standing in her yard. Her eyes dart toward the gun, and then I swear she screams even louder than before, causing every hair on my neck to rise.

"Lady! Would you stop screaming!"

If she keeps this up, I'm certain the whole town will hear her and come racing up the mountain with pitchforks raised to avenge whatever they think is happening to her.

"Get off my property!" she yells at me while pulling on the sleeve of her robe. With all her flailing, she's got it caught on the thorns of the blackberry bush, leaving it wide open and giving me the perfect view of her breasts and the most incredible body I've ever seen.

Not that I'd admit to looking to anyone.

"Why are you screaming? Are you hurt?" I look past her and around her to see if I might spot what has made her so worked up, but I don't find anything. There are no bears, no panthers, and no snakes slithering off into the bushes.

At the question of what's happening, her focus shifts back to the bush, where a strangled sound comes out of her, and she again pulls hard on her robe with a shaking hand.

When I march toward her, her already pale face turns even whiter. She's so spooked at whatever she saw, and then with me here as well, she cringes as I toss the gun to the ground and move into her space. I try not to look at her, but her creamy skin, tiny light pink underwear, and the smell drifting off her is so mouthwatering that I can't help but lock eyes with her. Her cheeks flush red, and time suspends as we both size each other up until the bush shakes, and she jerks so hard while letting out a strangled cry that the sleeve of the robe rips and propels her backward.

Instinct has me grabbing her to keep her from falling, but she wrenches herself free and moves away from me while pulling her robe tight around her and closing off the view.

"There!" She points, eyeing the bush like it personally offended her but standing taller and feeling justified for her crazy behavior.

I glance down into the bush and see two white furry faces with a black mask covering their eyes.

"For fuck's sake, they're just raccoons!" I look at her like she's lost her mind.

"What do you mean 'just raccoons'? They're rabid, they growled at me! Kill them!" she demands, still pointing at the bush.

If I wasn't so annoyed at this moment, I would laugh.

Tilting my head, I'm less subtle this time as I take her in from head to toe. Her tiny black robe barely covers her ass, which leaves her long shapely legs on full display. She's tall, but not quite as tall as me, and by the time my eyes make it back to hers, she's crossed her arms over her chest in a defensive pose and frowning hard.

Suddenly, my annoyance turns to irritation that I'm here, barefoot in the dirt where there are ticks, and I'm annoyed that my new neighbor clearly can't handle the mountain life if she's screaming over raccoons on day one of her being here.

I'm also irritated that I find her so freaking gorgeous it's hard to breathe.

"Where is your husband?" I bark at her.

"My what?" she yells back at me.

I glance quickly at her hands and find all ten fingers bare of rings. That doesn't mean she isn't with someone, but at the present, there's no clue to help me out.

"You're not the brightest, are you?" I ask, taking a step back and scanning over the yard. Not that I think any animal will come within a two-mile radius of her house now after all that screaming, but you never know. Curiosity could win out.

"Excuse me?" She drops her arms, and her entire posture shifts. Her back straightens, her hands fist by her sides, and the robe drops open.

My mouth waters.

Did she forget that is all she's wearing? I'm so

blinded by just how naked and stunning she is that it never even occurs to me to turn away.

"Just who do you think you are?" she asks in a tone that's so severe, lesser men would cower.

There's an air of sophistication to her. She's definitely not some townie who came upon some money and bought this place. There has to be someone else with her, right? Why would this woman buy this house?

"Who am I? I'm the guy who just came over here to save your ass when clearly I should be thinking about saving my own because you're crazy. Screaming over raccoons. Dancing around half naked. Who decided it was a good idea to sell you this house?"

"What?" Her eyes narrow, and she tips her chin up just a tad. "You've got some nerve. You don't even know me," she seethes, pieces of her blonde hair falling across her face.

"You're right, and based on this little episode, I don't want to. Rocky and Bullwinkle..." I wave my hand toward the bush to address the raccoons who are now peeking their heads out to see if the coast is clear. "Meet your new landlord."

"Rocky and Bullwinkle?" She looks between the raccoons and me, and then takes another step away from the bush in case they decide to charge at her.

"Yes. These two raccoons have lived here for a long

time. Longer than the two of us. Don't leave garbage out, and they won't bother you. What they do like, however, is fruit. You know because they are wild animals. Deer and bears also like fruit." I scowl at her.

"I wasn't aware there would be raccoons here," she says, pulling on the robe again. This time, she closes it and ties the belt around her waist. It's then I see that her arm is scratched from the bush, and I'm immediately annoyed even further that she's somehow managed to blemish her perfect skin.

"Wasn't aware? You weren't aware there would be animals that live in the forest of the mountains?" My brows pop up with sarcasm.

At this, she pinches her lips together and then looks me over from head to toe. I'm wearing a black T-shirt, a pair of gray joggers, and no socks or shoes. I didn't even think to put any on. I just needed to get here and see what the problem was. Her gaze flips to one of disapproval, and then she looks at the gun.

"I take it you live in the other house on the mountain," she says, ignoring the way I just condescendingly spoke to her. She brushes her hair back off her face and runs her hand through it. I don't know how she does it, but given the show she just put on, it somehow looks perfect, falling just past her shoulders and framing her large brown eyes, high cheekbones, and bee-stung lips.

This is just what I don't need.

Feeling that anger rise again, I don't answer, and this causes her to bristle. Silence and shadows fall around us as the sun has dropped behind the western tree line across the lake and is close to setting.

"Well, thank you for coming over so quickly, but you can leave now."

She's dismissing me.

Her eyes return to mine, and we stare at each other in complete disdain. I can see how she might not think favorably of me after I insulted her, but seriously, who buys a house in the mountains, wanders around barefoot without a care at all for ticks, and screams like the world is ending over raccoons? Raccoons.

Not needing to respond to her, I bend down to retrieve my gun. I've never needed to use this gun, but everyone knows it's better to be safe than sorry. Brushing it off, I turn to leave and just shake my head.

"Un-fucking-believable," I mutter to myself.

"And would you stop swearing?" she all but demands. "It's rude."

Rude?

Rude is the very indecent thoughts I'm having about my new neighbor and what I'd like to do to her without that tiny robe on. The way I talk is the last thing that she needs to be concerned with.

Stopping, I turn and glare at her one last time and then drop my eyes to her feet. Her feet that look damn near perfect with their red-painted toenails. She bunches them under my scrutiny and digs them into the dirt.

"Goldie, don't forget to check for ticks."

And with that, I'm gone.

4

CORA

Could last night have possibly been any more humiliating?

I know I'm new to this home owning, live in the mountains, and fend-for-myself lifestyle, but I certainly didn't expect to meet my new neighbor under such horrible circumstances.

At least, I'm assuming he's my neighbor. He didn't answer my question, but only one other person lives up here on the mountainside. I also remember Ash and Clay talking about a guy named Briggs, so that must be him, the one they're friends with. They seem to think he's a stand-up guy, and while I can appreciate how he came over here with guns blazing, literally, to help someone he doesn't know, his personality and his manners are severely lacking.

I can't believe the way he spoke to me.

Someone he doesn't know yet but ultimately will, considering we're neighbors. And that question about where's my husband, he has some nerve. Just replaying that conversation in my mind has my hackles rising.

And as it is, I've been waiting all morning for my friends to call and laugh. After all, if the situation had been reversed, I would have been on the phone with them immediately and told them about what had happened, just like I expected him to, but my phone hasn't rung. Yet.

I mean, who does that guy think he is?

While I really do appreciate him racing over here to help me if I had needed it, the second he opened his mouth, he was either swearing at me or talking down to me as if I'm some idiot. I'm sorry, but no one talks to me this way and gets away with it.

And what is with calling me Goldie?

I'll admit, I might have overreacted about the raccoons, but at the time, I didn't know they were raccoons. It could have been a wild boar or a wolf. I also didn't know about the ticks. Of all the times we've stayed at Emma's, she's never mentioned ticks, but you'd better believe the first thing I did last night was hit up the internet for research.

It turns out that ticks live in North Carolina year-round and are most prevalent now during late summer. Rashes, pain, fatigue, trouble thinking, Lyme disease—getting bit sounds horrible, and now I can't help but wonder what else he knows that I don't. Immediately, I ordered some permethrin spray for my clothes. I'm not going to be afraid of going outside. I just need to have my yard treated and have a set of standard outside clothes and boots that I slip on when heading out.

The question I have to ask myself now is do I do the right thing and go over there and thank him, or do I pretend last night never happened and ignore him?

Looking around my house, I settle on a recent ZZ plant that I propagated and potted. The plant is small, and the pot is white. It makes a perfect thank-you gift, as well as a perfect "hello, I'm your new neighbor" gift.

A lot of people don't understand my love of plants, but that's okay. They don't need to.

When I was eight, my nanny and I were walking through the city when we came upon a farmers' market. My mother never walked anywhere. We always took the car, even if we were only going a few blocks.

Both entrances of the block were closed, and there were so many people shopping that it was hard to see the white tents that lined both sides of the road. Of course I'd seen a market before, from the back seat of the car, but this was the first time I had ever visited one. There were vendors with produce, soaps, honey, artwork, jewelry, bread, orchids, and plants.

I don't know why, but I was called to the plants. They were so pretty, and there were so many kinds, most of which were meant for city living. There were big plants, small plants, ones with big leaves, and others with leaves so small they were smaller than my fingernails. Some needed to be on a balcony or in a window with light, but others didn't. Some let off herbaceous smells, while others would have flowers bloom. I was obsessed and wanted to touch every one.

The plant vendor was a nice young lady, younger than my nanny, but she told me the ZZ plant was the perfect first plant for me. We talked about how it is a succulent, and I needed to put an alarm on my phone to remind me to water it on the first of each month. That was the only day I was to water it, and if my plant got too much water, I would know because the leaves would droop and turn yellow. Also, this plant could not sit in direct sunlight, so it was perfect for anywhere in my room.

When we got home, I put my new plant on my desk and just stared at it. I wasn't allowed to have pets, so this was the first time I felt the pull of responsibility to care for something. I had a beautiful, live green plant in my room.

After this, plants became an obsession.

Begrudgingly, I suck up my pride. I know what I have to do. I was raised to do the right thing and I plan on living here for a long time, so I need to be the bigger person. It's now lunchtime, and I've waited long enough. I shove my feet into a pair of tall rubber rain boots to keep the ticks off, and I grab the small plant.

Making my way down my gravel driveway, I pause for a minute when I pop out onto the road to take in his house.

It's similar to mine in style, with the white siding, the brick fireplace, and the wraparound porch. However, it's larger and has a massive oak tree sitting next to it. I don't know why he would need a house this big. Then again, maybe he's married and has a wife who knows how to control him.

Taking a deep breath, I trudge up the front steps and knock on the door. A loud bark booms from inside the house. Of course this man would have a large, scary dog. That cliché fits him perfectly.

Eventually, the heavy tread of footsteps gets stronger as he approaches the door, then it stops, a few seconds pass, and then he whips open the door. The smell of bacon comes tumbling out, and my stomach growls.

It might have been daylight when he was over last night, but it was dusk, and he did not look like this in my memories. If I was anywhere else, with anyone else, my jaw would drop.

This guy is the classic definition of a mountain man. He's tall, broad-shouldered, has a full head of dark hair, and scruff across his sharp jawline. His eyes are brown, and they're on the darker side. He has freckles splattered across the bridge of his nose, and although I shouldn't find them endearing, I do. Dropping my gaze to run down the length of him, I get stuck on the fact that he's wearing flannel with the sleeves rolled up.

Flannel.

When he clears his throat, my eyes fly back to his and his brows drop, forcing two little lines to strike between his eyes, and he frowns.

So it's going to be like that. Hours later and he's still grumpy.

Instantly, I feel emboldened.

"Good morning," I say to him with a chipper voice.

His frown deepens, and he pulls the door closer to him to keep me from seeing the inside. So much for being invited in.

The big scary dog pops his head out between this guy's legs, and I realize he's not so scary at all. He's a chocolate lab, and he's old. He has white hair all over his face and looks like just the sweetest thing ever. I can't help but smile at him and bend down to pet his head.

"Well, hi there," I say to the dog, ignoring the frowning grumpy man. The dog sits, and his tail starts thumping on the floor.

My mood instantly improves. Maybe this won't go bad after all. I mean he has a nice dog. Nice people have nice dogs.

Standing back up, I smile at him. "I just wanted to come over here and say I'm sorry for how we met last night. Thank you for coming in case something was wrong. I appreciate it. My name is Cora, and obviously, I'm your new neighbor."

Now, while most normal people would introduce themselves back, he does not. Instead, his eyes narrow and then they drop to take me in from head to toe. To embrace my new mountain life, I'm wearing shortalls with a white T-shirt underneath and my tall rubber boots. His gaze stops on the boots, and his lips press together.

"I take it you're Briggs?"

His gaze shoots back to mine. There's surprise there that I know who he is as well as wariness. That's right, pal, you can just stand there all you want and wonder what it is that you think I know about you. I might know nothing, but he doesn't know that, and at the moment, I feel like I have the upper hand.

"Anyway, I just wanted to bring you this as a thank you for last night. I really do appreciate you coming over as quickly as you did."

I hold the plant out, but instead of taking it, he looks at it as if it's poisonous.

"What am I supposed to do with that?"

His voice is gruff like he hasn't used it much today, and I can't tell if I like it or not. Part of me wants to because I want to be friends with my new neighbor, but part of me doesn't after the way he yelled at me last night. I feel like I should still be on guard.

"Whatever you want."

There's no point in telling him that studies show having plants increases mental health and happiness. That constantly seeing them, being around them, and smelling them can help us feel more relaxed and less anxious.

"Well, I don't want it."

"Oh."

It never occurred to me that he wouldn't want the plant. I thought it was a nice gesture and I feel a blush of uncertainty heat my chest and climb into my neck.

"It's a really easy plant to take care of. You only water it once a month."

He somehow straightens and makes himself taller. "Do I look like someone who wants to take care of a plant?"

He has to be joking. Ash and Clay told me he owned this property, and there are signs for the business in multiple places, including the road and right in front of his house.

"You are the owner of an orchard," I say to him slowly because clearly one screw must be loose.

His hand tightens on the door, and his knuckles turn white. "By that, you mean it's a business where I make a profit."

"Maybe you should give it to your wife," I toss at him, suddenly feeling defensive. After all, he made assumptions about me.

"I'm not married," he spits out.

"I can see why." My tone is exasperated, and I hate that he's turned me into this.

His jaw tics as he clenches it.

"Please, just take the plant." I hold it out to him. If he takes it, then I can go back home, pretend he doesn't exist, and never see him again.

"No thanks. I'm not one for clutter lying around my house."

"Clutter!"

I look down at the plant in my hands, and my heart

pinches. He just insulted something that means a great deal to me, and anger diffuses from my bones into my muscles. The devil and the angel appear on each shoulder. The devil says, "Throw it at his head," and the angel says, "Just take it home and be done with this."

I came over here with the best of intentions. It never occurred to me that he would be just as horrible and grumpy today. I understand how last night could be situational, but I've done nothing to this guy for him to be so unfriendly.

"You've got some nerve," I say to him as I take a step backward. Righteous indignation has my heart rate picking up.

"You're the one standing on my doorstep uninvited," he growls at me.

My jaw drops open, and the old sweet dog between his feet lets out a small whine. Even the dog is aware of how inappropriate this guy is being. I mean seriously, what is his problem?

"Wow. Are you always this insufferable to people you just meet? I mean, I hope your investors keep you from paying customers at this orchard. With the likes of you, I would never return."

"If we're done now," he says in a flat tone as he shuffles the dog backward.

Oh yes, we are done. So done, we never even began.

Setting the plant on his top step, I whip around and storm down the stairs to leave. I'm so offended by this guy that I don't even know which emotion to settle on first! Arrogant, condescending prick. He may think his gruff and rude attitude will sway me to stay away, but he's got another thing coming. No one treats me badly and gets away with it. I am not the type of girl who will just sit back and let him think he's running this show. I may be new to this town and this mountain, but he just inadvertently declared war.

Turning back, I see he hasn't closed the door and gone inside. He's watching me with his arms crossed over his chest. Only this time, his expression is one of curiosity and not annoyance, but then, just as quick as it's there, it's gone.

A warm breeze blows, and I breathe in the sweet smell of the mountain. It clears my head, and I know my eyes have brightened with mischief. In the sweetest voice I can muster, I say to him, "I'll see you around, Briggs."

My smile is more like a smirk, and I know he sees it. He frowns again, and those two little lines I'm becoming familiar with strike deeper between his eyes. I've confused him with the one-eighty of my emotions, and the devil sitting on my left shoulder laughs. Good. I give him a little finger wave and then turn to head back to my house.

This will be fun.

He doesn't know we've gone into battle, but he will soon enough. And if there's one thing I know for certain, I will not lose.

5

BRIGGS

It's been a week since I've seen my new neighbor. And even though we've had zero interaction, I still feel her presence on the mountain as a part of each day, and I hate it.

I hate knowing she's just on the other side of that tree line and down the driveway. I hate knowing that she's over there by herself even though I shouldn't care, and I hate wondering if she needs any help. I've only seen one car come and go from the house, so most of the time, she's alone.

I can admit I was an ass to her. I had just gotten off the phone with my brother, who's demanding I be at the board meeting next month as we approach closing out the fiscal year, and even though I'm not an employee, just a shareholder, he loves to remind me that I owe it to him and my father to participate.

I hate these meetings.

With a passion.

Too many suits in one room with too many opinions and none of them align with mine. Of course I keep my mouth shut. There's no point in me saying anything. I don't participate in the day-to-day structure of running the business. I'm just the third largest shareholder, and it would be in bad taste not to show up and show solidarity with the family among the others.

Then all of a sudden there she was looking like a fucking ray of sunshine, petting Duke all sweetly and trying to gift me a plant.

A plant.

A plant that now sits on my kitchen table because I couldn't just leave it on the front porch indefinitely, and sunshine that blinded me from perfectly highlighted blonde hair, large diamonds in her ears, a denim jumper with the Prada logo on it which showed off her long legs, and black and gray Gucci boots.

The girl was dripping in brand names, and from head to toe, the amount of money she wore roiled my stomach. The mystery of her buying this house all the way up here instantly increased. Did she go through a divorce? Is this some kind of therapy where she needs to find herself? Did someone die, and she inherited a lot of money? I must admit I am a little bit curious. Add in the fact that she knew my name, and that curiosity turns to suspicion. It wouldn't be the first time a girl did something outlandish to force themselves into my orbit. Especially gold diggers, and at the present, I haven't ruled her out.

What are her intentions? It just makes no sense.

And the final look she gave me as a parting gift made every hair on the back of my neck stand to attention. Something deep down tells me that was not the last I'll see of her. Only, it's been a week, and nothing has happened.

What exactly is she doing over there?

"Hey," Cole says, catching Duke and me just as we're leaving the cider house. He has an office in the loft that overlooks the cider production, and it's where he spends most of his days. "Graham from Route 11 called and said they just tapped out on the hard cider and wants to know if we can run him down a keg?"

This is great news.

"Absolutely. We have six kegs left from last year's harvest, so it's good to move through those as we start kegging and bottling this year's next week."

Five years ago, I bought this orchard. The man who owned it before me had it for about twenty years. He purchased it right about the time Mrs. Benson's husband died. I think it was a midlife crisis dream of his, but once he was ready to retire, he was ready to be done with the demands and upkeep of this property.

It was an easy decision for me. My mother always loved Horizons Valley. She used to bring us here to go skiing in the winter, for lake fun in the summer, and hiking in the fall. She spoke so frequently of our time spent here that when she was diagnosed with cancer, I knew she didn't want to be in Charlotte. At twenty-five, I bought the property, and except for when she was receiving treatments, she basically left behind her life and moved into the house.

Needless to say, that did not go over well with my father or my brother.

"All right. I can run it down there on my way home," Cole says, dragging a hand through his blond hair.

"I appreciate it. Just let him know I'll send him an invoice."

Cole is a few years younger than me. He's my right-hand man at the orchard and has become my best friend. He's from North Carolina. He went to school for marketing at Appalachian State University and wanted to settle down somewhere in the mountains. That's the thing about North Carolina. People who are from here love it and stay here. I wanted to rebrand Red Barn Orchard and put in the cidery, and he was on board with everything I had planned from the first interview. For as much as he loves his creative side, he has no problem getting his hands dirty and picking apples with me when we're in season.

"Any plans tonight?" I ask him, already knowing exactly what they are. It's a little more than a tenth of a mile back to the house, and sweat slowly rolls down my back from the late afternoon humidity.

A goofy smile takes over his face. "Nothing too much. Amelia is cooking dinner, and we'll probably go for a walk somewhere. She loves this time of the year when everything is lush and green."

Cole and Amelia got married last month. She's a school teacher he met in town at the coffee shop Bean There. It was love at first sight, and we all knew it.

"Sounds like a great night," I tell him even though I cringe inside. While I'm happy for him, marriage and commitment after dealing with my ex Adele make me want to hurl myself off this mountain to drown at the bottom of the lake.

We're halfway back to the house when music drifts our way and floats around us. Music I've never heard before here on the mountain. I stop dead in my tracks as it's so out of place—it's deep, it's soulful, it's beautiful.

It's inconsistent.

Cole and I look at each other, both bewildered as gravel from underneath our feet kicks up dust at the abrupt halt.

This isn't coming from an album or a playlist, and that's when it dawns on me. My new neighbor must be playing it.

"What instrument is that?" he quietly asks, not wanting to disturb the moment.

"Pretty sure it's the cello."

I've been to my fair share of charity galas and benefits and spent plenty of unwanted time listening to stringed instruments.

"Sure sounds nice," he says, and I hum in agreement.

Slowly, we continue walking. Both of us are lost in thought over the music, and poor old Duke, he's just moseying along, happy to be with us. I've never considered myself an expert on music, but there is no question she is an expert. And from how it sounds, she's been heavily trained and playing for a long time.

Something warm diffuses its way into my chest cavity. Of all the annoying things that neighbors can do, this is not one of them. I will have no problem listening to her play night after night. My mother would have loved it.

We're almost to the house when she starts playing the theme song for *Indiana Jones*. While it sounds beautiful, it's not what I expected, and my lips twitch. Is playing a hobby for her? Does she belong to an orchestra? As much as I don't want to be intrigued by this new detail of hers, I am. She's apparently a rich woman who lives alone, is secluded on a mountain, likes plants, has no pets I've seen, and plays the cello. I'm no detective, but something here doesn't add up.

We're about to walk up the back steps to the house when Cole grabs me forcefully by the arm. Duke and I stop.

"Are those snakes by your door?" he whispers animatedly.

The breath in my lungs stalls. "What? Where?" I start scanning the ground around us. I'm not wearing boots. I'm wearing plain old tennis shoes, so if it were to strike, it would get me in the leg.

"Right there." He points toward the door, and my eyes follow.

Sure enough, I see two large brown snakes. One is lying on the doormat, and the other is half hidden behind the grill.

Oh. My. God.

While not many people know this about me, as I don't find it a habit to pass around my fears, I just don't do snakes. At. All. My heart rate takes off, my hands start tingling, and at this moment, I want to burn the whole house down.

"What kind do you think they are?" I ask him, swallowing roughly.

"If I had to guess, I'd say cottonmouth. They're dark and have those black strike markings. Briggs, these are poisonous. We can't go near them," he says, taking another step back.

I move back with him and pull on Duke's collar to keep him from wandering up the steps and meeting his fate.

I think I'm going to throw up.

"Well, we certainly can't leave them on the porch. I don't need them lingering around as we get ready to open for the season," I tell him as I panic internally.

A shiver runs through me, just thinking about them lingering outside my doors. Every time I open one now, I'm going to have anxiety and need to check it first.

"Stay here. I'll be right back," he says, running off and around to the front of the house.

Looking around, I'm suddenly distressed that more are just waiting to jump out at me. Do they have babies somewhere? Or eggs and they're just waiting to hatch.

It's like that weird sensation when you're watching a movie and someone has spiders crawling on them. You can feel them crawling on you too.

This isn't the first time we've encountered snakes on the property, but Cole knows how I feel about them, and he's the one who always takes care of it. Usually with a big shovel in hand, he twists so it's edge down, and he strikes like it's a sword, cutting their heads right off. However, this time, he's running back toward me with my shotgun in hand.

"You're going to shoot them?" I almost yell but pull back at the last second so as not to startle the snakes. My eyes dart back and forth between him and them. What if they start to slither away?

Oh. My. God.

I just can't.

"Well, I'm definitely not going to go near them. You have any other suggestions?"

Fuck no.

I step back a few more paces as he widens his stance and raises the gun. It looks like this gun is finally going to get used after all. Cole's elbow is almost ninety degrees to the ground, the butt is secured tightly against his shoulder, he aims, and without hesitating, he fires.

The crack of the weapon lets off a bang so loud that

my ears ring for a minute as the sound echoes across the mountain.

The music stops.

Both of us stare at the snake on the doorstep. He aimed perfectly and shot the damn thing in two pieces. I'm certain the bullet is lodged somewhere in the doormat, too. But there's no blood, gore, or last-minute twitches, and the other snake behind the grill didn't move at all.

What the hell?

Both of us slowly move to the steps to take a closer look.

"Is that a . . ." Cole mumbles before closing the distance and picking up a piece of the snake. It flops over in his hand, and I watch him squeeze it. Nothing happens, and nothing comes out of it.

"It's rubber." He looks at me, one hundred percent confused.

Rubber?

And that's when it hits me. *She* did this.

Indiana Jones also hated snakes! She never would have played that song had she not been involved.

That witch.

A chuckle leaves me, and Cole's confused gaze jumps from looking at the fake snake behind the grill to me.

At this, I openly laugh, and his gaze switches to looking at me like I've lost my damn mind.

That mischievous gleam she had in her eye as she stormed off last week? Well, now I know what she was thinking. She declared war, and shots were fired, literally. Only now it's my turn, and she had better watch her back because two can play this game.

6

CORA

It's the second week of August, and I am officially over the heat. I don't know why I thought it would be cooler living in the mountains versus the city, and I know the weather will begin to change next month, but these past couple of weeks have been miserable. Don't get me wrong, I still think it's beautiful, as everything is so green and ripe, but it's hot. Hot, sticky, and sometimes downright stifling.

I thought I would spend more time outside building and growing a garden. After all, that is why I bought this house, but with the heat and the summer coming to a close next month, I've decided to wait until next year before I plant anything. Planting anything in the ground out back, that is. In the meantime, my front porch has exploded with greenery, flowers, herbs, and lavender. I even planted blue hydrangeas along both sides of the porch stairs and the front edge, so the shrubs will be large and plentiful in a couple of years.

I hear the car coming up the road before I see it, and I know it's Juliet. Today is back to school for Bryce, so her days are officially free. Well, free outside of work, that is.

Juliet is Clay and Ash's sister, and I wasn't the only one who decided to return to Horizons Valley. She'd been living in Nashville, where she met her husband and had their son, Bryce, until he decided he didn't want to be her husband anymore. While what she's gone through is sad, and I know she didn't want to have to move back home, I'm glad she's here.

Excited to greet her, I walk out to the porch and jump at the sight of not one or two deer in my front yard, but as I count them, there are eighteen.

Eighteen!

Yes, I've seen a few over the past two weeks, but this is entirely different. Some are female, but the males point their antlers right at me as they have frozen at my sudden intrusion and are staring at me.

Oh my God.

What are they doing here?

The one with the largest antlers starts walking toward me, so I take a step back toward the door.

Fear, similar to the night with the raccoons, explodes inside me. My chest tightens to the point of not being able to breathe, and I let out a strangled sound that echoes around me and over the yard.

The big one stops walking, and I now truly understand the expression, "Like a deer in headlights." I imagine I look just like them. Big eyes, on edge, but still frozen.

"Morning, Goldie," someone calls out from the direction of my neighbor's house and that's when I know this is his doing. It has to be.

Son of a . . .

I also know he never would have sent them to my yard if he thought they would put me in danger. He's the one who came barreling over here with his big gun to save the day.

So this is how it's going to be? He's risen to the challenge. At least I had the decency to use fake rubber snakes, but no, he had to go and lure every deer off the mountain to my front yard! I know nothing about deer! But he doesn't know this, or does he?

At this point, Juliet's car turns down my driveway and comes to a complete halt as she takes in the scene before her. All eighteen deer turn and look at her. She looks at me with her jaw dropped and eyes wide, and then back to them. And then she scares the bejesus out of me and them as she lays on her horn. All nineteen of us jump. One by one, they race off, and she pulls up next to the house and parks.

I'm so happy she's here. I wave and watch her laugh at me through the windshield.

This isn't her first time here since I've moved in, but it is the first time I have no boxes to unpack. For the most part, everything feels put together.

"What in the world was that?" she asks as she climbs out of her car, holding a drink carrier with two large lattes.

I jog down the steps to hug her, and we turn to look at the yard where the deer were. It's then I spot all the tiny yellow pieces in the grass. Going to investigate, I pick up what I'm certain is a corn kernel and show it to her.

"Why would you do that?" she asks, kind of horrified.

"Oh, I have my neighbor to thank for this." I throw the kernel down and wipe my hand on my pants.

"You know, if deer think they're going to be fed, they're like stray cats, and they'll keep coming back."

She looks out over the yard at all the little yellow pieces left behind.

"Really?" My yard really isn't that big, and the idea of them trampling it or, even worse, coming up onto the porch has me alarmed.

"Yes. Don't feed them. They'll be messing all over your yard and bringing ticks with them."

At the word tick, my skin crawls, and I look down at my bare feet. I didn't even think about putting on shoes as I ran down the steps to greet her. I have large stone tiles as my walkway, so I wasn't in the grass the whole time, but still.

"I come with a present," she says as she hands me the drink carrier with the lattes, then lifts her bag and shakes it.

"The lattes are present enough. But don't parents like to drink champagne when their kids go back to school? Like a ritual celebration thing?" I tease. "I do have some chilling."

She smiles but shakes her head as we make our way to the front door. "No champagne for me. I think maybe I'm not the norm. I certainly can see how some parents might be this way, but after drop-off, I might have shed a tear or two because I'm sad he'll be gone all day. I really do love having him home."

"I hear homeschooling is a thing now," I tell her, and she barks out a laugh like I've lost my mind.

"Let's not go crazy."

Once we get inside and the door clicks shut behind us, Juliet kicks off her shoes and looks around the house.

"Wow, it looks incredible in here. I mean, I knew it would, but it's come together so well."

"Thank you. At first, it felt like a lot, but once I got started, it really wasn't."

"You added a ceiling fan to this room," she says, glancing up and then out over the other decorations that have changed the living room. "That was smart. I think you'll really like that when it's warm outside."

This ceiling fan is a farmhouse fan, and it accents so well. While most of the house is a lighter wood color, this one is dark.

"I saw it online, and I had to have it. It wasn't that hard to install either." I set the lattes on the coffee table in front of the couch.

"Wait. You installed it?" She turns to look at me, confused.

"I did. I watched a YouTube video and was done in no time." I settle onto the couch, and she stares down at me.

"Cora, you shouldn't be messing with things like

this. There's a reason there are professionals out there called electricians. You know I have a full Rolodex of companies should you need to hire someone."

"I know, but it wasn't hard. The fan arrived, and I knew I could do it myself."

"Still," she says, eyeing me warily. "What if you got hurt?"

"You worry too much."

Setting her large bag on the table, she opens it and pulls out a box of Cheez-Its. "Ta-da!"

A grin splits my face. "You definitely know the way to my heart."

Cheez-Its are my favorite snack of all time. Growing up, my mother did not believe in snacks, sweets, junk food, you name it. She was very particular about what the chef on duty was allowed to cook and feed us. She refused to have children who did not have a refined palate, and she also watched every calorie and carb I put into my body.

Cheez-Its were the one exception.

My mother was also obsessed with ballet. While I may be talented on the cello, I'm certain I would have been a ballerina if she had her way. And she tried. I was forced through dance classes all the way until fifteen. I went up on pointe at thirteen and never could keep my balance. Much to my mother's disappointment, the teacher finally told her this dream of hers would not come true. Never mind the fact that I did not have the body shape for this—I'm too tall and my feet are too big —she sure tried to shove me into the role.

But there was this one afternoon when she actually came to class to pick me up instead of our driver, and she met the principal of the American Ballet Company. I've never seen my mother fangirl over anything or anyone, but that day, while she maintained her composure, her eyes were wide and bright. The principal stood there eating a handful of Cheez-Its. When my mother questioned her, she simply laughed and said, "There's no use in working this hard not to be able to enjoy a few things in life."

From then on, I was allowed to have them. Not in large quantities, but it didn't matter. I love them. Winston, being the suck-up that he is, declined the crackers, or he would sneak me his portion when she wasn't looking. Back when we were friends, that is.

"Explain to me why your hot neighbor threw corn into your yard," she says as she settles onto the couch, pulling her feet up underneath her and placing the box of crackers between us.

I turn to face her, clutching my latte and inhaling the delicious scent of caramel. "You think he's hot?"

"You don't?" she asks, her brows raised.

"Well, I guess I did notice that he's not unpleasant to look at if you're into that whole mountain lumberjack kind of thing, but then he opens his mouth, and it's like his whole body transforms into something else."

"What do you mean?" She takes a sip of her drink.

"He's not nice," I say bluntly.

Visions of him standing in my yard yelling and swearing at me flash to the forefront of my mind. Although, when I took him his plant, a lack of profanity spewed from his mouth. Maybe he listened to me when I asked him to stop.

She laughs. "How can that be? Everyone in town loves him."

Love him? Is that possible?

"Have you met him?" I ask incredulously.

"No, but I've seen him in passing over the past couple of years."

"Well, I've met him, and he's rude, swears at complete strangers, and I tried to give him a plant when I introduced myself as his new neighbor, and he told me he didn't want it."

She laughs again and pushes a few loose pieces of her dark hair behind her ear.

"That's odd."

"Right!"

We both take another sip of our drinks, and my gaze wanders out the front window to the yard.

"So what do I do about the deer?"

"When I was growing up, my mother always hung bars of Irish Spring soap from the trees around our property."

"What?" I chuckle.

"Deer are very sensitive to smells, and they don't like soap. It's a cheap way to keep them away from your yard, and you can hang them in a way where they are hidden."

"I suppose."

"Next year, you can also plant things around the edge of your yard, like chives, garlic, and lavender. They also hate sudden sounds. I've seen people buy pretty little wind chimes and stake them throughout their gardens. Hanging them in trees is nice too, but if they bump against them in the garden, they get startled and run off."

"That's interesting."

Little wind chimes. I'm certain I could find some beautiful ones that would go perfectly in my garden next year.

"You've been here for two weeks. Are you bored yet?" she asks, eyeing me over the rim of her cup. Emma had asked me the same question when I talked to her the other day. I'm not sure why they think I would be bored. I love it here.

"Nope. Not even a little bit."

"How is that possible? You barely leave this house, and there's not that much to do every day."

"That's not true. I do leave the house. I went to Main Street the other day and walked through all the shops. I found a farmers' market just on the edge of town where I bought some fresh fruit and vegetables. You know I've been to both nurseries in town, and I met you at Avery's for dinner last week."

"Yeah, but what about the rest of the time? Aren't you lonely up here?"

"Not at all. I've been very busy. I put together everything in this house that needed it. I bought a tool set and hung the curtain rods and other things that needed to be put into the walls. I've worked outside a little each day, and I'm teaching myself how to cook. I didn't realize how much I relied on take-out food and delivery. In fact, you have to try this." I jump up off the couch and go into the kitchen.

Several times over the past couple of days, I've sucked up my fear and gone back to the blackberry bushes. There are just so many berries, and I can't see letting them go to waste. So I've picked a bunch and have taught myself how to make jam and a blackberry pound cake. I slice her a piece of the cake and take it to her.

She takes the plate from me and stares at the slice. "You made this?"

"I did." I smile proudly at her and resume my place on the couch.

"It looks beautiful." She takes a bite and then moans. "Cora, this is amazing."

"Thank you."

Pride diffuses through me.

"I've also been writing some new music. The songs aren't complete, but concepts and sounds are coming to me. I feel inspired here."

And I do. I know that most of our music over the years has been more mainstream, pop music, but what's been coming to me lately is more relaxed, almost like trendy folk music. I can't wait for a jam session with Avery and Emma once Emma and Clay return to the lake.

"I'm glad you're settling in. Not gonna lie, I was a bit worried about you."

"I think all of you were. But really, I'm good. I like being by myself, and I'm capable of doing whatever needs to be done. I haven't had to ask for help once."

"You know it's okay to ask for help, right?"

"Sure, and I will if I need it, but something is to be said for being completely independent."

And by independent, I mean completely away from my forever-disappointed-in-me family.

"If you say so," she says, stuffing more cake into her mouth.

7

BRIGGS

It's been a few days since I threw the corn into Goldie's yard, and each morning, I hear her come out of her house and bang on a pan while yelling at them to scare them off. Of course, a grin stretches from ear to ear each time, and man, do I wish I had set up a camera to see her reaction. After the raccoon incident, I'm pretty certain she's never experienced deer either.

Are they a little invasive? Yes, but if I were a deer, I suppose I would be too if I had to hunt for my own food, and randomly, there was some lying in the grass. I'd keep going back and looking for more. Eventually, they'll eat all the corn and move on, but in the meantime, I think it's hilarious.

I've just walked into the back of the cider house to grab a drink when Goldie storms through the front door. It bangs against the wall, and she marches toward the two women sitting at my counter.

"Please explain to me why the two of you are here," she half yells at them.

Jane, my part-time employee who works the retail side of the barn, and I glance at each other and then back to the two women.

One of them, her name is Avery and she's married to my friend Ash, and the other I believe is his sister. They both stare at her like they know they are in trouble, but Avery takes a bite of her cider donut anyway and chews slowly.

It's then that I look over at Goldie and really take her in, ignoring how the sunlight is pouring in from behind her, illuminating her as if she's a blonde goddess.

She's wearing white shorts, a dark green shirt that is loose enough for me to see she has a tank top underneath it, and flip-flops. Her hair is pulled back into a ponytail, and I swear she has the largest emeralds I've ever seen in her ears. I can't help but laugh out loud at how out of place they are, and that's when she registers me.

Her eyes narrow, and her nostrils flare.

"And you," she says. I widen my arms on the counter

in front of her, and I suddenly realize they are her friends. I lean into them, anxious to hear what will come out of her mouth. "Don't talk to them." She points at me.

Gone is the girl who came to my door thanking me, introducing herself, and bringing a plant—in her place is a vixen.

The women's eyes widen in surprise at her outburst, and I just smirk at her. Her already angry composure levels up, and her cheeks flush red.

"I take it you've met," Avery says. She's the one married to my friend Will Ashton, and she's adorably pregnant. Good for them, I'm happy for them.

"Oh, we've met," she says, placing her hands on her hips and using a tone that has the two girls now sizing me up in a not-so-friendly way. "Juliet, what are you doing here?"

"Eating donuts?" she says, but it comes out more as a question. She holds up the donut in her hand and takes another huge bite.

"You can eat donuts in other places in town. You don't have to come here!" I think if she was anywhere else, she would have stomped her foot. "You know what he did to me just last week. You're both fraternizing with the enemy."

"The enemy?" I chuckle, and at that moment, I swear

if Goldie's eyes were laser beams, she would have flayed me on the spot when she pins them on me.

Her two friends look at each other, they look at Goldie, and then back at me.

Avery sets down her donut, and before me, her posture changes as she swipes her hands together to brush away any remaining crumbs.

"What did you do?" she asks very accusingly.

"Yeah, what did you do?" Jane asks. I'd forgotten she was standing next to me, and as I glance at her, I immediately see she's taken sides with them. Her arms are crossed over her chest, and her face is curious and displeased. Jane was a friend of my mother's, and ever since Mom passed, she's watched over me. Of course I don't need her to, but I allow it because I know it would make my mother happy.

"Nothing that Goldie here didn't do to me," I tell them all innocently.

"Ha! You can't compare two little rubber snakes to eighteen deer!" She flings her hand back toward her property.

"Is that how many eventually showed up?" I rub my chin and nod my head like I'm impressed with myself, when even I know that's a lot.

"Why would you attract deer to her yard?" Jane asks, and then she looks at Goldie. "By the way, I'm Jane, dear.

If you ever need anything, you just stop on by. I'm here Wednesday through Sunday, ten to three."

"Oh." Goldie's taken aback by her kindness. "Thank you. I'm Cora, the new neighbor across the road. It's nice to know that not everyone here is a Neanderthal." She shoots me another death glare, and Jane snorts.

"Explain yourself." Jane waves her hand at me like I'm to proceed, and I stand straight. My gaze finds Goldie's, and her cheeks splotch red.

"I was just returning the hospitality."

Her friend Juliet snorts while Avery silently picks up her donut and takes another bite.

Dismissing me, Goldie turns toward her friends. "I thought we were meeting at the nursery?"

"Well, Avery got a craving, so here we are. We figured you could meet us for a snack, and then we'd just all go together."

"And this is the snack you needed?" she asks Avery.

Avery just nods, her blonde curls moving with her head. "They're so good," she whispers as if we can't all hear her.

"Darn right, they are. Best in the county," Jane says. "I make them fresh to order. They're always warm and full of delicious flavors. You'll have to come back"—she glances at me and then over to Goldie—"another day when this one is working up the mountain, and we'll visit together."

"Okay," Goldie says to pacify her, but what she really means is when hell freezes over. I may not know her well, but I do know after the refusal of her plant and the deer, I doubt she'll ever come over here for a visit.

Surprisingly, an unknown, somber emotion flickers in my chest at that thought. This has me scowling, and Goldie misinterprets the expression, assuming I don't want her coming over to see Jane. She scowls right back.

"Are you two ready yet?"

They nod and pack up their donuts. Goldie storms out the door, not even giving me a second glance. Avery places a twenty dollar bill on the counter and waves off Jane as she attempts to get her change. She shoves a large bottle of water and her donuts into her bag, and the two shoot me one more glare as they leave.

Silence engulfs us, and next to me, Jane turns and pops up one brow.

I let out a deep sigh and lift my hat to run my hand through my hair before putting it back on.

"She had it coming," I tell her, defending myself.

"Did she?" She tilts her head, eyes narrowing.

Ignoring her, I grab the water I came in for, spin around, and storm out the back door. The last thing I need is another woman giving me a hard time.

I first met Will and Clay almost five years ago, not long after I bought the orchard. I had gone to Smokey's, the bar locals frequent at night, when they were just starting to become known. I'd watched them play a set, and when they wandered over to the bar to talk to the owner, Rich, he introduced us. Since then, I've run into them a few times, but that's it. They've made a big name for themselves and work hard to keep their lives private. I respect that one hundred percent.

I also know that Ash's wife, Avery, is in the music industry. While I don't listen to pop music very often, even I have heard of Avery, Emma, and Cora. My stomach tightens and then dips at the connection.

I'm an idiot.

One hundred percent a complete idiot.

I should have put it together sooner with all the cello music floating around the mountain.

As I pull my phone from my back pocket, I realize I don't know her last name, but it hits me to look at Avery's social media accounts. Since they're friends and work together, she'll certainly be tagged in one or two posts, but I'm surprised when the page finally opens, and she isn't in just a couple but at least half of them. Some of the pictures are casual, but some are from performances, and she looks so beautiful that it takes my breath away.

"No shit," I mumble to myself as I stop walking and stare at the images, feeling annoyed that I'm a little bit in awe of her.

Avery, Emma, and Cora, the superstar music trio.

How did I not put this together sooner? All signs were pointing and glaring at the obvious. In addition to Ash, I'd seen Emma around town with Clay. If someone told me Dan from Dan and Shay had moved to town, and I met someone named Shay, I'd do a double take. The same with the Avett Brothers. If Scott Avett moved to town, and suddenly, there was a newcomer named Seth, I'd question it. So why didn't I when I heard the name Cora? She even looks like a superstar with her long, toned legs and perfect blonde hair, and as much as I don't want to fan over her, in a way, I am.

My feet start moving again as I continue to walk back toward the trees and scroll through the pictures. There are so many of them that it's a feast for my eyes, and an out-of-character wave of remorse hits me. I'm trying hard not to feel inadequate about how I behaved around her or turned on by what I've seen, but I'm failing. I can't imagine very many people have seen her naked.

Well, almost naked.

But I have, and unconsciously, I wipe my hand over

my face and quickly let the flashbacks of her gorgeous body play through my mind.

Tapping on one of the images, I see she's tagged and click over to her page. Cora Rhodes. That's her name. Her buying a house here in Horizons Valley now makes complete sense. Both of her friends are here. But why didn't she buy down on the lake like every other vacationer?

Then I go to Google and type in her name. Alongside all of her music accolades are articles about her and her family.

I stop walking again.

Her father is Richard Rhodes. Son of Winston Rhodes Sr. It turns out I know their names as well. Richard became an American billionaire after being recently appointed chair and CEO of Rhodes, a privately held, family-run business that his father started in New York City that develops and manages real estate. He is said to be one of the biggest landlords in the New York Tri-State area. His son, also named Winston, is his number two.

Huh.

It takes a lot to surprise me, but this here did it. It's more plausible to me to have a music star living next door than this wealthy Upper East Side princess.

Maybe I don't feel so bad after all.

I can't help but shake my head. I'm not even sure what for either. It's not like we were going to be friends. And now my behavior makes more sense. I'm not usually unkind to people, but clearly, my instincts were taking over when it comes to her. Aside from the pop star fame, after years and years of living in the same type of world, I'm familiar with her type: rich, pretentious, fake.

8

CORA

I'm still fuming when we reach the nursery, and I don't know why. Is it because I was forced to see his face today, and I wasn't prepared? Is it a little because I feel like my friends betrayed me by consorting with the enemy? Or is it because my feelings are hurt that he's apparently nice to everyone else, just not me? I did nothing but try to be neighborly, and he's the worst neighbor ever.

As I breathe in the late summer air that's humid but clean, I realize after my run-in with him that being at a nursery is exactly what I need. This nursery is new to me. I thought the two I had found were it, but this one Juliet brought us to is just one town over, and it's so cute. The anger coursing through me suddenly drifts away, and my heart overflows with distraction by the potential for my yard and my porch.

"How did you find this place?" I ask her, looking at the sample back porch they have decorated and displayed. It's just calling me to go sit and stay a while.

"Don't forget, I'm from here," she says as she runs her fingers over the bright yellow petals of a mum plant. I already know I'll be back next month as I prepare to decorate for fall. The possibilities feel endless.

"You do realize there's not much summer left for plants. You're going to spend all this money, and then they'll die in just a few months," Avery says. She's not surprised that we're here. After all, she knows me, but she knows nothing about plants.

"We're not here for this summer. We're here for next spring. I want to buy some daffodil bulbs to plant at the entrance of my driveway. I'm also considering them for around the perimeter of the yard. I read that deer don't like them."

Juliet chuckles, and Avery turns away. After we left the cider house, Juliet filled her in on Briggs's prank, which she thought was hilarious.

"I know, I know. You think what he did was funny. And if I step back and stand in your shoes, I would think so too. But still, he's insufferable."

He had some nerve to stand there in front of my

friends and act like they were his. With his dumb hat on backward, his T-shirt perfectly molding to his chest, and his white teeth that peeked out every time he smirked at me . . . I want to punch him in his pretty face.

"You did start this," Juliet reminds me, and I hum in agreement.

"I would argue that he started it by being the rudest person on the planet. You should have seen the disgusted way he looked at my poor ZZ plant. I mean, what did the plant ever do to him?"

"Maybe he really doesn't like plants," Avery offers.

I stop and look at them both. "Did you not notice the two big cut-open wine barrels overflowing with flowers on his front porch or the ones next to the cider house doors?"

"Those repurposed wine barrels did look pretty good," Juliet says.

"Okay, well, maybe he has a groundskeeper, a lawn guy, or someone who maintains them?" Avery says.

"Or maybe we call a spade a spade. He's a grade A jerk." I frown.

Neither of them says anything after this. Instead, they watch me prowl around the nursery.

Eventually, Juliet asks, "So if we're just here for daffodils, then why are you grabbing all of these extra plants?"

I glance down at the flatbed cart to the two large Boston ferns and the large pot filled with rosemary. I didn't even realize I was picking up other plants, but how can I not? They all look so wonderful.

It's then, a light bulb goes off.

"You know what I need? A greenhouse!" I declare to both of them.

A greenhouse and a garden in the backyard sound like heaven to me, and with the greenhouse, I could have plants all year.

"A greenhouse?" Avery pops an eyebrow at me. "That would mean you plan on spending more time here than in the city. The maintenance would be hard. And what about if we're traveling for work?"

My gaze shifts down to Avery's stomach as she's unconsciously rubbing the tiny bump, and then it rises back to her face. I stare at her blankly, and she laughs.

"Yeah, maybe you're right. Quick trips. But don't you want to spend some time in the city? You've always loved it."

I have always loved it, but what did I love about it? Is it because I was raised there? Is it because it's familiar? Also, am I hanging on to how it felt when the three of us were there together? Things have been different since Avery moved here to be with Ash, and Emma to be with Clay.

I let out a deep sigh. Her question is a question I've been asking myself over the past couple of weeks. How much time do I plan to spend here? What is meant to be a vacation home is starting to feel more like a real home. Don't get me wrong, the condo and the house are about the same size in square footage, so it's not like I suddenly feel I have all this space, but I love how I'm not surrounded by others.

I've also been thinking about our schedules. Emma wants to be in the city in the summer and here at the lake in the winter. I want to be here in the summer and the city in the winter. How will that work if we're trying to write new music? And then I ask myself, do I really want to be in the city if they're both here? And the baby. I want to be a part of its life. How can I do that if I'm living there and Avery is here? I hate to admit it, but I already feel closer to Avery's child than I do to Winston's.

That's right, Winston has a son. But I only see him on our annual family trip between Christmas and New Year's. For the rest of the year, either I'm not invited to family functions or he's hidden. He's only four, but maybe they think I'll rub off on him.

"I do love the city, but I feel different here and like it," I tell them both without pouring out my soul.

"Besides, I could always hire someone to help if I needed it."

Hiring someone. Just the thought makes me cringe. I love my space, and I love that I'm able to do things on my own. Right now, the only thing I've hired out for is someone to mow the grass, but give me time. By next summer, I'll be able to do that too.

"You know he looks like your type," Avery says as we resume wandering and turn down a new row. This row has the tiny wind chimes, and my heart leaps.

"My type of what?" I ask her.

"Guy," she says as she pulls her water bottle from her bag and takes a sip.

At this, my heart stutters. I stop pushing the cart and turn to face her. "Please tell me you're joking."

She laughs. "I'm not. In fact, he kind of looks like that football player from the Tampa Tarpons you were with last year."

"He does not," I declare, a flush burning its way through my cheeks.

"Let's see." She holds up her hand to tick off her fingers. "Tall. Muscular. Dark haired. Scruffy beard."

I think about what she's saying, then shake my head. "Nope. Not similar at all. And Timothy was more like a teddy bear than an actual grumpy bear coming out of hibernation."

"You think Briggs is grumpy?" Juliet asks.

I turn to face her, shocked. "You don't?"

"No. He seemed fine today. I told you he's always friendly to the people in town, and the few times I've seen him, he's been super nice to Bryce and me."

"By that, you mean super phony and a fraud. He's not nice."

"I don't know, I've been living in this town longer than the two of you, and I've never heard anyone say anything bad about him."

I scoff and move to the wind chimes.

"Maybe it's just you." Avery laughs, her eyes twinkling like she's in on a private joke that I'm not privy to.

Maybe it is just me, but why? Usually, people love me, and other than the screaming the night we met, I haven't done anything wrong for him to react to me the way he has. Images of him scowling at me in my yard and at his front door flash through my mind.

"Do either of you know anything about him?" I ask, picking up a small chime with a dragonfly on it and suddenly feeling the need to know some dirt on him.

"Have you looked him up or looked at any of his social media pages?" Avery asks.

"He doesn't strike me as the type of person to post on Instagram." I place the wind chime on the cart.

It suddenly occurs to me that while I have been

keeping shovels and tools on the back porch, I need a shed. I'm actually surprised the house doesn't have one. Maybe it did at one point, but they got rid of it when they decided to sell.

"Well, he doesn't, but Cole does. Cole Mahoney works for him. He's a very nice guy, just got married and his wife is one of Bryce's teachers. Cole runs sales and marketing for the orchard. I follow the orchard, and I think there's a lot of information about him. A few news articles will pop up, too, with awards he's won for his ciders and the different charitable contributions he's made around town."

"He also doesn't strike me as the type of guy to hand out money." I glance at Avery.

"I think he comes from money," Juliet says.

"Perfect. Another strike in his column. I've known enough guys who come from money over the years to know that they are not worth the effort. Arrogant, always think they're right, and better than everyone else. No, thank you."

"I don't know. I feel like we're stereotyping him, and we don't even know him," Avery says, waving her hand in the air at a bee that's come too close to her. I hear what she's saying because I'm certain I could be stereo-typed too.

But still.

"If he comes from money, then I know enough. Don't forget, money is my world."

Just thinking about Winston and some of his friends I've endured over the years causes my stomach to clench from nausea. I know my parents don't realize this, but sending me to Juilliard and not some elite Ivy League college was one of the best things they've ever done. Being surrounded by people my age who didn't care about surname financial portfolios and whose yacht is bigger was like discovering a whole new world.

"What we need to do is come up with more pranks," I tell them, feeling a renewed purpose after our run-in with him this morning. "He may think I'm just some helpless woman after how we met that first night, but I'm not."

Returning the hospitality. I'll show him hospitality.

"We could butter his steps," Avery says like it's the most common thing ever.

Juliet and I both turn to look at her. "Butter his steps?"

I try to picture myself with a large tub of butter and rubber gloves, scooping out the butter and smearing it across his steps.

"Yeah, so when he walks out, he slips and falls."

Juliet and I laugh.

"Oh my God, but what if he hurts himself? I don't think I want to take it that far."

Or worse yet, what if that sweet little lady Jane was to attempt entering the house, and she slipped and fell. That would be awful.

Avery just shrugs.

"Oh, I know," Juliet says, all excited. "We could put a For Sale sign at the base of the road. I could also hang a listing in the window at the office on Main Street and maybe a few flyers around town."

A For Sale sign . . . hmm.

"I love that idea. There's also the classic 'honk and wave' bumper sticker. Can you imagine him driving around town and all these people honking at him? He's the least friendly person I've ever met, and with people waving at him, the scowl he apparently hides from everyone else would come out in full force, exposing him for the fraud he is."

"No, I can't imagine people constantly honking at me. I think I'd jump every time, afraid I was about to hit someone." Juliet grimaces.

"I think it's funny," Avery says, grinning. "Or you could send him a glitter bomb."

A laugh barks out of me at just the thought of him opening a pink and gold glitter bomb and it going off all over him and his porch. But then again, what if he didn't open it on the porch but in his house. That would be such a mess, but I don't dismiss the idea. Instead, I file it away for later.

"I say, let's start with the For Sale sign. Maybe he'll get an offer he can't refuse and take the hint and move."

BRIGGS

She thinks she's so smart.

I'll give her credit for the sale listing. It was genius, and I wish I had thought of it. I also wish it hadn't taken me so long to catch on to what was happening. I started receiving calls at the cider house asking if I was the person to speak to regarding the property for sale. Each time, I told them no, that they had the wrong number, thinking that there must be an error somewhere with my number, but after about the tenth call, I asked which property they were referring to, and they said mine. Of course, I was confused at first, but then I saw red and laughed.

Wouldn't she just love that so much? Little does she know that I have zero plans to move away from here anytime soon.

After that, Cole spotted the sign at the base of the road, and Graham saw the listing in the window at the real estate agent's office. He called me confused by what he was looking at, and then instead of storming the office demanding to know who did this, I politely called them and told them I'd changed my mind. I didn't want to get whoever hung it up in trouble, accomplice or not.

"Are you sure this is a good idea?" Cole whispers as he looks around Goldie's front yard. Although I don't know what he's whispering for. It's lunchtime, and he knows that no one else, besides her and me, lives here.

"Absolutely. She started this war, and I have no interest in waving the white flag and letting her win."

For the past two days, I've been anxiously waiting for her to leave her house, and she finally left fifteen minutes ago. I can no longer hear her car, so even if she was to return because she forgot something, we would hear her car coming up the road.

I've realized that she doesn't go to many places, and she spends a lot of time alone. I've wondered if she's dating anyone, but over the past couple of weeks, no one has come to see her other than her two friends or a delivery truck. Of course this means I'm paying way too much attention to her, but I can't seem to stop. I don't know what it is, but even knowing who she is and where she comes from, I'm still intrigued by her. I can't help but find myself wondering about her and wanting to know more.

Of course, this feeling absolutely aggravates me, as I vowed after Adele that I would never fall for a vapid princess again, which is another reason why I'm here right now. I want to piss her off too.

Walking up the front porch of Goldie's house, I do a sweep for any cameras she might have set up for personal safety. I find none and instantly feel irritated that she's bought this house, is living by herself, and hasn't felt the need to add this basic layer of protection.

Looking around the porch, she's done a nice job with it. It looks inviting and very homey, something I wouldn't expect from her, a rich princess. There are rocking chairs on both sides of the door. Each has a small table to hold a drink and a plate. She has plants hanging in the corners, flower baskets along the railing, and even a wind chime.

Just out of caution, I knock on her door even though I know she's not home.

Nothing.

Now, do I know if she has an alarm on the inside? No. But I guess we're about to find out.

I slip the key into the lock, and sure enough, the deadbolt slides, and the door rattles, letting me know it'll open.

This also pisses me off because she has no idea how many people might have a key to this house, and she didn't even have the afterthought to have the locks changed once she moved in.

"I'm thinking I shouldn't be here for this. I don't feel comfortable sneaking into her house," Cole says, looking around all nervously like a SWAT team is about to jump out and arrest us.

"You aren't supposed to be going into the house. You're on car watch," I remind him.

"But still, this feels wrong."

I let out a deep sigh.

"Then go ahead and leave," I tell him. My plan is to get in and out. I'm not going to be here long, and I definitely don't need any assistance. Besides, it's not like breaking and entering in North Carolina is a felony. It's just a misdemeanor. Even then, I'm not here with the intent to commit a felony. I'm just playing a prank with a key I already have to the house. I'm certain a judge would see my side. Especially if they knew what she had done.

"Yeah, okay. I'm out." He turns and skips down the steps and heads back down the driveway to my house. "I'll call you if I hear anything."

Rolling my eyes, I push the door open and stare inside. I'm not sure why in my mind the house still looked the same as when Mrs. Benson was here, but it doesn't. She's completely transformed the inside, modernized it, and although I don't know her well, it looks just like her.

It looks incredible.

The living room has a large black-and-white-patterned throw rug and a plush navy velvet couch. The fireplace has been whitewashed and perfectly placed details are everywhere: the curtains, the lights, the artwork, and the plants. She has more plants than I have time to count.

Does it look like too many plants? Not necessarily if you like that sort of thing, but seeing all this makes me understand why she brought me one.

My phone buzzes in my pocket. Pulling it out, I see it's Cole.

"What?" I ask him. It's been three minutes since he left, and instant adrenaline rushes through me to think that she might be headed back and he's spotted her.

"Where are you putting it?" he asks.

"That's why you're calling me?"

"Yes."

"Cole, if you wanted to know that, then you should have stayed." I look around the living room for the most inconspicuous place.

"Don't you feel just the slightest bit bad about this?"

"No. Why would I? It's not like I'm damaging or stealing anything."

"If you say so," he drawls out, and then he hangs up on me.

I roll my eyes.

Shoving my phone back into my pocket, I find my interest switches from get in and get out to one of curiosity. I would be lying if I said I hadn't researched her more, but it seems the more I learn about her, the more of a puzzle she is.

This doesn't look like the home I would expect from a rich New York socialite. It doesn't even look like a home I would expect from the wealthy Southern socialites I grew up with. It doesn't look like the home of a world-famous pop star cellist, nor does it look like a home for a single person.

What does a house look like in all of these scenarios? I don't know, but it's not this. This house looks straight out of an upscale farmhouse magazine.

Stopping, I stare at the painting on the wall. The navy-blue couch is really the only thing that's bright with color. It's a painting of a garden. There are some vegetables, but there are a lot of flowers too. The sky is a pale shade of blue, and my heart twinges because I know that my mother would have loved this painting too.

Of course her personal belongings are lying around everywhere, but aside from the painting, what catches my eye is the cello lying across the couch and the music sheets haphazardly strewn across the table in front of it. Some are blank, and some have handwritten notes scratched onto the page.

Outside of the first night when I heard her playing the theme song for *Indiana Jones*, she's played every night since then. Some are full pieces and others are broken up sections, and now I know why. She's composing.

I've never known a musician, at least not one like this, who is a professional. Is it difficult to write music, or does it just come to her? Aside from her shrieking and, in general, being a pain in my ass and wondering what stunt she's going to pull next, I do have a large amount of admiration and respect for her and her chosen profession. She may be a rich princess, but she's not sitting around being lazy or pampered and spending exorbitant amounts of money. She's got some drive and ambition that's not normally found in girls of her class. Even my ex, when I think about her existence now, she was lazy and kind of a waste of space.

Moving from the living room, I walk into her kitchen and open her refrigerator. She's got fruits, vegetables, eggs, bags of salad, a few Tupperware containers that look like leftovers, a hodgepodge of random things, and cans of sparkling water. Her counter is clean, but there's a bowl of blackberries, and I can't help but smirk.

"So she went back out there after all. Good for her."

When I open her pantry, I find a bunch of regular stored items and four large boxes of Cheez-Its. I glance back toward the living room and find a box there as well.

My phone buzzes, and again, my heart jumps into my throat.

"Cole," I answer.

"Are you still there?"

A wave of guilt passes by me as I remember why I'm here and that I definitely should not still be in her house snooping around.

"I'm almost done. Is she coming back?"

"No. Just curious, where did you hide it?"

"You know, if you had just stayed, you would know."

But then again, if he had stayed, I wouldn't have had this opportunity to take a peek into her life.

Glancing around the living room, I zero in on a large plant she has in the corner. Perfect. It'll echo.

"Plant. I have to go." This time, I hang up before he can say anything else.

Crossing the room, I glance toward the stairs, and my eyes stick on the pictures hanging on the wall. At least two dozen, all in bronze frames, must climb with the stairs. Not being able to help myself, I make my way over and inspect each one. Most of the pictures are of her and her friends performing, winning awards, on vacation, and at Ash's wedding. There's one of her solo performing in black concert attire, there are two of her family, where none of them look happy, and there's one of a little girl sitting on her lap.

Of course Goldie is beautiful in all of these pictures.

Looking around, I can't help but think that maybe over the last couple of weeks, I've misjudged her. I know how that feels and should probably attempt to do better.

But even then, doing better will not stop me from planting this device.

Moving to the corner plant, I pull the small white device from my pocket and flip the switch on. It chirps, and my lips curve up in a victory. The battery will only last a few days, but I can sneak back in to replace it every now and then. Peeling the paper off the back to free the adhesive, I lean down and press it to the back side of the planter. It chirps again, and I chuckle. Is there anything more annoying than a cricket you can't find? With the sound playing irregularly every two to fifteen minutes, it'll be hard to find.

Standing back, I look around one more time, then get the hell out.

10

CORA

All morning, I've been hearing cars going up and down the road and people laughing. Juliet mentioned she was coming up this weekend to bring Bryce to Briggs's opening weekend, and I had to admit I had no idea what she was talking about. Of course this is when she teased me about being a recluse and not in touch with reality. Apparently, there are advertisements for his orchard all over town and a large sign at the base of our road, right where our For Sale sign was. She explained that he throws this party every year to promote his "You Pick" apple orchard.

I'll admit it's a great idea and a good way to gain some publicity, but it sounds like Briggs is having the biggest party ever, and it's only ten in the morning. Wandering outside, I stand on the porch and glance toward his house. Of course I can't see anything since the trees line the road and block the view, but it doesn't stop me from staring in that general direction. The weather is mildly warm, and there's no cloud in sight. The perfect day for this.

"The perfect day not to be inside my house," I say to myself as I settle into one of the rocking chairs. It seems a cricket has found its way in, and I can't find it. It's not making a lot of noise, but it's frequent enough to make me want to pull my hair out. I've looked for it, but I can't find it. It's a shame too because I would rescue it and set it free. As it is, I suspect it's in my house until it dies.

Was I planning on going to the party? No. But by the time Juliet and Bryce arrive, I'll admit, I'd grown to be fifty-fifty annoyed and intrigued. The murmuring voices sound happy, and the children are laughing. Throwing in the towel, I decide to go, so together, the three of us walk down the driveway toward my nemesis.

Will I see him?

Will he ask me to leave?

At this point, I would say that's a viable option.

"Mom, I'm so excited for the donuts," Bryce says as he skips ahead of us. "Do you think he'll have caramel apples like last year?"

Bryce has gotten taller. Every time I see this kid, it's like his legs get lankier, and his feet get bigger.

"I'm not sure, but this is an apple orchard, so I'd say the odds are high," she tells him, ruffling his hair.

It's been a little over a week since the last time I was here, and every morning around ten, I think of Jane's offer to come over and visit with her. I do wonder about the donuts, and by now, I'm not sure if I'm avoiding them out of principle or stubbornness.

"You know I haven't had any of these famous donuts yet," I tell them, and they both turn to look at me like I'm crazy.

"Ms. Cora, you are missin' out," Bryce says at the same time Juliet says, "Why not? You basically have direct access to them twenty-four seven. I can't imagine living this close to them. We would be eating them every morning, and well, the hips don't lie. Everyone would know why I look the way I do."

I laugh.

"Stop. First off, you are beautiful. Second, you know you'd eventually get sick of them." Although, if they're as good as everyone says, I can see how craving them daily with a hot cup of coffee could become problematic.

"Ms. Cora, no one could ever get sick of these donuts."

Rounding the corner, I'm shocked to see so many cars. There must be at least fifty, and they are parked up and down the road in a field he opened on his side of the mountain just before his house. Usually, our mountain is so quiet, but today, it's bustling with people and just feels strange. I've gotten so used to the quiet and the lack of people that I'm not sure about this. I know it's wrong to feel like this is an invasion. After all, this is his business, and I don't own the whole mountain, but still.

"I can't believe how many people are here for this," I tell her as we step onto his property and head toward the cider house, where there seems to be a crowd.

"Yeah, it was like this last year, too. Bryce and I were in town deciding whether to move back or not, and I needed an escape from my parents' house. Before that, I don't know. We were still in Nashville."

"Do you miss it?" I ask her, watching her to see her reaction.

She pauses and then says, "I'm not sure. I've been thinking about that a lot lately. When I first left, I wanted excitement and the freedom of a new place and living in a big city, but I don't feel like I'm missing that now. I thought I would. Yes, I love Nashville, but there's something about being here with my family and friends, and having Bryce grow up in a town like this."

I completely understand what she's saying. I grew up in a giant city, went to a wealthy private school, and had everything money could afford, but I didn't have this.

This place makes the heart feel different, warmer, at ease.

The quote, "Home isn't a place, it's a feeling," I finally understand it.

"Mom, can I go play?" Bryce asks, breaking me from my thoughts. He's pulling on her hand and points toward some kiddie activities set up on the other side of the main house and in an open part of the orchard.

"Yep, just let me know where you're going if you decide to do something different and check in frequently, so I don't worry."

"Okay. I'm going to go jump. Nathan's there."

Juliet glances toward the bounce houses and sees a woman she recognizes. They wave at each other, and Bryce runs toward her.

"A friend from school?"

"Yes, a new friend. The family is nice. She's only asked me about my brothers and y'all maybe three times." She laughs.

I grab her arm and stop her.

"People ask you about us?"

She shrugs one shoulder. "Of course they do."

I frown. "It never even occurred to me that they would. I'm sorry."

"Nah, no biggie. I'm used to it. Just you wait. The

mom will find her way over here at some point to meet you."

"Should I feel flattered or annoyed?" I ask as we resume walking. I'm glad I'm wearing sunglasses, as the later in the morning it gets, the brighter it gets, and they give me a little bit of a secure feeling like I'm hiding. Ridiculous, I know, but still effective.

"Let's go with flattered. From what I've seen over the years, people tend to gawk more than approach, so if she actually has the nerve to come over, then good for her."

"I suppose, you just tell me what you need," I say to her. Yes, we've had fans over the years approach us, but not so much recently. We've slowed down on performances over this last year, so mostly people just stare, and here in Horizons Valley, they've respected our privacy.

"Thank you," she says. "Oh, look! There's your favorite person being interviewed."

Speaking of staring, it's a shame that I dislike him so much because now that Avery has planted the seed, I think she's right. He is my type, and he looks good today. Standing just outside of the cider house, he's tall, commanding, and appears comfortable at the same time. He's wearing black denim pants, black work boots, and a white button-down untucked with the Red Barn Orchard logo embroidered over his heart and the sleeves rolled up. His hair is styled, and his beard is trimmed. He looks straight out of a *Men's Journal* mountain man magazine.

Briggs's eyes flicker over the reporter's shoulder and lock on me. Usually, this is when the scowl drops in place, but today, all I get is a twitch, a once-over as his gaze drags over the length of me, and a neutral expression. So that's how it's going to be. He has to play nice to maintain his businessman image. He can't see my eyes behind these shades, but a slow smile twists onto my lips, and his nostrils flare in response.

The news anchor interviewing him realizes she's being momentarily ignored and turns to see what's caught his attention. Her face lights up. "Well, if it isn't Cora Rhodes," she beams loudly. The cameraman whips around to follow her lead, and I swear so does everyone else in a twenty-yard radius. She quickly walks to where she's standing directly in front of me and forcefully extends her hand. "I'm Jessica Smith from channel eight news. We're here to capture Briggs's opening weekend event for an around-town segment we're airing tonight. Do you mind if I ask you a few questions?"

Pasting on a smile I perfected at a young age, I return her handshake and tell her, "Of course. Ask away."

Briggs then moves to stand next to me, halfway

scowling. Maybe more like grimacing. It's not like I'm purposely trying to steal his thunder, but I don't hate that this is an in-his-face moment where he sees that people actually like me. I smile up at him, as he's perfectly angled behind me, and he wipes the expression off his face. Removing my sunglasses to make this interview more genuine, deep brown eyes bore into mine, and unwittingly, my stomach swirls at his nearness.

Juliet squeezes my hand to pull my attention. I totally forgot she was there. Actually, I forgot everyone was here at the moment. "I'm going to go find Bryce. I'll see you in a bit."

"Okay." I nod at her, and as she walks away, she turns back once to grin at me and wiggle her brows.

And just what is she grinning at? I narrow my eyes.

"All right," Jessica says, turning to face the camera-man. He shifts into place to capture all three of us, and she shimmies her body to make sure her outfit is lying flat.

"Joining the festivities today is Cora Rhodes. You may know her from the musical group Avery, Emma, and Cora, and we are delighted to catch a few moments with her." She angles toward me and shoves her micro-phone in my face. "Cora, we hear you recently moved to Horizons Valley. How are you finding it so far?"

Annoyance flashes under my skin. What does this have to do with anything? She's out here because she's supposed to be showcasing Red Barn Orchard, and with this one question, this suddenly feels like a different kind of interview. Briggs must think the same as the air stiffens between us.

"I love it. The town and the people have been *so* welcoming." I tilt my head and smile sweetly up at Briggs. He smirks at my sarcasm, thinking I'm funny. Then again, only he would pick up on the sarcasm as it's directed to him. I turn back to face her. "And I love events like this. I first heard of Red Barn Orchard from my friend Will Ashton on the Fourth of July, and of course I had to come and try their famous cider donuts. They're delicious, and I'd be lying if I said I haven't been here more than once."

Her eyes flare at the mention of Ash, and she's so proud of herself for talking to me. You can see she's like the cat who got the cream.

"So would you say that Red Barn Orchard has become one of your favorite local spots?" she asks, digging. Should I say yes? I don't know. I do want to so that maybe Briggs will get more business, but at the same time, I don't. I don't really want a bunch of strangers wandering up our mountain because they've discovered where I live.

I glance at him quickly, but he gives nothing away.

"I would say that Jane, who runs the cider house and makes the delicious donuts, is the sweetest person here, and everyone should definitely come out and see her."

My tone lets her know I don't want to be asked any more questions. This was quite possibly the fastest interview ever, but she crossed a line twice. Seeing the tension suddenly emanating from the two of us, she takes her cue.

"Thank you, Cora, and there you have it! Jane and her cider donuts are some of the best and sweetest in town. But don't forget to sample the hard ciders, grab some apple butter or other pastries, and pick some apples while you're at Red Barn Orchard. 'Tis the season, and I don't know about you, but it's time for a hand pie." She winks at the camera, and then it's lowered.

"Wow, that was perfect timing." She turns to beam at me.

"Sure was," I say back, still smiling but dripping with sarcasm.

Something brushes my lower back, and I glance down to see it's Briggs's hand. With the few interactions we've had, the only time he's touched me is when he tried to keep me from falling by the blackberry bush. While I don't remember much of that, I certainly feel his fingertips now sparking a weird sensation through my thin shirt and into my skin.

"I'm glad you're here. I have your order," he says, gently pushing me to move. "Thank you, Jessica, for stopping by," he says to her. Without waiting for a reply, we leave those standing around watching and start walking away.

"It was nice to meet you, Cora," she calls after us, and I wave my hand in return without looking back. The crowd around us has grown, and a twinge of unease makes me momentarily nervous. Is it a problem for him that I'm here? Does he feel the need to shuffle me away to prevent any kind of fangirl scene?

Then I hear her tell the cameraman that they need to get a few seconds of clips of people picking apples, drinking the cider, and the kids playing.

The moment is over.

"Rude much?" I mumble to him as he steers me not into the cider house but around the outside of it. I could be talking about him or her, or both, I don't know.

He doesn't answer, but as we keep moving, I'm not unaware of his long muscular legs as they walk next to mine or the heat of his large hand as it remains on my back. I don't know where we're going, and surprisingly, whether he was rude or not, I'm not unhappy about it.

11

———

BRIGGS

I love the opening weekend of the "You Pick" season. Every year, we spend months getting ready with the different flavors of cider, the take-home jams, jellies, and butters, and making sure the property is in tip-top shape. We also plan a few extra fun things to entice people to come out, like food trucks, live music, and three bounce houses for kids. Outside of the fall festival weekend, this is our second-largest revenue day.

What I don't love is being ambushed by reporters.

I know this is the wrong attitude to take, that Jessica coming out here really had good intentions, but she's irritating, and I hate running into her around town. I also just, in general, loathe reporters.

Growing up, my family was frequently followed and always photographed. It would be one thing if what they reported was accurate, but the content was almost always grossly inflated or just fake news. And unfortunately, too many people believe what they say.

Goldie is silent as she walks next to me. Then again, I'm not sure what I expect her to say. She did me a solid by not talking about herself and bringing the story back to the orchard. Who knows, maybe if I'm lucky, this clip with her will reach beyond Horizons Valley and bring in more customers.

As we round the cider house, maybe thirty yards away, is the large red barn that warehouses the cider production. It wasn't originally red, but I figured with the name and the branding, it should be.

"Thank you," I say to her as we walk by a few people who've been to tour it, and I hope she hears the sincerity.

She glances my way, and I watch her pinch her lips together out of the corner of my eye.

"I'm surprised they let you out of the house today to actually speak with people."

I can't tell if she's teasing or if she's serious. Then again, I've never given her a reason to think differently.

"Me?" I smile down at her. "You're the one who instantly drew a crowd. Do you have this problem everywhere you go? Is that why you never leave your house?"

It never occurred to me not to let her know that I

know her comings and goings, but when her head jerks to look up at me, I think maybe I should have kept that to myself. Her eyes trail over my face, and then she peels them off me to look straight ahead.

"How do you know when I leave? Have you been watching out for me?" she teases, pink dots blooming on her cheeks.

I don't say anything because the truth is, I have. Don't ask me why, but I've paid unnecessary attention to any movement that comes from her house.

"Or should I say stalking me?"

"Don't flatter yourself. You know as well as I do that sounds echo around the mountain. A car engine can be heard from a mile away."

"Charming as always," she mutters.

"I'll have you know I have a special superpower where I can charm anyone," I tell her, and I do. It's part of the reason my father and my brother all but demand I stick around. Maybe it's my height or size, or maybe it's my don't-give-a-shit attitude, but whatever it is, people gravitate toward me, and I've mastered how to play the game.

"Is that what you were doing while swearing at me the night we met, charming me? Tsk tsk, Warren, someone lied to you."

Of course she would bring up that night.

"I'll admit, that wasn't me at my finest."

She snorts. "You can say that again."

My hand drops from her back, and she steps away, eyeing me suspiciously.

Deciding to change the subject, I ask with a smirk, "You've eaten my donuts?"

"Of course not." She scoffs, and my smirk falls.

"So you lied?"

She tucks a piece of her hair behind her ear, and this time, my eyes catch on the large gold flower earring. It's probably the size of a nickel and undoubtedly costs a fortune.

It's then I allow myself to take in the rest of her again.

When I first spotted her over Jessica's shoulder, I couldn't tear my eyes away. It's like the sun had cast a spotlight, and along with my eyes, both followed her. She isn't wearing anything flashy. On the contrary, she's in a denim button-down shirt with rolled sleeves, white shorts, and short worn cowboy boots. She's meant to look like everyone else here, only she doesn't. She shines.

"I don't know. Maybe I did; maybe I didn't. Everyone else seems to love them, so what does it matter if I just repeated their sentiment instead of voicing mine?"

An unwanted twinge pinches me in the chest. She's

been just across the street for a month and has yet to taste the donuts. Then again, if I had been a nicer neighbor, I would have brought some to her. It's not like they're hard to make.

My lips flatten together, and I hum instead of answering her.

"Where are we going?" she asks just as we're about to enter the barn.

"I thought I would give you a tour." I wave my hand toward the inside of the barn.

She stops to look at me. "Now?"

"Yes, now. Is that a problem for you?"

"No, it's fine," she says warily. "But don't you think you're needed somewhere else?" She resumes walking, and I follow.

I shrug. "We won't be gone all day. It's fine. Besides, I should have offered it to you sooner."

She mock gasps. "Briggs Warren, is this an apology for being a terrible neighbor?"

Listening to her say my full name does something to me. A swirling whips through my chest, and I'm not sure why.

"Listen, Goldie, I have nothing to apologize for," I spit out, feeling a rush of annoyance. Then again, I'm not sure if I'm annoyed with her or with me.

She looks over, and I look back. I've never given much thought to eye color before, especially not brown ones, but on her, I can't imagine anything else. Her brows draw down in a way that lets me know she didn't like my answer, but her eyes tell me her feelings are hurt.

Shit.

"And what do you have against plants?" she snaps, her hands falling to her hips.

"Nothing."

"Then why didn't you take mine?"

"I don't know."

When really I do know. Everyone has neighbors. I just wasn't prepared for my new one to look like her. I figured a nice older couple or a young family would be moving in, not this twentysomething bombshell who's created a mental distraction for me.

"Well, that's a dumb answer."

I let out a sigh.

"Literally, your job is trees. It's not like you have an aversion to green things. And a plant is nice. It's not one of those things you eat or drink, and then it's gone. You can appreciate the sentimentality of where it came from and who gave it to you."

I don't argue with her because she's not wrong.

I should have taken the plant.

"For what it's worth, the plant is safe and sound in the house. I didn't leave it out there or throw it away."

She looks at me and then looks away. "Maybe you have a few redeeming qualities after all."

"Hey, man. How did it go with Jessica?" Cole asks. He's standing just inside the barn to greet whoever may come in. He too is wearing a button-down with the orchard logo.

I glance at Goldie, and she blushes. I understand what it is like to go places and suddenly become the center of attention. It's happened enough during my lifetime back in Charlotte.

"It went well," I tell him as he comes to stand next to us. He's smiling at us like he knows a secret that we don't know, and his eyes skip back and forth between the two of us. I clear my throat.

"Cole, this is Cora. Cora, this is Cole."

"It's nice to meet you," he says, taking a step forward to shake her hand. He's got this nervous edge to him, and I can't tell if it's because of the cricket chirper or because of who she is.

"It's nice to meet you, too," she replies kindly.

Inwardly, I groan. She is kind. Kind to everyone but me. Then again, I deserve that.

"Cole and I work together here at Red Barn." I know a lot of business owners like to clout their title, but Cole has always gone above and beyond. Although technically, he does work for me, he's poured himself into the place, and it feels more appropriate to say he works with me. "He mainly focuses on parts of the business that I have no interest in, like marketing."

"Oh, that's great. I've looked at the website and the social media pages for the orchard. They look really good," she tells him.

And the idiot beams.

"Thank you," he says.

"I'm going to show her around. You can head up to the front for a bit if you want."

"Sounds good. I want to see if Amelia is here yet, too. Amelia is my wife." He smiles again like he's telling her he won the lottery. I can't imagine being that in love with someone. Truthfully, I can't imagine being in love at all. I've been down that road once, and in the end, I couldn't change directions fast enough.

I clap him on the shoulder, and he says goodbye as he jogs off.

"He seems nice," she taunts, watching him leave.

He is nice. The best. And he puts up with me.

"Come on, Goldie, let me show you around."

Inside the cidery, we walk to the wall where I have six stainless-steel fermentation vessels and a few smaller ones where we test out different flavors.

"It takes twelve to fifteen pounds of apples to make one gallon of cider. Fermented apple juice is called hard cider, while freshly pressed, non-alcoholic cider is called sweet cider. Currently, we have four standard flavors that come from Red Barn Orchard, and then we experiment with seasonal flavors to see how well they're received by the public."

"What made you want to start this venture in the first place?"

It's a good question, one that I've been asked many times, and whereas my usual go-to answer is because I saw an opportunity, the unexpected need to tell her the truth instead spills out.

"When I was a kid, my mom used to bring me here for the donuts. She loved coming here. I don't even know why, but she did. Truthfully, you can get cider donuts almost anywhere around here, but whatever it was, she just loved this place."

"Your family vacationed here?"

"Yes, we have a lake home."

"Who lives there now?"

"No one. It's empty until my father or brother comes up to stay. Although lately, the visits have been less frequent, which is fine with me."

She thinks about this.

"Where is your mom?"

"She passed away about three years ago from cancer."

"I'm sorry."

I shrug and let the grief of her memory wave through me.

"You bought this property and said to yourself, 'Let's make cider'?"

"Basically. I was walking through town, and for no reason, I stopped in front of the real estate agency next to the coffee shop to look at all the postings they had taped up on the inside of the window, and that's when I saw the property was for sale. Like your house, the family who owned it had attempted to be a homesteader, but the couple couldn't keep it anymore, and the adult kids didn't want it. To this day, I'm not sure what came over me, but I walked into the office and made an offer. I couldn't stomach the idea of them turning the mountain into another golf community."

"When was this?"

"Five years ago."

"So before your mom passed?"

"Yes."

"I see."

What does she see?

"Yep. I am the proud owner of one hundred and

eighty acres, forty-five of which are a fruit orchard, and last year we added the pasture for some animals."

"Did the previous owner make cider?"

"I'm sure they did, but they didn't on the scale that we do and commercially sell it."

"So you built this brewery?"

I move her along and take her to the back wall of the barn. Here, I have glass vessels showing off the color of a few different ciders in their fermenting process, as well as where we keep the kegs, bottles, and cans.

"Well, the barn was already here. I just painted it red, and we don't brew anything. Brewing involves boiling or cooking. For example, to make beer, the 'brewer' steeps barley or wheat grains, which converts the starches into sugar. We are a cidery like wines are to wineries."

"No cooking?"

"Nope. Harvesting, washing, milling, fermenting, bottling. The fermentation process will take care of any harmful bacteria."

"That's interesting. I didn't know that."

"We have over one thousand apple trees and almost three dozen varieties. Cole and I have traveled all over the state to taste different ciders at different farms to see which we like best. It's interesting how each apple can taste so different. It's like they have their own personalities. We've also begun experimenting with other fruits, honey, and spices like cinnamon to see what flavors we can develop."

"How many people do you have working here?"

"Full time, it's just Cole and me. Then we have Jane. During the season when we need the apples picked, I hire kids from the high school to help out. Here is where we package the cider. Mostly, this is just Cole and me."

"Is it hard?"

"No. I like working with my hands, and I'm proud of what we make."

"Who designs the labels?" She's looking at the large framed labels we have hanging, almost like a trophy wall.

"I designed the orchard logo, but the labels are a combination of ideas between me and Cole. He's really good at what he does."

I walk her over to the last wall, where I have a small bar set up for people who ask about tours. It's not a lot, but I have four taps running year-round where people can sample the different flavors and then relax if they want to on one of the four leather chairs sitting nearby.

"Want to taste?" I ask her.

She looks around the barn and then back at me. Her face is blank, and she is right. I probably should be out there shaking hands and kissing babies, but I just want to be here with her for some unknown reason.

"Absolutely," she says, sliding onto one of the stools. Have I imagined watching her drink my ciders? Yes. But having her sitting here, I hate that I notice how she brightens the whole place.

I grab four small glasses used for a tasting flight, fill each halfway with the different flavors, and then turn to set them in front of her. I find I'm nervous about her reaction, which is ridiculous, but deep down, I want her to like them.

She picks up the first glass and takes a sip. It's our signature cider coming from the mature apple trees here on the mountain. Hell, she even has a few of these trees over in the back portion of her yard. This cider is what made me want to take a deeper dive. I made it the first year and knew I was on to something.

"This is good."

My heart expands in my chest, and I press my lips together and smile at her.

"Is this something you dreamed about, or is this like a hobby?"

I think about my father's reaction when I told him. At first, he thought I did this as an investment, which he was fine with. But as I spent more and more time here and began expanding the production, the disdain crept in, as well as his opinions of my life choices.

Ask me how I feel about his opinions as I breathe in this fresh mountain air and watch my feisty new neighbor drink my ciders.

"Well, it wasn't in the plans, but the moment I saw it was for sale, something in me clicked. I didn't even question it either."

"So what's next?"

"The donuts are great, and I love the you-pick season, but I'd like to expand the operation a bit more. Twelve ciders on tap and build out a tasting room."

"Tasting rooms mean more people," she says, eyeing me.

"That it does."

She drops her gaze to the next glass and subtly nods her head. I know what she's thinking. I've thought it too.

"Does that bother you?"

She picks up the second glass and takes a sip. Her brows rise in acknowledgment of the flavor, and then she puts the glass back down. This one has cinnamon infused.

"I don't know. It's not my place to say anything to you. This is your business and your land."

She's not wrong, and while I also shouldn't care what she thinks about this, I find I do.

Looking over her shoulder, my gaze drifts over the equipment we have. I am proud of what we make. "I don't have a huge production here, but we do supply cider for a few of the local bars in town, like Route 11. I've been in talks with a few other orchards about cross-promotion, putting a few of theirs on tap and vice versa to create awareness when the time comes."

She picks up the third glass. Her face twitches, and I have to suppress my laughter. This one has sour cherry mixed in.

She licks her lips. "I think that's a great idea. You could even do something like a passport book with the other orchards. If everyone hands it out, you'll help each other, and maybe once they get so many stamps from the visits, they get a prize or something."

I don't respond right away. I just stare at her, and her cheeks turn red.

"Whatever, it was just an idea," she says, trying to downplay her thoughts.

"No, it's a great idea. My mind went three steps ahead to Cole designing this. Sorry."

She picks up the last glass and takes a sip.

No reaction this time.

She sets it down, points at the first glass, and says, "This one."

12

CORA

*I*t's just after lunch when there's a scratching on the front door. My heart rate picks up, as it's not a soft scratching either. It's loud and kind of rough.

Seriously, what kind of animal has shown up now?

I move closer to the door, wait, and sure enough, the scratching starts again.

Oh my God.

Are the deer trying to come into the house now? Is that scratching the big one with the horns? Are they all standing out there in solidarity, demanding food? Or maybe it's not the deer. Perhaps it's the raccoons or some other wild animal.

Slinking off to the side, I move to the living room window that overlooks the porch and peek out to see what's there. The yard is empty, so whatever it is, it's on the porch. Straining, I'm just barely able to make out a brown furry butt with a long tail that's wagging.

A laugh bursts out of me as I think about all the other possibilities my mind went to.

Opening the door, I find a very old but happy brown Labrador.

"Hey there, buddy."

I bend down to pet him and see the name Duke stitched into his collar. He wags his tail at the attention, then walks past me to the carpet in the living room and lays down.

Well then.

I close the door and move to the kitchen to watch him.

It's weird to have an animal in the house.

Sure, I've been to other people's houses where they have pets, like Avery's, Ash's, and Clay's, but I've never had one in mine.

I move about the kitchen and make a cup of tea, all the while watching this dog sleep. People talk about how pets keep you company, and they're not wrong. Even though he's asleep, I no longer feel alone in the house.

Briggs must be wondering where he is. Then again,

maybe with all of the people around today and the noise, Duke just wanted a moment of peace.

I can appreciate that.

Briggs was different with me today. I didn't expect him to give me the tour or be so open. He talked to me like we were new friends, but I've seen the other side to him, the more dominant side, so I know it's more like frenemies.

As the sunlight wanes and the hours pass, the low chatter from across the street dies down. I know today was the exception, as it's opening day, but I can't help but wonder exactly how many people will be coming up the road over the next two months. It surprised me when he asked me what I thought about him expanding, but I'm certain my preferences don't really matter in the end.

It's just after dinnertime when Duke gets up, comes over to where I'm at on the couch, and stands next to me, wagging his tail. He's so cute, with white hairs dotting his face. I pet him a few times, and then he makes his way to the door and stands by it.

"Ready to go home, are you?" I ask him, and he huffs as if he can understand me.

"Well, how about I walk you back so I know you make it to your grumpy owner."

Slipping on my tall rubber boots, I open the door,

and Duke wanders out. He doesn't run or sprint off. Instead, he slowly meanders down the stairs and then turns to look back at me to see if I'm coming.

Together, we make the trek up my driveway and over to Briggs's house. Today's activity is gone, and the mountain is again silent.

I like it.

In fact, it makes me wonder how I'll do back in the city with all the noise.

At his house, I trudge up the front steps and knock on his door. A few moments later, I hear his heavy footsteps. The door flies open, and there he is, freshly showered and surprised to see me here.

"Umm," I mumble as I'm stuck staring at his damp hair, his skin which has that freshly cleaned look, muscular tanned arms as his T-shirt is loving him perfectly, and his pink lips, which are not scowling at me. "I had a visitor." I wave my hand toward Duke, and his eyes, which were pinned on me, drop to his dog.

Surprising me even further, he drops down where he's crouching on the balls of his feet and pulls the dog into a hug.

"Too much for you today?" he asks, and the dog nuzzles into him. "I was wondering where you got off to. How long was he with you?" he asks, glancing up at me.

"Just a couple of hours."

Standing, he scratches Duke behind the ears, and then Duke leaves us to go into the house.

"That makes sense," he says.

"What does?"

"That he would go to your house. He was Mrs. Benson's dog. After she passed, he just came over here and stayed."

"So he's not your dog?"

"Well, he is now. She's dead."

My cheeks heat, and I narrow my eyes at him.

"I just meant that he belongs to that family. No one came and got him?"

"One of her sons checked in with me, but Duke was happy here, and I don't think they wanted him. It's fine. This was a little before my mom died, and he would lay by her side. He made her happy."

I don't know what to say to this. Keeping a dog because it lay next to his mother while she was sick is a very selfless thing. Between buying the orchard and the dog, I've quickly realized that he loved his mother very much.

And that's when his words hit me. "My house sat empty for over three years?"

"Yes."

"Wow, I didn't realize that. It wasn't in that bad of shape when I bought it, so I just assumed it was a recent thing."

"Nope, it just sat there. At one time, there was a small barn, but they didn't maintain it, and it was old, so they tore it down and threw down some grass seed."

"Where was it?"

He glances toward my house. "Far northeast corner."

"That makes sense." It's exactly where I want to put my garden.

He pauses, eyes me warily, and then asks, "How do you feel about blackberry cheesecake?"

I want to ask if this is a trick question or if he's got an inside joke due to how we met, but somehow I think it's not.

"I feel pretty good about it," I tell him, watching him closely.

"Come on in, I was just about to have some. Mrs. Wheeler, she owns Bean There in town, brought it up for me. She brings baked goods with her wherever she goes."

He opens the door wider to let me in, and I'm instantly struck with how homey his house is. I don't know what I thought—bachelor pad, poorly thrown-together decor, or whatever—but this house has been professionally decorated. He closes the door, and I slowly follow him.

"I love that place, and she sounds like Avery. Avery

just can't help herself with the baking. It makes her happy, and then she's doubly happy when she gets to give it away. Ash is too." I grin. He loves to harass her about all the extra calories, but he gladly consumes everything she makes him.

"For as many of my donuts as she's eaten, she hasn't brought me anything yet."

"Just you wait," I tell him, thinking that if we actually become neighborly, he will certainly find himself on the list.

As we walk toward the back of the house, the first thing I notice is that he has a lot more windows than I do. Windows without curtains. While I'm certain it's amazing during the day when the natural light is pouring in, the idea that someone could be outside staring in, no thank you.

In the kitchen, my jaw drops. This isn't your run-of-the-mill house kitchen. It's top-of-the-line, a chef and photographer's dream kitchen. A flicker of Juliet saying that he comes from money suddenly has me questioning him a little more. Where did the money come from, and how much exactly?

I watch him as he moves around, grabbing two plates and some silverware.

"How was your day?" I ask. Not sure what one calls this type of day. It wasn't really a party. Well, I guess it kind of was with the bounce houses and food trucks. "Everything go as planned? Are you pleased?"

He cuts me a slice and hands me the plate.

"Today was great. So far from what I've seen, it's the best opening day we've had since taking over this place."

"That's amazing! I'm happy for you." I smile at him as his eyes find mine. They're a dark shade and filled with mystery. Who are you, Briggs Warren?

He nods and leans a hip against the counter. Then, awkwardly, we both start eating the cheesecake. It's delicious and makes me wonder if I should invite Mrs. Wheeler over.

"It was odd to have all of these people up here. It's usually so quiet, but today was not quiet."

He sets his plate down on the counter. "I don't know if I should be apologizing or not for this," he says, looking at me cautiously.

"I'm not saying it's a bad thing, just different."

He hums as we both finish, and he takes the plates and puts them in the sink. It's then I look over toward the dining room and see my plant sitting right in the middle of the table. A smile spreads from one side of my face to the other.

He instantly looks uneasy.

I point toward the plant. He follows and then rolls his eyes.

"Did you think I threw it away?"

"Well, from what I know of you, it wouldn't surprise me."

"I would argue that you don't know me at all," he says as we walk back to the living room.

"Jury's still out, but I do feel a little bit like I've entered the twilight zone."

"Why?"

I glance around the room and see three framed photos on the fireplace mantel. In one, he is with an older woman, who I'm assuming is his mom. In the second, he and Cole hold up a bottle of cider and a trophy, and in the third is a family of four. I'm not close enough to get a good look, but the boys look younger.

"Well, this whole day, you've been . . . nice, and your home is beautiful."

He laughs, and my heart stutters as it's the best, most unexpected sound.

"Then let me be the first to warn you, don't get used to it. Being nice ruins my image."

I turn to face him. "And what image is that?"

"Badass mountain man," he says, very matter-of-factly.

At this, I can't help but grin.

"I thought you said you were charming. Now you're a badass?" I tilt my head.

"Can't I be both?"

My eyes again flicker to the photos.

"My mother lived here with me for a while, and I gave her free rein to do whatever she wanted to do at the house. It made her happy."

"Well, it looks amazing in here," I tell him as I again look around. And it really does. Cream colors and rustic dark wood. If I had to describe everything I've seen, from the kitchen to the dining room to the living room, I would call it chic farmhouse. It's then I see tiny flickers just outside the window.

"Wait, are those fireflies?" I move closer to the window and peer outside. Briggs moves to stand behind me, glances out, and then he looks down at me like I have three heads.

"Yes. Have you not seen any since you've been here?"

I'm a little stunned by his nearness and over-whelmed by not only his size but also the way he smells. It's a mixture of sandalwood, bergamot, and cinnamon apples. He smells a little like his orchard, and that fits him perfectly.

"No, I haven't."

Silently, we watch them float just above the ground and around the shrubs. The heat from his body envelops mine, and I seem to soak up every pheromone he gives off. I've always thought he was kind of good-looking, but how I feel now borders on dangerous.

I can not be attracted to my neighbor.

After a moment, he steps away, and my body sags in relief.

"That surprises me because they are all along the back edge of your property. With your evening escapes to the blackberry bushes, I'm surprised you haven't seen them."

"I haven't been back outside at night, and it didn't even occur to me to look for them."

"Goldie, they are everywhere. Even if you were to sit in that fancy rocking chair on your front porch, you should have seen them."

He's teasing and mocking me at the same time. I might have spent a little money on them, but in the cooler months, I plan to put them to good use, and I wanted comfortable chairs that will last.

"Well, now I'm sad that I haven't, and how do you know what my rocking chairs look like?"

He smirks, and then it dawns on me that he was at my house when he threw out the corn.

"Season is over too. I'm surprised these are even still here. Mostly, they are here in May, June, and the beginning of July. And I just do."

"Maybe there aren't as many in my backyard as you say there are, seeing as I moved in at the end of July."

"Maybe," he mutters with a shrug, but he's clearly just pacifying me.

And for reasons like this, I have to remember that he's a frenemy.

Turning away from him, I look back out the window to see if I can spot any more of the little flickers of light.

"Just wait until May," he says.

"What happens in May?"

"The blue ghost fireflies make an appearance."

"What are blue ghost fireflies?" I turn to look at him. He's intrigued me, and the smirk on his face lets me know he knows it.

"They are a rare and beautiful type of firefly. It's a unique species that, for some reason, is located here in western Carolina. They've been spotted in a few other places, but primarily they're here. For just a couple of weeks, usually in May, they arrive. They glow blue-green instead of the gold-white light we see the rest of the summer."

"Wow."

"My mother loved them. She would sit outside every night and wait for them."

Silence fills the space between us as I think of what

to say. He's mentioned her several times tonight. It's easy to see that he misses her.

"Well, I'll have to make sure I'm here in May so I can see them too."

"Where else would you be?" he asks.

It's then I realize that while I don't know much about him, he doesn't really know anything about me either.

"New York."

BRIGGS

Stripping off my suit jacket, I drape it across the back of the couch in my brother's library and make my way to the bar. He invited me over, as he said he needed to discuss something privately with me, so I found myself in Eastover, already dreading whatever he had to say. Coming from him, it could be anything from it's time you take on more of a role again with the company to don't you think it's time to apologize to our father for taking his wife away. What the two of them have never understood is that my mother did what she wanted. Her choosing to live and, in the end, pass away in Horizons Valley was her choice.

I let out a defeated sigh, just wishing this day was over.

This past week has been exhausting, and I had

forgotten this from previous years. Picking the apples, washing them, milling or grinding them, and then crushing and pressing to extract the juice. While the apples don't need to be ground immediately to get the quantities we want for each flavor, it must be done all at once and not slowly.

Scanning over the bottles in front of me, I may make ciders, but I certainly appreciate the flavors of an old single malt whiskey. My brother doesn't disappoint, as there's a full bottle of Macallan Enigma. I open it with zero regard to whether or not he wanted me to.

After today's meeting, it's needed.

My family owns the largest private equity firm in North Carolina, totaling just over five billion dollars. We're approaching our sixtieth anniversary, and they're already worried about how we can use this to our advantage from the PR sector. Quite frankly, I feel like it's not as important as they think it is, and it's definitely not something I should have to listen to, especially since we've all heard the story repeatedly.

My grandfather met my grandmother during the civil rights movement in Greensboro in 1960. He joined in at the sit-ins with several baseball friends as he played with the Greensboro Yankees, a minor league team. While Jackie Robinson was the first player to enter the Major Leagues in 1951, almost ten years later, the teams in North Carolina were still mainly segregated. No one really knows why my grandmother was there. Did she believe in the cause, was she rebelling from her parents, or as a socialite, was she looking to be photographed and have her picture printed in the papers? It's never been really clear, but what did happen was they met and ultimately fell in love.

My grandmother came from a prominent family who found their fortune during the Carolina gold rush. Their property produced one of the largest gold nuggets found in the state, in addition to numerous other gems such as amethyst, ruby, sapphire, and emerald. My grandfather didn't come from much at all. All he really had going for him was being able to play baseball and hustle people with money. If you gave him two quarters, he'd make a dollar.

Little by little, he would use my grandmother's inheritance to invest in people and companies he thought had potential, and in turn, he made a nice amount of money. It wasn't long after that he was approached by other wealthy individuals. They wondered if he invested their money, could he make them a profit too? For years, he focused on the industrial growth of the Carolina market and surrounding areas of the South. He ultimately revolutionized several cities, resulting in many jobs, and he became someone to the people of North Carolina. It's what I'm most proud of when I think about our company's history.

It was after my father took over that things began to change. He began to work less with the companies and their shareholders and instead pulled the control strings. He's stopped listening to them and declared he knew best. He has become ruthless in cost-cutting over the past ten years or so and has done more layoffs than in the rest of the years combined with the company. Instead of trying to improve our overall economy, he's changing its landscape and adding more industries such as business and tech-enabled services and healthcare. I understand learning, growing, and adapting to change, but there's a reason some view PE firms as evil. There's something to be said for the quote, "With power comes great responsibility." In my opinion, he's been irresponsible, and quarter after quarter, I cringe listening to him.

Filling my glass with two fingers, I throw back the contents and welcome the burn as it goes down.

The front door opens, and I hear heels clicking across the floor. The sound is faintly triggering and takes me back to a time when I looked forward to that nightly.

Leaving my glass on the bar, I turn and experience a moment of déjà vu as I'm staring into the hazel eyes of my past.

"Adele, what are you doing here?" I ask sharply.

I can't imagine a reason for her to be here. I made it very clear that we were over a year and a half ago.

When I take in her appearance, she looks like she always does, polished and perfectly put together, but it's the lines around her eyes that give away her nervousness or wariness.

Strange.

It's then I hear my brother's voice from behind her. I didn't even realize he had come in as well.

"Right. I know this might seem awkward for you . . ."

Awkward for me?

My eyes connect with his. They're closed off and cold. This has me raising my brows in question as I look back and forth between the two of them, and then it seems my body recognizes before my brain does what he's about to tell me, and ice water plunges into my stomach.

"There's no real easy way to break the news to you other than just getting it over with. Adele and I are getting married."

From somewhere in the house, the ticking of a wall clock echoes through the silence that has taken over the room. After that, it's like a freight train as everything in my brain screams.

Jaxon reaches for Adele's right hand and intertwines

their fingers as her left hand comes up and clutches the string of pearls around her neck. That's her tell of when she's distressed, and it's then I spot the ring. She's wildly uncomfortable with this, as she should be. What a bitch. As I stare at the ring, the only thing I can think of at this moment is that it's obnoxious in size and unnecessary, and although I shouldn't, deep down, I hate them both.

Adele and I dated for over three years. I knew the type of girl she was when I met her, but I was still drawn to her. We ran with the same crowd. Our families had worked together for years, and I was bewitched by her laughter and ability to go with the flow. She didn't seem to mind that I had just bought the orchard and split my time between Charlotte and Horizons Valley, and she even told me she liked spending time in the mountains. But it was after my mother died that things began to change.

I knew she wanted to get married. We'd been together long enough, but I just couldn't. I was grieving the loss of my mother, I'd officially given up my position with the firm and became a silent shareholder, and much to her horror, I moved to the orchard full time. She thought I would sell the orchard and move home after my mother passed, but she was wrong. She tried giving me an ultimatum to get me back to Charlotte, and I did consider it for a split second, but then I picked up her iPad one day, as it was lying on the island in the kitchen, and text messages from my brother flashed across the home screen.

Did you talk to him yet?

Remember our deal.

I didn't even need to know what the deal was, but I did know that speaking to him about anything was a betrayal. She knew I wasn't on board with how he and my father had been doing things. There was a rift between my family and me, and whether she thought she could close it, I didn't care. It wasn't her place. In addition to taking a good long look at my life in Charlotte, I had been taking a good long look at what a life with her would have been like too. And as the days dragged on, it became less and less of what I wanted. She wanted my name and what being married to me would mean for her, but only if I was going to keep up with the Warren society image. Those texts were the final push I needed to firmly sever everyone from that life.

"You're fucking joking," I say to both of them, but my eyes are firmly on her. Jaxon is my younger brother. He's always felt he had something to prove and wanted to get ahead. I understand his reasoning for wanting to marry her, as really he is marrying up, but what is hers? First off, he's breaking an unspoken brother code where you don't double dip, and second, her because she always expressed to me that he made her uncomfortable. From what I remember, she never really liked him, but then again, maybe she did. Maybe that's just what she told me. Perhaps they always had something, and I just didn't see it.

A disgusted shiver works its way through me.

"No," he says, breaking the intense stare down she and I are having. Jaxon has to feel the tension in this room. It's pouring off me, and my hands tighten into fists. "Here is your invitation to our engagement party. I don't need to express how poorly it would be for the family if you chose not to attend."

And the hits just keep coming.

"How poorly does it look for you both to be the sloppy seconds? I mean, really, Jax, what the fuck?"

Adele gasps.

He doesn't answer but instead holds up the invitation for me and forces me to take the few steps between us to get it. The envelope is thick and silver. My name is calligraphed perfectly on the front, and then it hits me. Everyone knows about them but me. Everyone in the meeting, including my father and who knows who else.

Once an asshole, always an asshole. I shake my head in disappointment as my arm drops.

Returning to the bar, I lift the bottle, pour another

finger, and toss it back. The sound of crystal almost breaking echoes through the room when I not so lightly slam the glass down.

"Was any of it ever real?" I ask her as I turn to face them again.

Instead of responding, she keeps her chin high and angles her face toward my brother to dismiss me.

There's my answer.

Over three years.

Of. My. Life.

I think some part of me always knew the real reason she was with me, but seeing the proof of this confirms my suspicions.

I'm surprised to feel pain from this.

It's not that I'm not over her because I am. I just feel betrayed by both of them.

"You understand she will never love you, right? This is only about the money," I say to Jaxon, and he just smirks at me.

"Who said anything about love?"

And it feels like he's slapped me. I was in love with her. Love wasn't just a fairy tale. It was a real thing I had hoped I had found but unfortunately didn't.

Then again, if this is her version of love, no fucking thank you.

At this, her gaze drops to the floor, and where a

better man might feel some sort of sympathy toward her, I do not. I hope she feels shame and regret. What a horrible life Jaxon is going to give her. Then again, she knows how to play the game, and I'm certain she'll always have the upper hand with him.

Glancing back and forth between the two of them, I see nothing but years of unhappiness and infidelity. Years of weight, years of darkness, and years I'm grateful not to be experiencing myself.

It's feeling the dread and darkness for a life I almost had that suddenly has me craving the light. Gold light. Gold light where the sounds of a cello whisper to my ears. My breath stalls as I'm hit with this realization. I should be asking myself why, as I've firmly slotted her into the neighbor category, but at this moment, I can't and won't. I don't know what this means, but there's only one place I want to be right now and only one person who I want to be with. It's time to go.

Without another word, I place my glass on the bar, grab my jacket, and brush past them as I head for the door.

"Briggs," Jaxon calls after me. "You will be there, right?"

The only answer I give him is the backside of my middle finger.

14

CORA

A knock on the door downstairs startles me. I reach over and grab my phone off the night- stand to see that it's almost midnight. A sudden moment of panic has me internally berating myself for not getting an outside camera set up yet.

Who would come here this late?

Then again, I only know a few people in this town, and I'm certain all of them would have called first.

There's another knock on the door. This time it's harsher, louder, and it has me slinking out of bed toward the stairs.

"Goldie, answer the door," someone calls from the outside.

Relief and curiosity hit me at the same time.

What is he doing here?

And then panic.

What if something happened, and he needs my help?

Groaning, I make my way down the stairs to the front door. I flip on the porch light, throw it open, glare at him with my most severe face, and am about to very forcefully ask what he wants when I take in his attire. White dress shirt, loose tie, suit slacks that perfectly hug his hips and thighs, and dress shoes. These clothes are tailored and custom-fit for him, and I'm shocked he owns them. He looks like every fantasy a girl like me from the Upper East Side dreams about and also every nightmare.

"What are you wearing?" I ask even though that shouldn't be the first question coming out of my mouth. Instead, I admire how even though his look is a look I've always claimed I hated, secretly, I don't.

And especially on him.

He rolls his eyes and then lets them trail over the length of me. Slowly.

My stomach tightens at his blatant perusal.

"I could say the same for you," he says, his voice rough and tired.

I know what I'm wearing is small and slightly indecent, but I'm over caring when it comes to him. After all, he basically saw me naked.

"They're called pajamas. You know something you wear to bed. For sleeping. Which is what I was doing before you so rudely showed up in the middle of the night. What do you want?"

"Sleep. Sounds great. Let's go." He waves his hand toward my room inside the house.

I know it makes no sense, but I turn and look at the back of the house like there's something there when I know there's not. "What do you mean?" I spin back to him.

"Goldie," he says in that stern way that he does, and it has my toes curling.

But that's all he says. Not why he's here, not what's wrong with his house or his bed, or why he's wearing these clothes. He just stares at me with an expression that he expects me to obey, and that doesn't work for me.

Instead of moving to allow him to pass, I lean one side of my hip into the doorframe and cross my arms over my chest. Could he barge right past? Yes, but he won't. I return his look with one of my own, and he lets out the deepest breath I've ever heard.

"Not tonight," he tells me, shaking his head, and that's when I take a closer look at the pleading in his face. He has tension lines around his eyes, shadows underneath them, and his shoulders curl in as he slouches forward. I feel slightly alarmed, and then he says, "Please."

While I've concluded that I don't really think he has something acutely wrong with him, there must be something big enough for him to come here and ask for this. And he used the word please. We both know this is out of character for him. Meanwhile, my character is flaring again to do the right thing. Clearly, he needs someone tonight, but I'm curious as to how he decided on me.

"Fine, but don't get any ideas." I look him straight in the eye. "I always wondered what it would be like to take a stray in." Turning my back to him, I make my way across the room.

Behind me, I hear the door shut, lock, and his footsteps as he follows me.

"Goldie, trust me, I have zero ideas or thoughts tonight."

Then what is this? He just had a wild idea when he decided he needed to come over here for a sleepover? Who does that? Who just shows up at someone's house and demands a sleepover?

"You do realize tomorrow you're going to hate yourself for this," I toss over my shoulder. He doesn't answer, and my stomach dips with concern. "Can I get you anything?" I ask him, stalling at the bottom of the stairs.

"Some painkillers and a water?" he asks, his gaze

wandering over my face. And then he does the oddest thing—he reaches up and rubs a piece of my hair that's fallen from the messy ponytail through his fingers, then tucks it behind my ear.

I stare at him as he stares at me, the awkward tension at this moment growing, and then he blinks, breaking the spell.

"Sure," I tell him.

"Thanks," he says, moving past me to trudge up the stairs.

What in the world happened to him tonight? And what in the world has possessed him to come here? Was he nice to me last weekend? Yes. But that doesn't actually mean we're friends. If one is to stack up all our interactions together and rate them, I'd say last weekend was the anomaly. Then again, technically, he wasn't rude to me the day the girls were at the cider house eating his donuts.

Ugh. Confusing. Contradictory. Man.

Back in my room, I find him sitting on the opposite side of the bed from my phone charger staring out the window. During the day, you can see the lake clearly. It's a nice view, but maybe not as nice as the view before me now.

Briggs is shirtless and pantless—his clothes draped over a chair I have in the corner—and I can't help but let my eyes briefly wander over the long smooth lines of his muscles as he sits in just a pair of boxer briefs. He really is a handsome man. Only at this moment, he just looks miserable.

Miserable and annoyed.

"Here," I blurt, moving to stand in front of him, where I hold out the glass and the medicine.

"Thanks," he mumbles as he takes them from me. He swallows the pills and the whole glass of water, then hands me back the glass. Rolling my eyes, I place it on the nightstand on his side of the bed.

Walking off, I move around to what I guess will be my side of the bed and climb in.

Both of us settle in as I turn the light off, the only noise being that of the still night and the ceiling fan.

Briggs Warren is in my bed.

I never let people sleep in my bed.

Somewhere, somehow, pigs must be flying.

Briggs lets out another sigh and runs his hand over his face. I wouldn't say his body is tense, but it's definitely something.

"Do you want to talk about it?" I ask.

"No," he grumbles.

Is it wrong for me to think he should at least be telling me something? The way he was dressed, my mind runs wild. Did someone die? Did he gamble away all of his money and have to go meet with a lawyer? Was he out on a date that turned terrible? Just thinking about all of the things that might have happened to him cause my anxiety to slowly creep up.

"Are you okay?" I ask, unable to help myself.

Rolling to his side to face me, he stretches the arm underneath him across the bed until his hand brushes my shoulder. But instead of moving it, he leaves it there and exhales the words, "I am now."

What does this mean?

I've lived here for six weeks. I've barely had any interaction with him, and even then, half of those were not good. Yet here he is, saying he's better just because he's near me. I've never made anyone better, so this is confusing.

"Where were you?" I ask him.

He's quiet before he answers, and then he says, "Charlotte."

Charlotte must be where he's from.

I did look him up on social media, but only the orchard. It never occurred to me to do an internet search and learn more. Juliet said she thought he came from money. Well, what kind of money? Charlotte is a huge financial city, and it's home to several banking centers.

"Is that home?"

"No. It used to be. Home has been here for the past five years."

"I see."

And I do. Visits with my family back in New York always leave me feeling exhausted and less than who I know I am, too. It's stupid really, how much we allow other people to influence us, especially those who call themselves family.

"Yeah."

His fingers brush against my skin again, like this tiny connection somehow makes him feel better. So I roll over onto my side, facing away from him, and scoot in his direction just a little until his hand touches my back.

It's warm.

It's nice.

Tomorrow, when the sun is out, and we're both thinking more clearly, I will have to revisit these last fifteen minutes. Him wanting to come here. Me allowing him in. Him wanting to touch me. And me liking when he does.

15

BRIGGS

The sun peeking through the curtains is what wakes me. It's blinding, bright, and disorients me because I always sleep with the room-darkening shades closed. Squinting, it takes me a moment to remember where I am, and that's when I feel the heat of her body burning down my entire right side.

Immediately, my heart rate picks up, but I can't discern if it's because I'm in her bed and she's next to me or if it's because I'm mad at myself for showing up here in the first place.

I mean, what the hell was I thinking coming here?

She called it. She said I would be mad at myself this morning, but I'm not sure yet if I am. And for reasons I don't understand, I really did want to be with her last night.

Today, now, that's a different story.

When I look over at her, she's facing away from me, but she's curled up on her side. She's scooted all the way over onto my side of the bed to press up against me. I don't know if she's the type who gets cold and drifts toward heat or if she just normally sleeps in the middle of the bed and ended up next to me. My eyes trail over her essentially bare shoulder, sans the tiny strap of her top, and I take in the long length of her neck. She really is a beautiful woman, and with that thought, I squeeze my eyes shut and mentally smack my palm against my forehead.

She's my neighbor.

I don't know why all I wanted was her or really why I'm even thinking about this. And now I just made things uncomfortably complicated with her.

Neighbors don't seek out each other for comfort in the middle of the night. Neighbors don't slip into each other's beds. Neighbors definitely don't lose self-control when it comes to physical touch. Why did I so desperately need to touch her last night?

Shaking my head, I slide out of the bed. She rolls to her back, and I can't help but stand here and stare at her again. Her shirt has risen up just a little, her hair is wild and all over the pillows, and her face looks different.

Different, I realize, because she's not scowling at me and being a harpy.

Quietly sighing, I slip back into my clothes, shoving the tie in my pocket, and I make my way down the stairs. I didn't notice it last night, but she's doing something with the space under the stairs. She's got a drop cloth on the floor, a hole cut into the wall where I'm assuming she's going to put a door, and there are a bunch of tools on the ground. From there, I can't help but pause to stare at the painting in her living room. While I have mixed opinions on what I know of her so far, from the cello-playing superstar and the rich New Yorker to the woman who buys a mountain house to live in alone, I can see how the garden's brightness and colors suit her. Given that her front porch and her house are overrun with plants, I guess she wants a garden like this one day too.

I also glance toward the plant where I hid the cricket chirper and smirk to myself because she still hasn't found it. It's right there. She'd find it if she moved the leaves and looked for it. Meanwhile, it probably needs new batteries. I'll have to run over here and change them the next time she's gone.

The cool air hits me the second I open her front door, and I deeply inhale the scent of the mountain. It's always grounded me. It reminds me that I'm no longer in Charlotte, and apparently, I need that.

What an absolute shit show the whole day was, from the meeting topics to the men in the room who I've lost respect for over the past several years, and then to my brother. Even after the drive home, I'm still processing the fact that I'll have to see Adele at every family function going forward. I'll also have to see my brother's smug face as he actually thinks he one-upped me by marrying her.

Then again, I guess they really are perfect for each other.

After a quick stop at the house to let Duke out, I make my way to the cider house. I know I can't pull a Houdini after I just showed up at her door, so I fire up the donut maker. We bake our donuts instead of frying them. This machine can make up to nine at one time, and each batch takes less than five minutes to complete. Jane loves how they can be made upon order, and Goldie might have declared that she would never eat one, but I think I can persuade her to change her mind this morning.

What's so special about these donuts? The batter is infused with cinnamon, nutmeg, and apple cider. They are warm, filled with spices and fruit, and then rolled around in cinnamon sugar before being served.

My mother loved these donuts, and while they aren't my favorite to make and sell, and you can find them at just about any orchard in the fall, I keep them in memory of her.

Packing up the newly made donuts, I make my way back to her house. I don't know if she's up or not. If she isn't, I'll just leave them in the kitchen. That should be a good enough thank you for last night. That is, until she demands a reason for my late-night appearance.

I open the door without knocking, and immediately, her eyes connect with mine. She's standing in the kitchen, holding a cup of coffee, and she's wearing that little black robe from the night when we met.

Of course I can't get a reprieve and have her still be sleeping.

"You don't knock anymore?" she asks, popping one brow up.

I close the door behind me and make my way toward her. Clearing my throat, I tell her, "If you were still sleeping, I didn't want to wake you. Again."

"How considerate of you," she teases. Her eyes run over the length of me, and I suddenly wonder if I should have changed too before returning. "Want a cup of coffee?"

"Yes, please."

I set the donuts on the counter as she turns and

opens the cabinet for another cup. She then sits down on the second island chair while pushing the first to the end of the counter so she can sit perpendicular to me. The robe rides high as she stretches, and I drop my gaze. I've already seen her once. I don't need to see her again even though I'm starting to think I might want to.

How dumb and even more complicated would that make things?

I watch as she picks up an almost full pot and pours me a cup. Does she make a full pot daily, or was she wondering if I would come back?

Turning around, she slides the cup across the island to me and eyes the bag.

"Cream or sugar?"

"No. Black is fine. Thank you."

Her eyes again drop to the bag. I open it and hand it over to her. She takes it and peers inside. I know the smell has just assaulted her senses.

Her brows pull down in confusion. "You got up and went to make donuts?"

"Yes," I grumble.

"By all means, sound angrier about this," she says as she rolls her eyes and reaches in for one of them. "There sure are a lot in here."

Then she places the bag down, and while holding one, she gets out two plates and takes the offered seat.

Her robe again slides up the thighs of her long legs, and I mentally sigh.

I watch her as she takes the first bite of the donut, pauses as the flavors sink in, and then chews.

"Okay, Warren, even I'll admit these are pretty darn good."

Pride swells in my chest. Stupid, I know, they're just donuts, but still.

I reach into the bag, get one for myself, and eat it.

I'm stalling, I know I am, and then she calls me out.

"Are you just going to sit here in silence while you stare at me, or are you going to explain?"

I run my hand over the back of my head and then over my face, letting out a deep sigh.

"I had a meeting in Charlotte yesterday, which was fu—" I stop saying what I really want to say, remembering she asked me not to swear at her. "Terrible, and then afterward my brother invites me over to his house, where he introduces me to his fiancée."

She tilts her head. "And?"

I swallow. I'm embarrassed by what I'm about to tell her, and I don't know why. I didn't do anything wrong. Their the ones who should be embarrassed.

"She's my ex. My only ex."

Her eyes grow wide. "And here I thought I took the prize for having the worst brother ever."

"You have a brother?" I ask, forgetting that I know she does. Not because she told me, but because I went snooping, and he's in a lot of the photos with her and her family online.

"More like a second father, and they love to remind me how much of a disappointment I am."

My brows pull down. How can anyone possibly think she is a disappointment? She's smart, talented, successful, and independent. Other than moving away, I can't imagine anything she's done wrong.

"I've heard the same story before." I pick up my coffee and take a sip. "But I'm confused. How could they possibly be disappointed in you?"

She picks at the second donut she's put on her plate and plops a piece of it in her mouth.

"With my family, it's all about appearances. And don't you know, my place is married to the person they've chosen for me and playing for the New York Philharmonic."

Anger pushes down on me.

"That makes no sense." And it really doesn't. I do understand that some people still adopt the philosophy of advantageous marriages, but her family is so wealthy. What would be the point?

She shrugs.

"It does in the world where I come from."

We sit in silence with our thoughts while eating more donuts and drinking the coffee.

"Are you expected to go to this wedding?" she asks.

"Unfortunately." I shake my head with disgust.

A person shouldn't know the ins and outs of their sibling's spouse, or what they taste like, for that matter. It's not normal.

"I have to return to Charlotte for the engagement party in a few weeks. Don't you know it will look bad if I'm not there?"

"Trust me, I know," she says, studying my face.

Doing the same to her, I take in the fact that she's not wearing any makeup. She's got freckles dusted across the bridge of her nose, her skin looks clean and youthful, and her lips are the perfect shade of pink. Goldie in the morning, just out of bed, might be my favorite version of her.

"Do you still love her?" she asks, pulling me from my thoughts.

"Hell. No."

"How long were you with her?"

"Over three years."

Her jaw drops just a little. "Yikes. That's a long time. I'm surprised your brother went there."

"I wouldn't put anything past him. He's younger and tries every day to prove he's better. Only he's never seemed to realize that I'm not in competition with him."

"Must be a miserable way to live life."

"I don't get it either. My mother was a very loving person. She didn't raise us to feel slighted one way or the other by each other."

"He's always been this way?"

"To some degree, yes. But now that you mention it, he has gotten significantly worse since she died."

I probably should think about this more and figure out why, but I'm not sure it would matter.

"So why did it end?" she asks, leaning back in her chair.

"I know this is bad to say, but after my mother died, I changed. And maybe if she had been willing to change with me, we'd still be together, but honestly, I just stopped loving her. I didn't want the life that she did, and we grew apart."

"Hmm," she mumbles as she looks at her plate and thinks about this.

"What are you doing over there?" I turn and look at the construction mess so she knows what I'm asking about.

"Oh, I decided I wanted to build a small wine cellar, and that's a great space to do it."

"A wine cellar?"

"Yeah, I saw one in an architectural magazine, and my mind took off. I've looked at so many, and while I originally thought I could just put in the door and build out the space underneath, now I've decided to make most of the wall glass."

"Do you drink that much wine?"

She rolls her eyes at me.

"Yes, I do like a glass of wine every now and then, but the cellar won't be that large. It's the perfect space, and then I'm installing the cooling system against the back. It vents through the downstairs bathroom, which is fine. No one sees that anyway."

I eye her project, visualizing what she's trying to accomplish, and she's right. This is a great space for it. It has me thinking this would be a great addition for my house too. While I do drink a lot of the cider, my staircase is tall enough and long enough that I could incorporate beer taps as well.

"Do you need any help?"

She looks at me strangely, then shakes her head. "No, I can do it."

"All right. You know how to find me if you do," I offer. My lips curl up to smile at her, and after her cheeks turn a nice shade of pink, mine do the same.

Then, out of nowhere, she says, "I'll be your date to

the party if you want one. If there's one thing I know for certain, it's how to present in a social setting."

My eyes lock onto hers and this is when I decide I should be adding selflessness to her long list of qualities, too, that definitely don't point toward disappointment. I should be surprised that she's offering, but I find I'm not. Warmth from her sunshine seeps under my skin.

My smile turns into a smirk. "Yeah, I might have researched my new neighbor just a little and discovered a few things about you, Ms. Rhodes Corporation."

She laughs.

"Just a little, huh? And it's not mine. It's all my father's. Well, his and Winston's."

"Winston is your brother?"

"Yep." She pops the p.

While I did research her, I paid more attention to the images I found of her over the years than I did to the printed information.

"So what's his deal?" I pick up my coffee and take another sip.

"He's three years older, married, and has a son. We used to be friends, but the older he got, the more he slipped into my father's shoes. Everything, and I do mean everything, is identical. From the way they stand with their left hand in their pants pocket to the way they chew like a cow with the jaw not going up and down, but more around, to the way they crack their neck. They talk alike, they dress alike, and the way they frown at me is alike. It's eerie."

"I'm sorry," I tell her, and I am. It's one thing to constantly have your parents judge you, but it's another to have the parents and the sibling judge you. Jaxon may judge me, but only in the way that he thinks it's crazy that I don't want their lifestyle. Something tells me it's different for her.

"I actually have to head back to New York next month. My parents host a fundraiser event every year, and I'm expected to be there."

She looks down at the plate and drags her fingers through the remaining crumbs, smushing them on her fingertip, then sucking them off. Not a visual I need in my head, and I shove it into the mental box I've now titled Goldie.

"Okay. How about this . . . if you come with me to my brother's engagement party, then I'll go to New York with you for your parents' event?"

Having just picked up her coffee cup, she peers at me over the rim with her big brown eyes. I have no idea what she's thinking, but I can see the thoughts running through her mind.

"You do realize the scale wouldn't be balanced. A

trip to New York is a lot different from a car ride to Charlotte."

I shrug. "Whatever. It is if I say it is. Besides, if this works out well, you can be my date to the wedding, too." I grin.

She ponders this, sets her cup down, and leans back in her chair as her lips twist up in a mischievous smile. Then, for an unknown reason, my heart leaps when she says, "Deal."

16

CORA

September in the mountains is vastly different from the end of July. It's almost as if overnight, the humidity dissipated, and the days and nights cooled. I mean, I know fall is coming, but this morning was the first time I felt it. Excitement coursed through me as I thought about mums, hay bales, and dried cornstalks. Driving through the cute little town of Horizons Valley as I was off to meet my friends, I fully felt the shift as shop owners and homeowners have begun making the changes.

Since Bryce returned to school, Juliet, Avery, and I have set a regular coffee date every Friday. Only this week, we've decided to go hiking after coffee since Juliet has no appointments scheduled. The weather is just so beautiful, so we're spending the day outside exploring the national forest that bumps up against Horizons Valley.

"Are you sure this is a good idea?" I ask Avery as she straps on her water pack and tightens it across her chest. I glance down at her stomach. This morning, she announced that the baby was the size of a head of cauliflower.

"Of course! Just because I'm pregnant doesn't mean I'm not allowed outside. I still run just about every day on the trail around the lake."

I know nothing about pregnant people or babies, but hearing that she's still doing this makes me want to cringe. And I'm surprised that Ash allows this. Not that he tells her what to do, but he is the father and her husband, and I feel like he should have some say in the health and well-being of both of them.

"Yes, I know you do, which I still don't understand, but what if you trip?"

"Then I trip," she says matter-of-factly, looking at Juliet and me. "I'll be fine. I promise."

The last time she tripped, she broke her wrist, and we had to cancel shows because she couldn't play.

"But you're not just a little bit pregnant. You're a lot pregnant. Third trimester pregnant. You're putting my future godchild at risk." It's so strange to see her looking like this. I mean, I know this is what happens—the belly grows—but it looks so out of place.

She laughs. "You're not Catholic."

"And you're missing the point. You're carrying precious cargo in there," I say as I pick up the backpack carrying some essentials we may need, like food, bug spray, chafing cream, and a whistle. Not that we'll get lost or need help, but you never know.

"Precious cargo that loves fresh air and sunshine." She holds out her arms and squeezes her eyes shut as she tips her head back to soak up some sun. Meanwhile, I slip on a pair of sunglasses. It's bright out here today.

"When I was pregnant, all I wanted to do was lie on the couch and eat SpaghettiOs," Juliet says as she closes the trunk of her car, locks it, and slips the key into her own small backpack.

"Really?" I look at her, surprised. "I've never had those. I've heard people talk about them before, but I've never eaten them."

Juliet laughs. "I don't know what to say right now. You missed out on one of childhood's greatest meals."

Together, the three of us move to the trailhead. Only two other cars are here, which means it's not crowded and will be a nice hike. All three of us are wearing hats, so should we encounter people, they will not likely recognize us.

"Are you kidding? My mother would never have let me eat that pasta out of a can. Don't you know it's beneath us? Then again, we had a chef who prepared our food. If she actually had to do it herself, things might have been different."

Speaking of my mother, internally, I laugh at her reaction to knowing Juliet, Avery, and I are going hiking. Hiking for my mother is the walk from her chauffeured car to meet her personal shopper at Bergdorf's.

"Well, if you ever decide to try them, I want to be with you when you do." She laughs.

We set off on a trail that's a four-mile loop. It's supposed to be easy, meaning no roots for Avery to trip over and no drastic changes in elevation.

"Speaking of pasta, have either of you eaten at Bella's Italian restaurant yet? The new one on Main Street?" Avery asks.

"No, is it any good?" Juliet asks.

"It's to die for, and I'm not just saying that because I'm pregnant, and most things taste good. Even Ash was impressed. The pasta, the sauces, and the bread are made fresh daily, and the place will make a killing with all of the tourists who come into town year-round."

"Sounds delicious. Maybe we should go there for a late lunch?" I chime in. We figured, at the most, we'd be out for about an hour and a half, and even though I have

Cheez-Its and protein bars, it's never too early to start talking about lunch.

"Or maybe you invite your hot neighbor and see if he'd like to go?"

I glance back at Avery, and she wiggles her eyebrows suggestively.

"Like on a date?" I scrunch my nose.

Visions of Briggs and me sitting in the dark at a tiny two-top table at a restaurant with a red-and-white-plaid tablecloth, a candle, and Italian music in the background have me shuddering. He would hate that just as much as I would.

"Semantics." She shrugs her shoulders.

Then my vision changes to a large comfy booth with bright lighting, gorgeous blue-and-white Italian plates, and a bottle of limoncello on the table. That he might go for, but then the fog clears because what am I thinking? Briggs and I will never go on a date. We aren't like that. At all.

But what are we?

We were enemies, sort of.

Then we were cordial to each other, and he was kind of nice.

And now we're what, friends? Friendly? Acquaintances? I wouldn't call us business partners, but we did kind of make a deal.

"Speaking of my hot, annoying neighbor, I have a bit of random news to share."

"Ooo, gossip. I love it," Avery calls from behind. The trail has narrowed, and we're in a line instead of walking next to each other. She has to be in the middle so I can see if there are any uneven areas, and Juliet is behind in case she needs to catch her.

"Well, I wouldn't call it gossip if it happened to me."

"Now I'm even more curious."

Nerves creep into my stomach. Why am I nervous about telling them this? It's not like it needs to be a secret, and nothing happened, and no salacious acts occurred. Although, I haven't forgotten the way he looked sitting on the edge of my bed in just his underwear. His size alone swallowed up space and air in the room, and I didn't hate having the heat pour off him as he slept. A few times, I did wonder what would happen if I made a move. But then I laughed to myself and eventually fell asleep.

"This past Saturday, Briggs showed up at my door at midnight."

Avery gasps.

"What for?" Juliet calls from the back.

"He wanted to sleep with me."

The noise behind me ceases. Both girls have stopped walking, and I turn to find them looking at me, jaws dropped. A blush burns through my cheeks at how that sounded.

"No! Not like sex, just sleep. Next to me. In my bed."

Oh my God.

"He spent the night at your house?" Avery asks, her brows pulled down in confusion.

"Yes! He showed up wearing business attire and demanded we go to bed. He stripped off his clothes, climbed right in, and went to sleep. It was so out of character for him I didn't even know what to think. I just let it happen."

"But you never let people sleep with you. Even me. If we're on the road, you all demand your own bed."

"I know! But there he was. He took off his clothes, and I became tongue-tied. I'm twenty-nine years old, and I've seen plenty of men undressed for one reason or another, but with him, I didn't know what to do with myself."

"Describe. In detail," Juliet says, taking a step forward.

"I don't know. He's a tall, lean but muscular, somehow tanned even though I've never seen him outside shirtless, bearded, mountain man. If his shirts were plaid, he'd remind me of a hot lumberjack."

"But you said he was in business attire."

"Yes, and that almost makes it worse. At least in

jeans and an orchard shirt, he looks like he belongs here. Toss on a pair of tailored slacks and a button-down, and he looks like he belongs in my world, which is something I've always said I never wanted. You should have seen him," I groan.

"I'll tell you what I think. He likes you." Avery grins.

"What I think is you need to burn some sage and rid his aura from your house," Juliet says, and we all laugh.

"You do realize, if I did that, it would be just my luck to have an allergy attack. Meaning I'm the evil spirit here, not him."

Juliet laughs.

"So what happened to him? Why did he come over?" Avery asks as we start walking again.

"I can't make this up. You're going to die. He said he was at a meeting and then went to his brother's house, where his brother announced he is getting married. To. Briggs's. Ex-girlfriend."

"What?"

"That's horrible."

They both speak at the same time.

"How long did he date her?" Juliet asks.

"Over three years."

Three years. I've thought a lot about this, and even though he says he doesn't love her anymore, and I do believe that, three years is a long time. I've never met anyone I wanted to be with longer than three weeks, but he chose her. This has to hurt him at least a little on some level. Of course all of this makes me wonder what kind of woman she is. What was it that he originally fell for? Is she the same now, or is she different? He's obviously different based on what he's told me, but do people really change who they are? I don't think I've changed from who I am on the inside, even if on the outside I've made decisions for me that appear different. Like buying this house.

"No. Just no." She shakes her head.

"I don't understand," Avery says, still looking at me with confusion.

"From what I gather, I think his family is a lot like mine."

What is it about wealthy people caring more about appearances than they do about being genuine?

"Not possible." Avery frowns.

"I don't know," I tell them, each of us lost in our own thoughts as we weave through the trees.

This trail is really nice. Now that we're out here, and I see that it isn't difficult or in any way dangerous, I feel better about Avery. We've exited the tree line and have come upon a small field. It's full of white, yellow, and purple wildflowers. I pull out my phone to take a picture. These would look lovely spread between the trees in the bare patches back on the mountain. Those patches must have been crops for the family that lived in my house before me, but these would be a nice addition.

"I should have known you'd be taking pictures of plants while we're out here," Avery teases.

"I can't help myself."

"What are you going to do about Briggs? Do you think he'll come over again? Is this going to become a thing?" Avery asks, adjusting the hat on her head, long curly blonde hair pulled into a ponytail out the back.

"He hasn't come back since last weekend. There's been a lot of activity over at the orchard. He's got workers out collecting apples. In addition, customers are coming to pick the apples and taste the ciders. I hear cars coming and going all day long."

"Do you want him to come back?"

"I don't know. It was kind of nice having him there. I didn't feel like my space was being invaded, which is how I've felt with other people. We did kind of make a deal with each other."

"And what is that?"

"I offered to go with him to his brother's engagement party, and in return, he'll go home with me in October to my parents' event."

"You're going to take him to New York?" Avery asks, shocked.

"Yep."

"Oh, to be a fly on the wall when he walks in and meets the rest of the Rhodes family." She grimaces.

"Emma and Clay are going, too. I'm sure she'll give you a very detailed rundown."

"I don't know why you still go to those."

"Because I have to."

"No, you don't," she says.

Avery didn't come from money like I do, but in the small town where she grew up, her family was a prominent one. She tried to be their perfect daughter until one day she said, "No more." I understand what she's saying—technically, I don't have to—but her situation was different from mine. They're my family, and I do like making them happy.

"Maybe one day I'll stop going, but how can I pass up the opportunity to take the mountain man home?"

Behind us, Juliet gasps.

"What?" We turn and look at her, and her face is lit up.

"I just had the best idea for your next prank." She grins.

17

BRIGGS

"I think we should talk," Cole says, coming from his office upstairs.

The hair on the back of my neck immediately stands up. I don't think he's planning on leaving me anytime soon, but you never know, and the way he just said that sounds ominous. Even though we're best friends, it's not like he would have discussed it with me beforehand.

Wiping my hands, I set down the towel and turn to face him. I've worked nonstop in the orchard over the past few weeks. Between collecting and picking apples, getting them washed and stored in the large walk-in coolers for later use, then in the mill, pressing them and the juice sent to the fermentation tanks, I'm just beat. Everyone has been all hands on deck, even Goldie. I've seen her up on the mountain helping Jane, but being the owner, I feel it's my responsibility to put in the most time and go above and beyond.

"All right. What's up?" I place my hands on my hips.

He pauses, and his face pales. "This is awkward."

"What is? Spit it out."

Anxiety creeps in a little as I suddenly think I should be alarmed at what he's about to tell me.

He rolls his lips into his teeth, lets out a deep sigh, and says, "I didn't realize you were ready to start dating again."

Huh?

"What do you mean?" I ask, examining him for clues as to what the hell he's talking about.

"Nothing! I mean nothing by that, and I think it's great," he says, taking a step away from me.

I tilt my head a little and stare at him. Did he find out I stayed at Goldie's? She must have mentioned it to Jane. Or maybe he found out about our deal? Does he think it's a real date? He must, and then I laugh while walking over to the bar to pour myself a glass. Cold, crisp, tart, and delicious.

"Cole, it's not what you think," I tell him, shaking my head. He knows all about my family and was appalled when I told him about Jaxon and Adele. Then he very vocally announced that he never liked Adele in the first place, and he had a few very specific choice words to say about them.

"It doesn't matter what I think," he says defensively.

"Yeah, I guess it doesn't, but something about this has you all worked up, so spit it out."

"Briggs"—he hesitates and then stands a little taller—"it's just not good for business."

I'm thoroughly confused. From the influx of people we had after the news segment, I can't see how being friends with her would ever be bad for business. Not that I plan on exploiting her in any way. Come to think of it, it still pisses me off that she hasn't installed a security system with all of the strangers rolling in up here.

"How so?" I ask, curious to hear how his mind works on the topic of Goldie. Although, when it comes to her, I'm not sure I care what he thinks.

"Well, for starters, you shouldn't have used the orchard's email address. I mean, to each their own, but have you seen how many emails have come in over the past week? There must be at least a hundred, and all with photos of people's feet. I think using a personal email address would be best."

I'd just taken another huge swig of cider, and instead of spewing it everywhere, half of it goes down the wrong pipe, and I start choking. Almost violently.

"Did you say feet?" I wheeze as he comes around the counter and slaps my back.

"Yes. It's nothing to be embarrassed about. Everyone has their fetishes. I mean just the other day, Amelia and I were talking about role-playing, and—"

"STOP!" I hold up my hands. "I don't want to know this," I tell him as I back away.

"But I just want you to know it's okay."

Is this a therapy session or something? He's somehow consoling me and scolding me at the same time. Only I'm clueless here!

"Cole! What the fuck are you talking about?"

"The emails." He throws his hands out.

"What emails?" I set the glass down and glare at him.

"From the dating website."

"I'm not on any dating sites." I shake my head like he's lost his damn mind.

"Yes, you are. Amelia and I looked you up after the first couple came in."

"You what! Where?"

"Binder."

"You've got to be fucking kidding me."

I see red.

"Nope. Are you saying you didn't set it up?"

"Hell, no. Can you imagine if word of this got out? What does it say?"

"That you like feet."

Oh. My. God.

Who would do this?

I start pacing back and forth, thinking of all the ramifications of this. Maybe someone just used my photo and is catfishing people, but that can't be right because they used the orchard's email address. And that's when it hits me.

I stop in front of Cole, and I can't help the volume of my words as they come pouring out of me.

"That little witch!"

"Who's a witch?" he asks, eyes big with excitement over me figuring this out.

"You know she did this, and she's just sitting over there in her house probably having a grand time laughing." I throw out my hand in her direction.

"You think Cora did this?"

"Well, I certainly didn't! What a fucking debacle."

Turning, I storm out of the barn. I'm halfway to her house when the curse of the mountain strikes again. Instead of the beautiful notes from the cello that I hear nightly, a high-pitched wail from Cora's smoke alarm stretches from across the trees to me. Instantly, my anger is gone, fear sweeps through me, and I take off for her.

Running through the open front door, I head straight for the kitchen and find Cora using a baking sheet to try to fan the smoke out of the window over the sink.

"What the hell happened?" I all but shout at her.

This moment is all too similar to the night I met her. Only this time, gray smoke pours out her front and back door, and she's fully dressed. Unfortunately, I'm emotionally involved. Well, emotionally pissed off.

She jumps at the sound of my voice.

"Geez, could you warn a girl or something? For someone so large, you are freakishly silent when coming and going."

She puts down the sheet pan, pulls her hair free of the messy knot it's in and redoes it. Her hair is always so golden and so shiny. Too often, I've thought about running my fingers through it, but it looks like a mess right now.

"I'm not sure how you didn't hear me come running through the door when I'm wearing boots."

At this, she looks me over from head to toe, but her gaze is slow. I don't think she's looking at me, and then it occurs to me that she's remembering. Her cheeks flush pink. Yeah, I understand better than she does. I actually saw her naked, except for the tiny underwear, and I can't forget that either.

Not that I want to.

Clearing her throat, she looks away from me and moves to the sink to wash her hands. "Why are you wearing boots?"

"Why am I wearing boots? I was working in the barn when I heard the alarm. The better question is, what happened? Are you hurt?"

When I look around her kitchen, it's like a bomb went off with how much stuff she has everywhere. There are bowls, mixing utensils, ingredients like flour and sugar, and a bowl of chopped apples. Clearly, she was trying to fry something as there's a mess all over the countertops, and don't get me started on the black smoke residue along the back of the range wall or the pot on the stove with the large fire blanket thrown over it.

"No, not hurt. Embarrassed, maybe."

I walk to the sink and grab her arms to look at them and her hands. She yanks them free and glares at me.

"Do you mind?" she asks, spinning around and going to the living room, where she picks up three plants and takes them outside.

"Yes, I mind!"

"Well, while you're over there not minding your own business, maybe make yourself useful and move the plants," she orders me.

As the smoke clears from my head, I realize she's trying to save her plants from the polluted air. I move to the one with the chirper, pocketing it so she can't see it, and grab the plant. This is a perfect opportunity to take it home and replace the battery. It also reminds me why I was coming here in the first place.

"I was trying to make some apple fritters with some apples I bought, but the oil got too hot," she says as she brushes by me, not looking at me, and picking up two more plants. "I didn't realize the oil could just burst into flames."

Bought? What?

"Didn't you see the smoke? That's the sign it's too hot."

"Thanks for the obvious lecture, but no. I was turned around and chopping the apples. I wasn't paying attention, and I should have been."

"Where did you buy apples? You can have all the apples you want from my trees. If you wander up, I think there are even a few left on your side."

"I bought them from you," she says, like I'm the dumbest person ever.

I recoil at this. I don't want to take her money. They're just apples.

"When?"

"Yesterday. I didn't see you, but Cole was there. I bought them from him."

Seems like Cole and I are going to have another little chat. I pick up one of her larger plants and take it to the porch and set it down so it can get a few moments of the afternoon sun. She brings out another, and after she sets it down, I embrace her arm to get her attention.

"Goldie, your money's no good to me. Just pick what you want. Always."

"I support my friends. I don't take from them."

Hearing her use the word friend has the anger in me calming, and she sees the change as the tension in her face relaxes too.

"Thank you, but next time, just pick them. Okay?"

"Okay," she says, and then glances down at my hand, more like she's surprised that I'm touching her instead of being repulsed that I am, and then back to my face. "Thanks."

I drop her arm. "Speaking of Cole, he and I had a very interesting chat just before I came over here."

Her eyes widen as she interprets my tone, and she whips around to put her back to me.

"Oh yeah. About what?" she asks, all innocently, scurrying away from me and into the house.

"You know what," I say as I follow her, allowing myself

to finally take her in completely. She's wearing tiny athletic shorts that appear much shorter on her long legs and hug her ass perfectly, a matching tank top, and an apron around her waist. Images of how my hands could perfectly squeeze her fill my mind until I hear her snicker.

"You think you're so funny," I all but snarl.

At this, she turns back to me, and her face is lit up like she just won the lottery. "Oh, I totally do."

She proceeds to walk directly into my personal space and run her foot down my shin and up the back of my calf while biting her bottom lip.

"Do you like that?" she teases in a seductive voice, and unfortunately, I do. I like it very much, and another part of me likes what it sees and is curious as to how it would feel. I've never given much thought to feet, but I'm thinking I could make it work if she was down for it.

My hands grab her. I pull her close and bend down so my lips fall just next to her ear. Her foot hooks behind my leg, and even through the burnt-tainted air, the lemony and vanilla scent from her shampoo tickles my nose.

"Goldie, cancel the account." My voice is rough as having her wrapped around me and being this near to her is dizzying.

Her hands move to my hips, and she pulls me a little closer. "And if I don't?"

I pull back a little to stare down into her face. "Don't forget, two are playing this game."

"Two, huh? As far as I can tell, you're behind." Her eyes sparkle.

"Am I, though?" I tuck a loose piece of her hair behind her ear and run my thumb down the length of her neck. She's so close, she smells so good, and the relief that I have knowing nothing happened to her almost has me closing the distance between us to kiss her. But instead, I watch as confusion and desire sweeps over her face, and an evil smirk tips my lips.

"I don't lose. Ever."

"Neither do I," she says, her eyes dropping to my lips.

The moment between us stalls, charges, and the air becomes heavy. If I tried to kiss her, would she let me? Would she part her lips and allow me to sink into her mouth to taste what I've been fantasizing about since the night we met? I know I shouldn't, but damn if I don't want to.

"I guess we'll see," I say, severing the thoughts in my head.

"I guess we will," she challenges, her cheeks flushing pink as her eyes again find mine.

"You sure you're still good to go with me this weekend?"

"Of course. You don't need to worry. I was born and raised for these scenarios." She squeezes my waist one more time, glances again at my lips almost like she's disappointed, and then drops her foot and steps back.

It's the right thing to do. We both know it.

"Do I need to be concerned?" I raise one brow at her.

"Of course not." She smiles. "Greedy, pretentious social climbers, you're speaking my language. I can one-up anyone in the room, including your brother."

"I don't know if we need to one-up him, but considering that he's marrying Adele, it might be fun," I say, considering what she's said. I love how she's game to be whatever I need her to be. Surprisingly, I'm not worried at all about bringing her and it seeming not real. She has this way about her that sucks you in, not pushes you away. I know as she charms the room, it will be enough to drive Jaxon crazy.

"Always wants what he can't have, right?"

"Pretty much."

"Then we've got this."

She walks past me and runs her hand down my arm.

"I'm starting to wonder if I should be afraid."

She laughs.

"Never." She winks at me, then moves to pick up another plant.

"All right, Goldie. Let's get you cleaned up."

"I can do it," she states, almost a little defensively.

"Never said you couldn't, but I'm here, and we can make this go away twice as fast."

I watch as emotions shift over her face as she thinks about this. I understand she does everything on her own, but she doesn't need to. I'm here, and I can help. Eventually, whatever wall she had thrown up slides back down, and she says, "Okay."

CORA

I swear, being here makes me feel just like it does when I'm at home. Only this time, I'm in a large mansion hidden behind a gate surrounded by a perfectly manicured lawn and a valet team parking the most expensive cars on the planet.

A part of me was surprised to hear that the party would be at Jaxon's house versus a venue. Then again, I've discovered that his brother is very concerned about what others think of him. He wants to show off his wealth, even if it's inherited and not earned.

"Do you have a house here?" I asked him when we pulled through the gate. Clearly, we were in a very affluent neighborhood.

He laughed. "Almost."

Briggs and I talked a lot about his family on the drive

in. I appreciated that he didn't purposely speak ill of them. He was just to the point about their characters and what I could expect. We also briefly spoke about Adele. Briggs explained that he didn't understand her angle with marrying his brother, but then again, her family expected the union between him and her, so maybe they were still pushing that agenda.

I looked them both up online so I knew what to expect when we arrived. We also spoke about a few other people who would most likely be in attendance, and much to Briggs's surprise, our worlds do overlap.

After the long drive, I beelined to the restroom, and I'm walking out of the library when I spot Briggs's dark head of hair above the others in the room. He's standing with several other men and a woman so blatantly looking at Briggs with complete longing that my body temperature rises a few degrees. I know I shouldn't be spying on him the way I am, but he brought me here as his date, so staring is justified.

Two of the men eventually walk off, leaving one man and the woman. He's shorter than Briggs, but just by a few inches, and taking in the way Briggs's back is ramrod straight and his hand is clenched around his glass, it doesn't take a genius to realize this guy isn't talking to Briggs, he's speaking at him.

His brother, Jaxon, and that's Adele.

I use this moment to study her. I guess you could say she looks like what one would expect from a Southern socialite—waif thin, long blonde hair perfectly curled, and her eye makeup is done in a way to make her eyes look big and doe-like. She's wearing a short tight off-white dress and pearls. She reminds me of a Barbie doll, and my stomach sours thinking that at one point, Briggs loved her. Three years is such a long time.

And now she's about to become his sister-in-law.

No thanks.

A server walks by with a platter of champagne glasses and offers me one. I decline, but we haven't been here nearly long enough, and well, first impressions are lasting impressions.

It's so interesting watching him in this setting and hard for me to connect the dots of our life back on the mountain to this one in front of me. There, Briggs is a force to be reckoned with. He works hard, and people have nothing but nice things to say about him. People flocked to him at the season kickoff party, outside of those few moments with the reporter. He's someone they want to know.

But I see here that although he silently commands the space around him, he's silent. It's odd to see him don this shell of indifference, but maybe this is his way of self-preservation. Heaven knows, I certainly do what I need to do with my family too.

Okay, I guess it's showtime.

Briggs spots me approaching, and he catches the up-to-no-good glint shining off me. He smirks in response. Unexpected butterflies swirl, and I just wink at him.

"There you are, darling," I say to Briggs as I slide up next to him, wrap my arms around him, and then stretch on my toes to kiss the corner of his mouth. He's shaved the usual scruff off his face, shocking me when he opened the door back home, but here and now, I hesitate as my lips settle against his warm skin and soft lips.

I like it. A lot.

And if I thought I would shock him, I don't. Instead, his arm smoothly wraps around my waist, his hand anchors to my hip to keep me connected to him, and after I pull back, his head drops a little to rest next to mine, and he returns the intimacy by pressing his lips into my forehead. I'm surrounded by his exquisite smell, and while I should be moving away, I lean in farther and breathe him in, just like he does to me. He took that kiss and then gave me one of his own, and instead of remembering that I'm supposed to be playing a part, I'm too busy wondering why being affectionate with him is so comfortable.

I can feel the eyes of his brother and the woman as they rake over me. I'm guessing neither expected me, or maybe they did because his brother nearly growls.

"Keeping it classy like always, I see."

As if this little display of PDA is noteworthy to anyone in this room. It's not. He's just being rude, and if I were a lesser woman, then the intended dig would probably hit its mark, but I'm not. In society and wealth, I completely outrank him, and it's assholes like this that I've had to deal with my entire life.

Taking a tiny step from his side, Briggs's large hand falls to my lower back while mine wraps around his waist.

From over my head, Briggs says, "You would know, wouldn't you? Till death do you part."

I glance at the two of them after his comment and then ignore them, as if they are simply nobodies, and turn back to Briggs. "Sorry I took so long. I ran into Donovan's wife, Kristie, and we got busy catching up."

Briggs doesn't actually know if I did or did not run into her, but a small smile forms on his lips as he stares down at me adoringly, and a small surprised noise comes from Adele. Kristie does not give her time freely to just anyone, and my guess is that Adele here has tried to stick her foot in the door to open that relationship and failed.

At this moment, my heart whispers, "What would it feel like to actually have this man looking at me fondly?"

"Donovan Daniels?" his brother blurts.

Tearing my eyes away from Briggs, I turn to face his brother, my composure and air demanding that my pure Upper East Side pedigree be recognized, and it is, given the way his brother's nostrils flare.

"Why, yes. Lovely couple."

I'm certain they want to know more, but this is a power move that I know how to play very well. Never overshare. Give them just enough to feel left out and want to know more. People are greedy for gossip and information, and it's in moments like this when they think they have the upper hand over us, over me, that their confidence wavers, and while I'm smiling at both of them, they feel as if I'm looking down my nose at them.

And I am.

Briggs's brother pulls his shoulders back a little as he tries to stand taller. Too bad we're eye to eye with me in these heels, and I watch as Adele's lips purse together, and her gaze takes inventory. Large diamond stud earrings and a single tennis bracelet, this shows wealth but not flamboyance. The simple square cut neckline of my Oscar de la Renta dress, which I had shipped in just for this event, that shows off the lean lines of my collarbone, the length of my neck, and wraps my frame perfectly, ending just at my knees. To my Valentino heels, recognizable by the one gold stud present on the strap of each ankle.

"I'm sorry, who are you?" his brother asks.

"Goldie, this is my brother, Jaxon Warren, and his soon-to-be wife Adele. Jaxon, my girlfriend, Cora Rhodes," Briggs says as he waves his free hand back and forth between us, the other still clamping down and holding me to him.

Girlfriend.

We said I'd be his date, so this is a new development. One that I don't mind, and I'll have no problems playing.

While Rhodes is a common name, it's also a name that, when mentioned in elite social circles, causes people to pause and wonder if I'm one of those Rhodes.

Which I am.

"I didn't realize you were dating anyone." He eyes me warily. Meanwhile, out of my peripheral vision, I watch as Adele stares at Briggs.

"And why would you? It's not like you care. I'm only here to be seen, right? Keep up those pretenses of a unified family."

His brother shifts uncomfortably, not liking that Briggs is publicly speaking about their fake image.

Jaxon's gaze whips back to me, and he says, "I'm sorry, have we met?"

I look him over head to toe, slip on a smile that's more condescending than pleasant, and tell him, "No, but congratulations to you both. Briggs tells me you're perfect for each other."

Sliding his hand to clasp mine, I intertwine our fingers, and he squeezes in approval. Then his thumb slowly begins to brush back and forth. Goose bumps race up my arm.

"Thank you," Adele says, stepping closer to Jaxon and ignoring the slight. She places her left hand on Jaxon's chest, flashing her giant ring. I don't even glance at it. I'm not playing her game. She's playing mine. A game that I find I don't like. I'm not myself anymore in these types of situations, and I have no problems admitting it.

Doesn't mean I can't or won't play the part, just that I'd prefer not to.

"So when's the big day?" I prompt, trying to keep up the pretense that we are actually happy for them.

"Christmas Eve," she states excitedly as if I should think that a wintery Christmas wedding is ideal.

I pause to allow the insecurity to slip in.

"How unfortunate for all of those who have children." I turn to look at Briggs. "I suppose we could delay our trip. You just let me know what you want to do."

"You weren't planning on being here for Christmas?" Jaxon asks.

Briggs's thumb never misses a beat.

"No. We were planning on spending it with her family in New York, and then we're headed to Nice the week between Christmas and New Year's."

I randomly mentioned this year's family trip to him on the drive in, but I didn't actually think he was listening to me. But by him saying this, he has me wondering if he would like to go? He certainly would make it more fun for me, and I've been there enough times where I could show him around and make it fun for him too.

A different server walks over to us, and he has two glasses of champagne and two glasses of scotch. We each take a drink and thank him.

"Where did you two meet?" Adele asks, looking only at Briggs.

"Horizons Valley," he says at the same moment Jaxon takes a sip. This surprises him, and he lets out a choked sound.

"I just love it there. It's quite possibly my favorite place on earth," I say, giving Adele a smile that speaks of many, many unmentionable moments with Briggs, and then I turn and smile up at him. His eyes lock with mine and very intimately roam over my face. In my stomach, tiny butterflies flap their wings.

"Hungry?" he asks, speaking to me as if they aren't even there.

"Starved," I tell him. "But maybe we should circle the room once. There are so many people we should say hello to. I saw Charlie Levitt, and I just adore him."

At this, Jaxon clears his throat in disbelief. Charlie Levitt is notoriously a ruthless businessman who's made his fortune in the shipping industry. He does business all up and down the East Coast, so I'm not surprised he's here mingling with the high rollers in Charlotte. He makes grown men shake in their shoes, and then they leave the room crying.

"You know Charlie Levitt?" he asks, not in a way that says he's surprised by our acquaintance, but in a way that's condescending, as if he thinks I'm lying.

"Of course. Our families are close friends, and I grew up with his youngest daughter, Lauren."

And with this statement, Jaxon knows. I am one of those Rhodes. His eyes widen and take in the two of us again. I smile up at Briggs like I think he hung the moon, and in return, he leans forward to again brush his lips across my forehead where he speaks gently, but audibly, next to my ear.

"Let's make those rounds so I can get you fed."

I nod in agreement.

"You're the best."

And with that, Briggs pins his brother with one last look, never glances in Adele's direction, and without saying another word, we walk away.

19

BRIGGS

Having Cora at my brother's engagement party was a thing of beauty. She worked the room like no one I have ever seen before, and it was not lost on me how often my father and my brother watched her. My father out of curiosity, in the way of how he can use knowing her to his advantage, and my brother out of pure envy.

We didn't even have to do anything to make him feel one-upped. Just the two of us together, united and happy, was enough.

Of course there's the small detail that she was quite possibly the richest person in the room. Combining her family's money with her music career is impressive to everyone, no matter who you are.

Regardless, she flitted around, introduced herself to

people, and even though her posture and air screamed class and sophistication, every time she laughed, light poured out of her like the blonde goddess that she is, casting a spell over the entire room.

And I have no problem admitting she enchanted me most of all.

Of course I wanted her even on the first night. What red-blooded man wouldn't have? But now it's bordering on a level that will drive me insane.

I've replayed her pressed up against me, her hand in mine, and her lips brushing my skin more times than any man should care to admit. Toss in her smart mouth, her long legs, and the fact that I know how incredible her breasts are, and my mouth waters, and well, parts of me farther south ache for attention.

It's a bad idea; it really is. She's my neighbor and has become my friend. Crossing the line would mess things up, but still, it's so tempting.

Tempting and also not the right time. Maybe one day, if she's on board, but I can't change things between us now because I owe her. After what she just did for me, I owe her that trip to New York, and I can't change any of the dynamics that might make it uncomfortable or impossible for us, so instead, I'm at the grocery store picking up what I need for my next prank.

"I don't understand why you still want to prank her. I

thought after last weekend, you'd called some type of truce or something," Cole says. He's a people pleaser all the way to his core, and he just doesn't understand anything that might rock the boat or cause someone to be unhappy with him.

"No, no truce was called. Besides, I can't let her have the last laugh. What she did with the dating profile . . . you think I should just let it go after that?"

Even though she took down the profile, I'm still getting emails. There are a few random new ones, but mostly they are follow-ups from the originals who sent them. All with more pictures of more feet.

"Yes. I think you should let it go," he says, and he would say that.

"Do you even know me?" I chuckle. After all these years, he should know better. I never back down from a challenge, and apparently, I don't from a prank either. However, I admit it's getting harder to come up with ideas. Some are funny, some are messy, and some are crossing the line, and I'm not interested in that.

"So you're at the grocery store? What are you getting?"

"Fish," I tell him as I stand in front of the seafood counter. While Horizons Valley is a great town, our grocery store is pretty basic. It's filled with essentials, primarily for tourists and not luxuries like you'd find at Whole Foods.

He makes a strangled sound. "I'm afraid to ask, what will you do with a fish?"

"Not one fish, but two." I eye the different fish behind the glass counter. Some are marinated filets, but then there are the whole fish, and excitement pierces through me.

This time, he lets out a deep sigh. "Okay, what are you going to do with two fish?"

"Hide one on the front porch and one on the back. This way, it'll keep her guessing where else I might have hidden one."

"Briggs. No," he chastises.

"Yes! The smell will drive her crazy."

"It will also drive wild animals crazy and bring them straight to her door. Did you forget that she did not do well with the raccoons or the deer? Why do you keep picking pranks that involve animals?"

It hasn't occurred to me that I do, but okay.

"Cole, she lives on a mountain. If she can't handle a couple of animals, then maybe she shouldn't be here." But just saying that causes an unknown ache to press on my chest, and I reach up to rub it. "It won't be that strong to attract animals. Maybe Rocky and Bullwinkle but within a day or two, she'll have found them and gotten rid of them. I don't foresee the fish being there too long, just long enough to piss her off."

"Why fish?"

"Because it's a thing."

"What thing?"

"Dead fish. Didn't you watch Mafia movies as a kid?"

"No, not really. I was more into Marvel and graphic novels."

Not surprising. Given his career choice, this makes sense.

I glance around to see if anyone I know stands near me, but there isn't. However, plenty of people are walking by, so I lower my voice not to attract attention. "Well, the Mafia, when they weren't happy with you, they would leave dead fish. It was a warning that if you didn't stop what you were doing or leave town, you would 'sleep with the fish'."

"As in they would put your feet in concrete and throw you overboard?" he asks, suddenly catching on.

"Yes. You would be kidnapped, sometimes tortured, and most definitely weighted down and tossed overboard."

"Huh. Dead fish. Learn something new every day. You think she watched Mafia movies and knows what this means?"

"I don't know, but the smell alone will be funny enough."

"Briggs." His disappointed tone has returned, but I'm over hearing it.

"Gotta go," I tell him and hang up as the guy behind the counter comes to stand in front of me.

I order two whole rainbow trout and can't help the smirk that sits on my face as he wraps them both in white paper, weighs them, and slaps the price sticker on them. While I wouldn't say these fish are large, they're definitely not small and will stink up the area.

"Thank you," I tell him as he hands them to me, and as I turn to head to check out, I almost run right into Will Ashton.

"Sorry, man. Didn't see you there."

"No worries. Just wanted to say hello. How's it going?" he asks me, leaning forward and clapping me on the shoulder. He's smiling at me like we're long-lost friends, and at this moment, I'm grateful for the beard as I can feel heat climbing into my cheeks. I feel busted, although I'm not sure why.

"It's going. So far, this season is better than last year, and Cole and I have started testing more flavors for the ciders."

"That's great. If you ever need an extra opinion, you just let me know."

"How's Avery feeling?" I ask. Everyone knows Avery Layne is pregnant. Even if I didn't know her as an acquaintance, which I do, when word got out, the world went crazy knowing she and Ash were having a baby. They're a power couple in the music industry, and this poor baby has no idea what world it will be born into.

"She's good. She's always had a bit of a sweet tooth, but it's been over the top lately. She's constantly talking about your donuts and sent me here to pick up these." He holds up two boxes of Little Debbie Nutty Buddy chocolate and peanut butter wafer cookies.

"That's it? That's all you're here for?"

"Yep." He smiles and glances around to see if people are looking at us, and they are. I know he can't help it. It's the downside to being famous, but it is a weird sensation to know that people are watching you. At least they aren't approaching us.

"Well, feel free to come get donuts anytime you want them. I'll even teach you how to make them if no one's there."

"Thank you. As much as she goes on and on about them, I can pretty much guarantee I'll be by. How's Cora doing? I hear she's letting you spend time with her." He grins, and I chuckle.

Just having him mention her name has my hand holding the fish starting to sweat.

"That's one way to put it, and from what I can tell, she's doing all right. I haven't seen or heard anything to think otherwise."

Very detailed images of her flash in my mind. The night we met, her storming into my cider house and yelling at me, seeing her lips wrapped around a glass in the barn as she drank my ciders, and her in a sleek black dress and tall sexy heels smiling at me like I hung the moon.

"Good. Avery gets worried about her."

"Why?" I tilt my head. This is an odd thing to say, and suddenly, I feel very defensive on Cora's behalf.

"Well, she's known for not being the best at asking for help when she needs it."

I think about what he's saying, but then I try to come up with scenarios of when she might have needed help. Other than the grease fire, which can happen to anyone and she had it under control, I haven't seen anything to cause any alarm.

I shrug. "She seems all right to me."

"Good. Coming from her New York condo life, we weren't sure how being a homeowner in the mountains would go. This is like a whole new world to her, and we're glad you're up there, near her, should she need someone."

I would be lying if I said this conversation didn't

confuse me a little. I knew she was from New York, but I guess I didn't really think about how the difference in living would be for her. I mean, why would I? She's an independent woman who bought a house. This isn't a new concept for people. Then again, if she's used to a vastly different white-collar lifestyle, then yeah, maybe I can see their concern, but she hasn't given me any reason to be.

It's then I think to ask, "Just out of curiosity, is she dating anyone?"

This isn't a topic that Cora and I have discussed. I mean why would we? But she is Cora Rhodes. Her superstar musician status alone could have her dating someone who lives anywhere.

He laughs. "Cora doesn't date."

"What do you mean?"

"She just doesn't. Every now and then, she'll drag someone along to an event with us, but mostly, she chooses to be on her own. Outside of the girls, she doesn't form attachments to people."

Outside of the girls. But what about me? We are neighbors, and I think we're friends, although I'm not sure how she's going to react over the fish, but given the fact that I can't seem to stay away from her or get her out of my head, doesn't that mean something too? Then again, maybe what I think and feel is one-sided.

"Strange. Why is that?"

"I'm not really sure, but from what I've gathered, her family does not treat her the best."

How can anyone not treat her well? She's amazing at everything I've seen her do so far, and she's kind and giving. I know she doesn't get along very well with her brother, but I didn't get the impression that they treated her badly, just that they give her a hard time because she's different from them.

Which I fully understand.

"Hmm," I answer, not really sure how to respond. Have I thought about Cora? Absolutely. Has she been a bit of a mystery? I didn't think so. I had pegged her as just another rich and famous person who bought a house in the same town as her friends to escape from the spotlight and get some peace, but with each new nugget of information I get about her, I'm starting to think there's a lot more to her than meets the eye.

"Well, I won't keep you. I just wanted to say hello. If you're up for it, when Clay gets back into town, maybe we can all get together for a cookout. I bought this new smoker, and I'm ready to show it off."

"Sounds good. Just tell me when, and I'll bring the cider."

"Perfect."

20

CORA

I'm avoiding my neighbor.

Why? Because he's an idiot.

I thought we had been working toward a friendship of sorts, but noooo. What he did, I'm still seeing red just thinking about it. Not only did he hide one big fish, but he hid two! One in the front and one in the back. It took me forever to figure out how to get them out from under the porch, and don't get me started on the bear scat I found at the bottom of my front steps. I know it's bear scat because I looked it up on the internet.

What was he thinking putting fish out to rot like that?

It smelled so bad, and I swear, not only did they attract bears to my yard, but every fly in a five-mile radius. So gross.

Once the fish were disposed of, I immediately got on the phone and called Juliet. She and I both agreed that it was time to place the order for his next prank, so that's what I did, and it'll be shipped straight to his house. If he wants to play dirty, then I am so down for it, and the minute I hit order, that anger shifted to evil retribution. This prank will keep on giving, and I can't wait to see his face.

Idiot.

Dumb, handsome idiot.

I might physically be avoiding him, but mentally, I'm not.

Every night since his brother's party, I've lain in bed and replayed different scenes of us together. The way we were together, no one would ever have suspected that we weren't an actual couple. He couldn't keep his hands off me, and I couldn't keep mine off him. Don't get me wrong, we were the epitome of class and sophistication, but together, we worked effortlessly. I've never been to an event where I had a partner in crime, and as the night dragged on, I became more and more excited to take him home with me to New York. If I had any reservations about how he would fit in, they evaporated almost instantly.

Just like my hesitation about touching him.

His broad shoulders, strong muscular arms, and

large hands were enough to keep me occupied, but toss in his handsome face, his dominance in a crowd like that, and him wrapped in a custom-tailored dark gray suit, and I could drool. Who am I kidding? I have drooled. Every. Night.

I'm not supposed to be this attracted to my neighbor.

"I was surprised you called and wanted to go to this today," Juliet says, pulling me from my thoughts as we walk out of Bean There onto Main Street. A line of people waits to get a cup of coffee, and it makes me happy for Mrs. Wheeler. "Avery gets so nervous and avoids these crowds, even if Blair is with her."

Blair is her personal security detail who always accompanies us when we travel.

"I know. But I do think she's better than she used to be. For as long as I've known her, she feels comfortable in only a few places. Now, though, add in the fact that she's pregnant and married to your brother and how the attention that comes her way has grown exponentially, she rarely leaves her house."

I've heard people talk about me over the years and how I'm a loner, and I want to point at Avery and ask if they've taken a look at her. She never goes anywhere. Granted, she has her reasons, but she's fine with it.

"Maybe we'll find something for her today that we can run over to her house afterward."

"Sounds good to me. She mentioned that Ash built the crib, and I'd like to see it."

"Does it seem surreal to you that she's having a baby?" I ask her as we round the corner and enter the crowd of the town fall festival.

"For me, it's not her, it's him. I can't believe that Ash is having a baby. I've known him for two decades and have seen him at so many different phases of life. This one to me is crazy. Ash as a dad."

"Just wait until it's Emma and Clay."

She groans.

"I can't. Not yet." She shakes her head but then grabs my arm. "Not because I think Emma will be a bad mother. I think she will be a wonderful mother. It's having Clay hold their tiny baby in his arms with love pouring off him. I'm not sure my heart can handle it."

I know what she means. My friends holding their little mini-mes that will undoubtedly look like them causes my heart to fill with joy too.

"Yeah, there are some good days to come." I smile at her and then look around. "Well, this is a lot larger than I expected it to be." White pop-up tents line both sides of the street. Fall decorations explode from every nook and cranny, and my heart overflows with happiness.

"Yeah, the town advertises this. It sucks in people who are looking for a place in North Carolina to go to see the leaves change. Our elevation is a little higher than towns like Asheville, so our leaves change a little earlier and then last a few weeks up to November. Of course the peak weekend for them always changes, but the festival brings in happy people."

"I know I'm certainly happy."

She eyes me suspiciously. "Honestly, I didn't peg you for a festival type of girl."

I bump my shoulder against hers. "Well, I am, so festival partner for life right here."

"That's good because Bryce would rather chew his arm off than be here, and he was so happy to go to Ash's house for a sleepover."

"I didn't know he was sleeping over. What are you doing tonight?"

"I haven't decided yet, but that's the beauty of it, right? I'm free." She laughs.

Slowly, we make our way through the booths. I wouldn't necessarily call it primarily an art festival, but there is a lot of art here. There are paintings, photography, pottery, and sculptures, but then there is jewelry, soaps, quilts, and an assortment of knickknacks and foods. I buy a welcome door wreath, some local honey, a hand-carved cutting board, and a kitchen towel with an apple fritter recipe on it. I may have failed the first time, but as they say, try, try again. Juliet buys a painting that supports the local high school and taste tests her way through all the booths offering samples.

"Hey, Cora," someone says from my left. Juliet and I turn to find Cole and Briggs standing under a red street tent. Quite a few of the vendors today have spilled over into the side streets, and while it didn't occur to me that they would be here, it should have.

Immediately, my heart pounds at the sight of Briggs. He looks better than any stupid memory my mind can conjure, but that doesn't stop me from frowning and shooting daggers his way.

Cole waves. He's the one who called my name. I politely smile back, then shift my gaze to glare at Briggs again.

He smirks, and my eyes narrow. He thinks he's gained an upper hand over me, but he hasn't. As far as I can tell, the score is not even. It's my three to his two. Smirk all you want.

Smug idiot.

Then again, if he knew what was coming his way, he definitely wouldn't be making that face right now.

"Hey, Cole," Juliet answers him politely, as it seems I've lost my ability to be social even though she knows what Briggs did. She elbows me in the arm to draw us closer and asks, "How's business today?"

Begrudgingly, I follow.

"It's great. We're almost sold out of sweet cider, and Amelia, who's working at the orchard, says we've had a lot of people stop in today to pick apples and taste the hard ciders."

"That's great! If they're eating Jane's donuts, then I'm certain you've got a customer for life."

He grins. "Yeah, she said Jane's been pretty busy too. Lots of people for her to talk to, which is great for her."

I again smile at Cole, thinking about Jane. She is the sweetest, but he's not wrong. She will talk your ear off.

"Have you tried the smoked trout dip yet over at Dan's booth? I hear it's delicious," Briggs chimes in, and Cole grimaces. Clearly, he knows what his boss and friend has been up to, and poor Juliet, who had to hear all about the fish fiasco, makes a squeaking noise next to me.

"You know, you really are just the worst," I deadpan while frowning at him.

"That's not what you said the other night." He grins.

Oh my God, I cannot believe he said that out loud, implying something different. I glance around to see if anyone is near us. There's no telling who just heard him.

Juliet gasps, and both she and Cole turn to look at me.

"Really?" I ask in a way that would make most cower. "What is wrong with you? And that's because the other night you were charming and well, whatever." I'm waving my free hand not holding a bag in front of him and not wanting him to know exactly what I thought of him after that event. "You must have conjured up your alter ego. It's unfortunate too. I like him better than you."

He laughs, and the sound sweeps over me. I haven't heard him laugh often, but it's such a nice sound, and I hate that I have a visceral reaction to it. I feel like a moth being drawn to the flame.

"Hey, I'm going to run over to Darby's candle booth and get Amelia a candle. She loves those candles as the wax is poured into repurposed pieces of wood, and I want to surprise her. Do you mind helping Briggs here for a few minutes?" Cole asks, stepping out from behind the booth.

"That's so sweet, she'll love it. And of course I'll stay and scare off the customers." I smile really big at him, and he wavers for a second as indecision flashes over his features. Then he shrugs and takes off. I glance at Juliet and see she's wrapped up in a conversation with someone she knows, so it's just us.

"Here, let me take those for you," Briggs says. He reaches for my bags, but I move my arms out of the way.

"It's okay, I've got them."

He frowns a little as his arms lower by his sides.

Moving behind the table in the booth, I set them down and turn to face him. He's smiling at me like the cat who got the cream. The scruff of his beard is back, and it looks good. He looks good. Handsome in a way that's natural and not forced and does not fuel the fire. I roll my eyes.

Big handsome idiot.

"I didn't know you planned on having a booth today," I tell him, looking down at his table and seeing his cute packages of donuts, jars of cider apple butter, and four-pack bottles of different flavors of sweet cider.

It's too bad that nothing is cute about him at this moment. He's a menace.

"I have every year since I bought the place. The booth helps the town and the tourists who come out learn about the orchard."

"Learn about the orchard. Maybe if they learned the truth about you, business would be so bad the town would ask you to leave."

He grins, clearly liking the banter with me. It's unsettling. Eighty percent of the time, I've had to deal with stiff and scowling Briggs, so to see him relax with me like this makes me feel like I'm in an alternate universe.

"Leave? Not a chance. Do you see that new gazebo over there?" He points at the one behind me, which is a prominent structure downtown. "That little donation came from Red Barn Orchard just last year. Since I took over, we've donated to the high school, the local food pantry, a pet rescue group, the 'Keep Horizons Valley Beautiful' organization, and last year, the gazebo. They're not asking me to leave."

"How sad for you that you have to pay these people to like you."

"Trust me, they like me. Everyone does." He winks, and I roll my eyes.

"Well, I don't like you," I tell him, and his small, amused smile stretches to become a large one. My breath catches, and my hands curl into fists. Why is he so attractive? Does he have this effect on everyone, or is it just me?

It's stupid.

"There's no reason to be salty, Goldie," he teases because we both know I don't mean it. I like him just fine. "What's that phrase? 'All's fair in love and war'? I think it fits, don't you?"

"Love. Is this your version of flirting with someone?"

"Do you want me to flirt with you?" he asks. His voice has gone deep, and his brown eyes, as they roam over the features of my face, have taken on this intimate, seductive quality. The butterflies in my stomach, or should I say moths, awaken and start fluttering their wings.

Ugh.

"Except there's no love. It's just war. A war which I will win."

His face shifts to give off an expression that says he knows something I don't. I'm not sure if he does or not, or if this is one of his methods of warfare. It's interesting that he said love and war. War stems from hate, and well, both emotions are so strong. I can see how easily love and hate toe the line with each other.

Shifting to stand closer to him, we look more approachable for anyone who's wandering by, and I'm hit with the distinct smell of him: pine and apples. My stomach tightens. This guy is going to be the death of me.

He bumps my shoulder with his. "Come on, you have to admit the fish was a good idea."

My jaw drops. "A good idea? Why do you keep bringing wild animals to my door? That's not funny, nor is it a good idea. It's scary."

His brows pull down, and the muscles across the top of his shoulders tense. "What wild animals?"

"Hello, as if the raccoons aren't bad enough, there's the deer and now the bears."

He crosses his arms over his chest, and unfortunately, my traitorous eyes travel over his biceps, which bulge out from under his short-sleeved orchard logoed T-shirt, and across his broad chest. I know what it feels like to be wrapped up in those arms, and as much as I'm angry with him, I kind of want to lean into him. "What do you mean, bears? We don't have bears on the mountain."

"Yes, we do. I have the bear scat to prove it."

His lips flatten into a straight line as he looks at me skeptically. "Are you sure that's what it is?"

"Do I look like an idiot to you?" I snap, and he unfurls his arms to run one hand over the scruff across his chin.

"Well, no, but you are new to mountain life."

"I may be new, but I'm perfectly capable of doing research." Pulling out my phone, I pull up the picture and hand it over to him so he can see what I saw. He frowns instantly.

"I haven't seen a bear on the mountain in years," he mumbles.

"Well, congratulations, your little stunt resurrected them. Into. My. Yard."

"Interesting," he says, looking at my phone again. "Do you know what to do if you're approached by a bear?"

Slowly, I feel all the blood drain from my face. It's

not that I haven't thought about this particular scenario, but actually being schooled on it like it's a real possibility scares me.

Seeing my reaction, he reaches for my arm to soothe me, but I snatch it back.

"Goldie."

"Don't Goldie me," I admonish him as I stare up into his stupid gorgeous face. "You created this problem, so you need to fix it. You need to find it and get rid of it."

"I'll work on it, but you need to know what to do if approached."

"If I'm approached, I'm going to tickle its belly." I smile widely at him. Meanwhile, his mouth turns down at my obvious attempt at humor. "Briggs, if I'm approached by a bear, I'm going to turn and run for my life."

"Wrong. That is not what you do. Stare it down, yell, and wave your arms. Make yourself loud and big, and if it's not coming any closer, then you slowly start backing away. Never ever turn and run. It will chase you."

My heart pounds at the thought of being chased by a bear. All I can envision is what we see in the movies, large, snarling, fiercely growling with its wide mouth open, and the claws swiping my way.

"You realize this is totally your fault."

Briggs drops his head a little and rolls his lips

between his teeth. He at least has the decency to look somewhat guilty.

"Sorry about that," Juliet says as she stands in front of the table and attempts to jump into our conversation. Only he and I are in another stare down.

I hate that I like his face so much. I also hate that I know exactly how those full lips feel pressed against my skin.

"Are you ready?" she asks me. "Or do you need us to stick around until Cole returns?"

"I'll be fine," he tells her, and this time, he beats me to my bags.

"I could have gotten them," I scold him.

"I know," he says, again smiling at me. "Thanks for hanging with me for a few minutes."

Instead of answering, I just nod and take my bags once I've moved out from behind the table.

"Text me if the bear comes back."

"I will," I tell him, and we turn to walk away. Looking back, I see he's watching us, or maybe just me, so I leave him saying, "Good luck with the rest of today."

He smiles, and the moths rejoice.

Juliet hooks her arm through mine. I glance at her and see she's smiling.

"Stop smiling like that."

"Smiling like what?" she says as her smile gets

bigger. She knows. I'm sure everyone knows at this point. Love and hate. Every day, I teeter more and more on the fence. Not that I'm in love with him, but I think I'm definitely becoming something.

"I swear I've gone from hating this guy to turning into a schoolgirl whenever he's near. I hate it, and it's stupid. He went from making my skin crawl to giving me these tingling feelings."

She laughs. "Those tingles, that's common sense leaving your body."

21

BRIGGS

Standing here on her porch, I'm nervous.

So ridiculous.

But given the way she looked at the festival, in a sundress with cowgirl boots, I can't stop thinking about her. I've already become somewhat obsessed with my neighbor, but her long legs and bright smile when she's happy make it hard to restrain myself from wondering if she wants to spend all her free time with me like I do her. I've never given much thought to a girl in boots before, and yes, I know that sounds unlikely since I live in a small mountain town, but it's the truth. Now that I've seen Goldie in them, I'd like to see her in the boots, but only the boots.

Instead, I'm here with my tail between my legs because I'm man enough to consider that maybe the dead fish took things a bit too far. I really didn't think they would attract bears. It was just two fish, but I was wrong. The thought that I might somehow put her in danger makes my insides want to shrivel up. My hands start sweating as I watch her through the door window as she walks through the house toward me. She's scowling, not that I blame her.

"What do you want?" she asks after she throws it open.

My mouth dries up as I take her in. Her tight outfit shows off her incredible body and what I've heard referred to as yoga clothes. Tiny shorts that show off her hot as fuck long legs, a sports bra, and a tiny apron. The image causes a problem south of my waist, a problem I've decided I'd like for her to fix.

Clearing my throat, I tell her, "Peace offering."

I whip the bouquet of sunflowers I have hidden out from behind my back and hold them out for her to take. Of course she doesn't do what I want her to, and instead, she narrows her eyes and scrunches up her face.

"What are those?"

"What do they look like?" I fire back and then take a deep breath. Be calm. "They're flowers. For you."

I can't remember the last time I gave a girl flowers. Most likely, it was my mother before she passed. She loved fresh flowers.

"What for?" She props her hands on her waist and frowns.

With my free hand, I reach up and rub the back of my neck. A strange feeling slithers over me that somewhat resembles shame.

I hate this.

Clearing my throat, I find her eyes. "I'm man enough to admit when I'm wrong, and well, the fish . . ." I shrug. "I also wanted to thank you again for coming with me to Charlotte. Not surprisingly, I've received several messages from my brother and father asking about you, and it seems I'm not the black sheep of the family for the moment."

She tilts her head and eyes me warily. After a moment, she reaches forward and snatches the flowers from me. These sunflowers are damn near perfect. I went to one of those farms just outside of town and hand cut each one. There are no bruises on the petals, the leaves aren't curling in to show the flower is already dying, and I felt like an idiot out there doing this by myself. Cole probably would have come with me, but for some reason, I felt I needed to eat crow by myself.

"You're welcome, but don't forget our deal. You have to come with me this weekend too," she says, giving me the perfect view of her ass in those tiny shorts as she heads toward the kitchen.

"I know." I follow her in and close the door behind me. Immediately, I notice a few changes to the house. She's completed the wine cellar project, which looks amazing, and in the dining room, she's split the wall with wainscoting and wallpaper. The wallpaper is bright with a floral pattern and very Goldie. She's also got her cello out and propped up against the couch, which now sits next to a brand-new piano. Lined music paper is scattered across the coffee table in front of it. Some of it she's scribbled all over, and others look professionally printed.

"And you're not forgiven for the fish." She reaches for a vase under the kitchen sink, fills it with water, and then gently places the flowers inside.

"We'll see." I smirk at her, and she gives me a scathing glance. "What are you making?" I ask, changing the subject and looking around her kitchen as I find a place next to the refrigerator to lean on the counter. For someone who keeps their house so clean, she really is a mess when it comes to the kitchen.

"Cupcakes." She waves toward a tin with twelve holes. Each is filled two-thirds of the way with batter and looks ready to go into the oven.

"Really?" It sure looks like there is a lot of stuff for some cupcakes. I can see flour, sugar, salt, eggs, butter, milk, vanilla, lemons, baking powder and soda, sour cream, multiple bowls, measuring cups, spoons all over the place, a spatula, and a hand mixer.

"Yes. I want to make some for Avery. Of the three of us, she's the baker, but Ash is gone with Clay performing somewhere, and I wanted to make these for her to cheer her up."

"That's nice of you."

"I'm a nice person," she says to me like she thinks I perceive her differently, as she walks the flowers to place them on the center of her kitchen table.

"I know you are," I tell her, lowering my voice so it's calm and affectionate. She is nice. Probably one of the nicest people I've ever met, and I'm not so stupid that I don't realize our problems stem from me.

She blushes, making me want to drag my fingers over her skin to see if it's heated. Every time I'm around her, staying away from her gets harder. Since Jaxon's party, I've asked myself why I wanted to in the first place. I understand that we're neighbors, and there's the potential fallout between us if things were to end badly, but I can't help but wonder why they would. I'm an adult, she's an adult, and there's no reason we can't continue to be adults in the end.

The oven beeps, and internally, I groan as she slips on an oven mitt and bends over to take out the first batch of cupcakes. The scent of cake batter and lemon fills the air. Delicious. I watch as she places it on the counter, grabs the next tin, and slides it into the oven. She sets the timer, throws the mitt on the counter, then turns to face me.

Silence passes between us as we stare at each other. I hope she's over being mad at me for the fish.

"The wine cellar looks great," I tell her as I point at it.

She glances at it and then smiles to herself, proud of it.

"Thanks. It turned out to be a bit harder to build out than I expected, but it looks so good."

"It really does."

It still amazes me that this gorgeous rich city girl spends all her time here in the house in the middle of nowhere doing projects by herself. I don't even need to ask about the dining room's new look—of course it was all her.

"Do you want a glass of wine?" she offers, almost like she's unsure if she wants me to stay or possibly go.

"No, I'm good, thanks, but I see the Cheez-It box. Do you like these crackers?"

She looks over at the open box. The few crumbs on the counter next to it tell me she's been eating them recently. Her cheeks flush as she rolls up the bag, seals the box, and pushes it up against the wall.

"I do. They're like my one vice. Always have been. What's yours?"

She's defensive, and I'm not sure why. I've seen the box or other boxes of them each time I've snuck in to change the chirper battery, but I don't want her to know that, and I see she's turned the question back around on me.

"Cider. Hard cider. I think it's delicious, and if it wasn't for the alcohol and sugar content, I'd drink it with every meal."

"It is pretty good," she says, making my heart flop in my chest. I work hard at the cidery to make each one delicious, so to hear that she thinks they're good makes me happy.

"How about you tell me what you're working on. I see you bought a piano." I look over in the direction of the music on the coffee table.

"I did. In the past, Avery, Emma, and I spent a lot of time together, whether we were on the road, in the city, or even here, but over the past two years, finding time for us to work on new music collectively has been hard."

"I hear you playing your cello every night," I tell her as I prop my hands behind me on the counter.

Her face jolts with surprise. "You do?"

I nod.

"I'm sorry." She fidgets with the edge of the apron and wipes her hands across it.

"Don't be. I love it. The sound echoes over the mountain, and it's beautiful. I wish my mother was still here to hear it too."

"That's sweet," she says, tucking a loose piece of hair behind her ear.

"What can I say? I'm a sweet guy." I shrug, and she laughs.

"Sweet and sour at best," she teases as she moves to the other counter to clean up some of the mess. My eyes drift down to her ass, the shorts are so tight and so tiny.

I clear my throat. "So you're working on new music?" I force my eyes away, and they skip to the plant with the cricket chirper. It's been moved a little to make room for the piano, and I don't know how she didn't see it, but she didn't because it's still there. I can see the edge of the sensor board sticking out.

"Yes," she says, looking over at the pages and smiling. She's proud of whatever she's working on, and it makes me proud for her.

"Tell me about it. I don't know much about the process of writing music, but I certainly appreciate it. Any titles?"

I want to keep her talking to me. I really have no reason to be here any longer since I gave her the flowers.

Speaking of talking, who does she talk to? Every day, I talk to Cole and Jane, but she's here by herself, and it's kind of strange.

"I'm leaning toward Gold Horizons for the album cover, but I need to discuss it with the girls first."

"Why that name?"

"Well, I love that it includes the town name, especially since we're all here now, and well gold for many reasons. Gold is still on par with a pop music look. It will market well even though I think this album will be a mixture of pop and bluegrass, and gold reminds me of sunrises. Sunrises inspire that moment when we reflect on what happened yesterday but are excited about the possibility of what the new day will bring. It's calm, warm, and hopeful."

"And here I thought you picked gold because I call you Goldie." I smirk.

"You wish." She smiles back as she moves toward her pantry to put away the dry goods.

"So bluegrass?"

"Yeah, I think it fits where we are right now." She moves to the refrigerator and takes out a cone-shaped plastic bag with some sort of tip and yellow cream. "In combination with American folk music, I want to combine the elements found in bluegrass music. There's old-time mountain music, fiddling that Emma can do, blues, gospel, and jazz. It's a different vibe from our other albums, but still us, and I think we can pull it off." She sets it on the counter next to the freshly baked cupcakes.

"I didn't realize you play the piano too."

She smiles brightly at me like I'm a dumbass while collecting the dirty dishes and then moves to the sink to drop them and grab a bottle of cleaner and paper towels.

"Most musicians can play the piano to some varying degree. The cello is the tenor voice of the instruments. It plays in the lower octave. Typically, it doesn't carry the main melody, it accompanies it. The piano helps me create the basic chord progression, the rift, the overall melody. This one is digital, so it records what I've come up with. I send it to Avery, and she does her thing from there."

"So how does it work? Songwriting. Is it hard?"

She begins wiping down the work area. "I don't know that I think it's easy, but I love it. We all do. Some of my favorite memories are when we can get together and have jam sessions. Usually, it all starts with a feeling. There's something that we each feel, and it resonates deep inside. This becomes the concept or theme. Like this time with the bluegrass. It just feels right. From there, we break off into two parts. We start jotting down story ideas for the lyrics and working on the chords. The best way I know to describe writing a song is like building a house. You put up the frame and then slowly build around it."

"That's good that you love it. Most people never find the thing that they love."

"Well, you should try telling my family that this weekend," she tosses out.

Hearing that they don't support her twists and shifts something inside me. Goldie is quickly becoming one of my favorite people, and I probably like her a lot more than I should. She should never feel any less worthy than who she is or what she does, and this wave of protectiveness blankets me.

"Is there anything I need to know before we go?"

"No. Clay and Emma are going with us. We're going to meet them for a quick bite beforehand. We're eating at one of my favorite places, and this way, you won't be led into the lion's den alone." She tosses the paper towels into the garbage and returns to the counter with the cupcakes, a bowl of icing, and the bag.

"I'm not worried. Consider me an elephant. They take out lions."

"An elephant?" She laughs while glancing at me. She's so pretty when she laughs. Hell, she's pretty when she's scowling at me too.

"Yes, you should see my trunk." I wiggle my brows, and her cheeks flush pink again.

"Oh. My. God. It's like you have no filter. None. You just say whatever you want, whenever you want."

I'm smiling so big, my cheeks hurt, and I watch as her eyes drift over my face and linger on my lips.

"Not whenever, just with those I feel comfortable with. Otherwise, I don't talk much at all."

She tilts her head as she thinks about this and maybe remembers our first few interactions. I'm not sure when I became comfortable with her, but it's been a while now, and like the night I crashed at her house, I'm constantly drawn to her and her light.

I lick my lips. Her eyes flare a tiny bit, then she spins to face the counter.

"Come taste this icing and tell me what you think. I'm going over to Avery's in a bit to take them to her, and I want to make sure it's not too sweet," she says, grabbing the wooden spoon in the bowl and stirring it a few times.

Hesitating just for a beat, I make a flash decision, and instead of moving next to her, I walk up behind her and crowd her into the counter. I want to be closer to her, and I want to feel her pressed up against me.

She lets out a small sound as my front leans into her back. I reach over her to stick my finger in the bowl, then put it in my mouth. She glances back at me over her shoulder to watch my reaction, but I don't give her one. It's the perfect buttercream, and filthy thoughts race through my mind about what I'd like to do with this icing, her, and my tongue.

Never breaking eye contact, I stick my finger back in the icing and hold it out in front of her in a silent challenge. She turns a little, looks at my finger, at me, and then back at my finger. My heart rate picks up as I'm dying to know what she will do.

And then, very slowly, she leans forward, wraps her lips around my finger, keeps her eyes locked on mine, swirls her warm tongue around me, and sucks it off.

It's probably the single most erotic moment of my life, and now all I can think about is her lips and tongue wrapped around other parts of me.

Maybe it's the scent of sugar, or perhaps it's the buildup that's been happening for weeks, but having just that tiny taste of her at my brother's house wasn't enough. The need to have her mouth fused with mine is so overwhelming, the only thing I can do after her lips pop free is lean down and breathe her in.

"Are you going to kiss me, or are you just going to stand there?" she asks, flashing me with a bit of that fire in her that I like so much.

"Just making sure you're on the same page, Goldie," I mumble against her bee-stung lips.

"Oh, I am."

And before she can say anything else, I silence her by sealing my mouth to hers.

I have never wanted a kiss as bad as I want this one, and I'm pissed with myself for waiting so long to get one.

I have no idea what it is about this woman that makes me this crazy, but if she's offering, then I am definitely taking.

Slipping my hand into her hair, I squeeze just a little and tilt her head to where I want it. She willingly leans closer to me. Her hand lands on my waist, and I push her further against the counter. Her lips open against mine, and I sink into the most delicious taste I've ever experienced. From the lingering sweetness of the icing to a flavor that is uniquely her, I instantly know that just one kiss from this woman will never be enough, and I need to be closer.

Picking her up, I set her on the counter without even breaking us apart. She moans into my mouth as I step between her legs and pull her hips flush with mine. Our age dictates that moments like this aren't new for either of us, and I have no problem pushing into her center so she knows exactly what she's doing to me. The heat of her sinking in through my joggers drives me insane, and I kiss her harder.

I want her, and she wants me. There's no hiding that at this moment. Our kiss is needy, and I wouldn't call it desperate, but it screams I've been waiting for this, for you, and now I can't get enough fast enough.

Her hands move from my shoulders to my hair, and she pulls aggressively as she fights for control. If she wants control, hell, I'll gladly give it to her, just as long as she doesn't stop rubbing her body against mine.

"Briggs," she whispers.

"I know, babe," I tell her as she twists my head in the other direction, and she sucks my bottom lip between hers and then bites down. My cock twitches violently, and I squeeze her ass even harder while holding her against me. I'm certain she feels it, and I want her to. I want her to know what she does to me.

Over and over, I ravish her mouth. I explore her teeth, the roof of her mouth, and every tiny speck of space in between. Eventually, she gasps for air, and I drag my lips over the line of her jaw to her neck, where I leave large open-mouthed kisses and suck just hard enough not to leave any marks. Not that I'm opposed to marking her up. I just won't do it without her approval first.

Having had enough, she pulls on my hair and brings my face back to hers. My beard is coming in after the weekend, but it's not long enough to be soft, and her skin is already red. If she'd let me, I'd bury my face between her legs and make her red there as well. Instead, I drink her in and kiss her as thoroughly as I can. I would kiss her for hours, no days, if I could, but that isn't what happens. When the timer to the oven goes off, cold water may as well have been thrown over both of us.

She gasps and pulls back to look me in the eyes. I know mine are hooded, and my cheeks are flushed, but I want her to see how much she affects me.

"That was . . ." she mumbles, her lips swollen and her fingers still in my hair.

"It was," I tell her, rubbing her against me one more time. As much as I don't want to let her go, I know I need to. We can not muddy the waters any more than this and risk making things awkward before we head to see her parents this weekend. Rich people are like vipers. They have heightened senses and strike the minute they detect weakness. I never want to put Goldie in a situation like this.

Stepping back, she jumps off the counter to pull her cupcakes out of the oven. I adjust myself as best I can and pull my shirt down until she bends over again, and I spot the line from the edge of the counter indented in her skin.

Inwardly, I groan.

"There," she says, switching off the timer and tossing the oven mitt. She turns to face me, and while there's a strength to her that keeps her composed and confident, I'm learning her cues. She subconsciously rubs her hands across the apron to smooth it out. I've seen her do this before, and I wonder if she even realizes she does it.

Reaching up, I tuck that one loose piece of hair back behind her ear. "I really am sorry about the fish," I tell her as my hand moves to the side of her neck, my thumb stroking along her jawline.

"No, you aren't," she says softly, looking up at me.

"Well, maybe not the fish, but definitely the side effect."

Her hand reaches up, and she runs it down my chest. Now she's smoothing out my shirt, but purposely. Does she crave to touch me like I crave to keep my hands on her?

"Yeah, and don't think I didn't pick up on your not-so-subtle hints. I'm from New York, so of course I know what a dead fish means." She pops a brow as if to challenge me to say differently.

I chuckle. "That's my girl."

And she is. She's become my girl, and I find I'm not

frightened by this or too much concerned over our neighborly proximity. Things are changing. What that means, I don't know. It's unexpected but entirely welcome.

She rolls her eyes.

"Just wait until you see what's coming for you. You won't be saying that, then." An evil, knowing grin takes over her face, and my eyes instantly drift to her lips.

"Should I be worried?" I ask, moving my thumb to drag across her bottom lip.

"Most definitely," she says as she pulls free and steps back.

22

CORA

Four days have passed without me seeing Briggs. It's crazy how that happens. You would think that since we live next door to each other, we'd bump into each other, like maybe on the road, but we don't. I took the cupcakes to Avery, which she devoured, and then I spent the night. We got caught up on working on new music since Ash was gone. She loved what I've come up with and have been creating. Toss in that the leaves have changed even more, and Briggs is super busy at the orchard, too. People seem to arrive at all times of the day to either pick apples or taste his ciders. I hear them up there, so I haven't ventured up. I don't want to disturb him.

Just thinking of him has me glancing his way. To save time, we took the family plane late this morning, and by the time we arrived in New York City, I had already slipped into my dress, and we were ready to go. Unbeknownst to us, my black dress matched perfectly with Briggs, as he's wrapped in a black suit with a black shirt and tie. I've had to swallow my tongue to keep it from rolling out of my mouth.

Guys in the city dress city. Unless they are working out, their wardrobe is pretty much always the same. Guys who are musicians, it's the same thing. I hate to stereotype, but clothes typically match the people. But with Briggs, he wears all kinds of styles. I've seen him in loungewear, workout wear, orchard professional clothes, working the mountain clothes, and dress clothes. I like that he doesn't fit in one box, just like I don't feel like I fit in one particular box. I like it a lot.

After my parents' party, our driver will take us back to my condo, where we'll spend the night. I'm already thinking about it because I know Briggs well enough to know he won't sleep in the guest bedroom. He'll climb right into my bed, just like last time.

Only last time we weren't at the place where we are now. Now, it seems we have crossed the line into more, and the possibilities are endless.

"I know I told you earlier, but just so you don't forget, you look beautiful tonight," Briggs says from beside me.

"Thank you. I don't hate that suit on you either," I

tell him, taking in the way the shoulders are cut and how the pants are smooth across his thighs. His legs are long and spread a little wide to accommodate our space in the back seat, and I just admire how good he looks. Good from head to shined shoes good.

One corner of his mouth tips up, and my gaze is drawn to his mouth. He's shaved again, showing off his perfect jawline, and his pink lips look even more delicious than usual. I know at some point tonight he will most likely kiss me. After the other day, I feel certain in my bones that it's inevitable, and the anticipation is painful. I should have kissed him the moment he climbed into the car back in North Carolina just to get it out of the way. Having his lips back on mine is all I can think about.

Does he think about me too?

"This is the second time you've worn a black dress. Is that your color?"

I look down and run my hand over the long skirt to smooth any wrinkles. "Don't you know, Neiman Marcus once said, 'Women who wear black lead colorful lives,' and I happen to agree."

His eyes connect with mine, and there's a heat in them that I might have seen glimpses of before but never like this. He likes my answer, and something heavy swirls in my stomach.

"Black definitely suits you."

At this, his hand slides across the seat between us and covers mine. He turns to look out the window like this isn't a big deal, but to me, it really is. I never hold hands with people. In fact, I've never been much of a touchy person. I didn't grow up getting hugs, kisses, or high fives, and outside of Avery and Emma, affection isn't something I'm familiar with.

Is he a touchy-feely person? Is touch a love language for him? For as much as I know of him, there's still twice as much that I don't.

City blocks pass as we sit in silence. Neighborhoods that I'm familiar with flash by, and instead of reminiscing about moments of my life, I almost overtly obsess about the man next to me. The man who was at one point my enemy but has now seemed to have become my friend.

I know this trip is just a quick twenty-four hours, but travel can be exhausting, and he didn't have to come. He could have backed out, and I would have said okay.

As we pull up to the restaurant, I see Emma and Clay waiting just outside the door. My heart leaps at the sight of her, but then again, I could spot her anywhere as she's wearing her signature color, purple. Her dress cuts off just below her knees, she's wearing four-inch heels, and Clay looks as sharp as ever, standing next to her in a charcoal-colored suit.

It's been over three months since I've seen Emma. That's the longest we've gone in years, and tears spring to my eyes. I didn't realize how much I needed to see her, but as we come to a stop and I throw open the door, not waiting for the driver, all I can think about is wrapping her in my arms and breathing her in.

"I can't believe you're in New York! I've missed you so much," Emma all but shouts as she returns my hug and squeezes me to death. Her enthusiasm matches mine, and I think we must look strange from the outside. She's so petite, and I'm so tall, but I don't care. I love her.

"You know I blame you for this, well, you and Avery. You somehow bewitch me into buying a mountain place, and then you leave."

She laughs and pulls back to look me over.

"There's something about that place, isn't there?" Her eyes cut to Briggs and then back to me. At this, her smile grows even larger. She's thrilled that he came with me, and I know she's dying to hear any details I want to share, which I don't. Not yet. It's hard to talk about, especially when I'm not really sure what is going on.

I laugh. "I've missed you, too."

"Hey, m-m-man. It's nice to see you," Clay says, and I glance over to see him shaking hands with Briggs.

"You too," he says, and seeing the two of them standing together makes my heart feel so full. I didn't think about whether Briggs would get along with Ash and Clay, but deep down, I hope he does.

Keeping me at arm's length, Emma takes in my dress and heels, laughs again, and says, "Nope, you don't look like a mountain woman. You still look like you."

I laugh again.

"You should see her in her boots," Briggs volunteers.

"You bought boots?"

"Yep, as someone here so eloquently schooled me on the importance of keeping my feet and legs away from the ticks."

"Oh, I didn't even think to warn you about those. We have our yard at the lake house sprayed, so they really aren't a problem."

"Well, I think my yard might be too large. I could look into just the area around the house, but I've also had deer hanging around too."

And with this comment, Emma moves back to Clay's side and now gives Briggs a once-over. In fact, we all turn to look at him because he knows what he did, and now he knows my friends do too. He smirks at me, which causes me to blush, and moves to stand next to me. His hand comes up to rest on my lower back, and I feel branded.

"So you're Briggs," she says, eyeing him like he's a rare bird being spotted in the wild.

"And you're Emma," he says politely.

They continue to eye each other in a stare down, and I laugh openly because I know both of them enough to know that neither will back down. But then Briggs does graciously, and Emma smiles victoriously.

"I made this for you," she says, holding out a silver gift bag to Briggs and shaking it. I don't know where it came from. Clay must have been holding it.

He takes it cautiously while uncomfortable at the same time. Internally, I rejoice because I'm certain he thinks this might be another prank. I made that comment the other day in the kitchen, and I know he's smart enough to be on the constant lookout.

"Do you want me to open it?" He looks between her and Clay.

"Sure." She beams up at him, and Clay just smirks. This has me smiling too because he for sure thinks it's a prank now.

Poor guy.

Moving the tissue paper to the side, he pulls out a small-to-medium-sized gray knitted sweater.

"It's for Duke," she says proudly.

"Thank you," he mutters, looking at it like he has no idea what it is.

I lean in close and whisper loudly, "It's a sweater."

"Oh," he mumbles, then smiles at her. It's one of those smiles that I've rarely seen from him. "He'll like it. We've already had a few very cool mornings, and winter hasn't even started. Thank you."

"You're welcome. I made it myself, so there might be a few imperfections, but whatever. Duke won't know." Emma is all smiles. She can't help herself; she's always happy and loves to knit gifts for people.

"Here, give it to me," I say to Briggs, walking the bag back to the car. The driver rolls down the window closest to me and leans across the passenger seat to take it. "There," I say. "He'll put it with our things at my condo while we're at my parents'."

At the mention of my condo, one corner of his mouth tips up, and his gaze drifts to my mouth. Oh, to be in his mind right now. My legs squeeze together just thinking about the night ahead of us.

Pivoting to face Emma and Clay, I need to turn off the sexy thoughts and turn the conversation to something new. "How many times has she dragged you here?" I ask Clay, and he just smiles.

"More than he probably cares to," Emma chimes in, but she doesn't look guilty over this; she looks triumphant.

"Nah, I think the food is good. I don't mind," he says, looking down at her affectionately.

People are passing us on the street. Whether or not they recognize any of us, no one says a thing or stops to take a photo. It's nice to be out and not feel that immense pressure. Then again, the clouds just rumbled, and the smell of rain is on its way, so they might be trying to get where they're going before the sky opens up.

"Lead the way," I tell them, and Clay and Emma turn for the door.

Briggs's hand stays securely on my back, and I like it. I wonder if he's going to touch me all evening? That's kind of how we interacted at his brother's party, so I imagine we will. Only this time, when he touches me, I won't be wondering what it feels like to have his fingers tangled in my hair. I'll be wondering what it's like to have them touch every other inch of me.

The four of us are seated in a nice booth in the back of the restaurant. I slide in first, and Briggs follows.

"Are you ready to head back to the lake?" I ask them as the hostess hands us our menus.

"Yes," she and Clay say simultaneously as they glance at each other and then back at me. "While it's been great to finish the summer here in the city, we are ready for space and the quietness of the lake. And I think Moose is ready for long walks uninterrupted by people and traffic lights. Plus we have Avery's baby shower coming up." She wiggles excitedly in her seat.

"That we do, and a wedding. Have you decided on anything?"

Four waters are placed on the table, and the four of us stop talking. It's not that we mind speaking freely in public, it's just that Emma and I learned early on to be wary of prying ears over topics we really don't want splashed across every media channel.

"Good evening, my name is Kyle, and I'll be your server this evening. Can I get you all something to drink?"

We each tell him our drink preference, and after he walks away, Emma shocks me.

"Actually, we have. We've decided to get married in February in Horizons Valley at the ski resort. A winter wedding just felt right for us. White fur, silver, lavender, snow on the trees, maybe in the air . . . I can just see the pictures now, and they'll be beautiful."

"February! I talk to you almost every day. Were you ever going to tell me?"

She laughs. "There's not much to tell. I was finalizing the big things before we announced, like renting out the resort. We hired Avery's wedding coordinator, and she's taking care of all the details. She'll tell you when it's time to buy your dress, and you just need to show up." She leans into Clay, and he wraps his arm around her to pull her close.

"This just feels so wrong! I feel like I need to do all the things for you."

She laughs.

"You really don't. I have it handled. Well, the planner does."

"Avery's coordinator was crazy. Crazy in the type A psycho kind of way. Are you sure that's what you want?" My mother knows people—well, her assistant does—so I'm sure I could find her someone else in a heartbeat.

"Yeah, we've talked about it and talked with her about how we need her to calm down a bit in order for us to agree to hiring her, and she said she understood and was on board. I mean, this is another celebrity wedding for her portfolio, so it's not like she was going to argue with us. And you have to admit, she really did a great job with Avery's."

"Yeah, she did. What about the band? Who are you hiring to do the music?" Because of course music is one of the most important questions for all of us.

"I asked Melanie Alverez if she and her band, The Druthers, wanted to come perform, and they said yes."

"Oh, I love Melanie. They really are perfect for your

wedding, especially since they were there for the engagement."

"That's what we were thinking." Emma and Clay smile at each other, that new, exciting kind of love still pouring off them.

"Are you ready to order?" the server asks, almost disrupting the moment. He's not returned with our drinks yet, but that's okay. I've been craving this place, and knowing we were coming, my stomach would growl on demand. Thai food is the one type of food Horizons Valley is missing. We've got so many other flavors, but not this one.

"He'll have the panang with crispy duck, and I'll have the hot basil with chicken," I tell the server.

Emma pipes up and says, "Same for us, and two orders of fried spring rolls for the table."

He glances briefly at the guys, Clay nods his head, and off he goes.

I catch Briggs looking at me as if he's just shocked that I ordered for him, but I don't care. This is my day. He glances at Clay, and Clay just shakes his head in a nonverbal way that says, "Don't even try. You'll lose."

Briggs huffs next to me, then leans back in the booth and angles my way. His smell flutters over to me, and I'm so busy inhaling the scent of apples and pine that it takes me a moment to realize his hand has drifted and found its way on top of my leg. I glance down and stare at his large fingers. He squeezes me once, and the fabric of my dress bunches just a little. Heat from my skin presses back in search of him, and my breathing picks up.

What is happening to me? You'd think a guy has never touched me before by the way my central nervous system reacts, and I'm too busy being shocked that he's touching me and thinking about what I should do when Emma starts talking, and I miss part of what she's said.

"How's the orchard doing this season?"

"It's doing well. In fact, Cole, who works with me, and I have just signed with a contractor to expand the cidery. Over the past couple of years, we've talked about increasing our cider production and adding a larger tasting room, and that's finally going to happen."

I twist to face him more. "You did? You didn't tell me this."

His eyes lock with mine. They're such a soulful brown, so warm. Not only is my leg soaking it up but it seems my chest is too. "Not yet, I didn't." He gives me a shy smile.

Shy? This guy is never shy. What gives?

"Why not?"

"I was a tad worried that you'd be pissed."

I pull back, stunned. "Why?"

"The construction will go on for months."

"So?"

He shrugs his shoulders. "I just know you like it quiet."

"Yes, I do. But I also want you to follow your dreams and succeed."

He should know this. We've talked enough about our lives, the expectations bestowed upon us, and the things we love. I can't believe he'd think I'd be anything other than supportive.

The table falls silent as Briggs stares at me. The crinkles next to his eyes and the way his lips press thin tell me he's feeling apologetic.

Good, he should. We're friends now, so expanding your business and large construction projects are definitely things friends talk about.

"Surprise," he says, and Clay chuckles.

I just shake my head at him.

"Tell me, Briggs, every year we perform at a charity event, and if Cora wanted you to be there, would you go?" Emma asks him. She doesn't understand that this thing between us is not really a thing. Or maybe it is. I just don't know yet. I glance down at his hand before sliding my gaze his way.

He glances at me. "Absolutely. If she wants me there,

then I'll go." No hesitation, just assuredness, and his thumb starts swiping back and forth over my leg.

"Really?" I'm surprised by his answer. It's never even occurred to me to ask him or assume he'd want to come.

He gives me a small smile, then squeezes my leg before turning back to face them. "Yes, I've actually watched several performances online."

"You have? Which ones?" I'm so shocked my jaw drops open.

"Madison Square Garden and that performance you did a few years ago at the Grammys."

"I had no idea. Why didn't you say anything?"

"Why would I? Did you look me up after we met? If so, you didn't tell me either."

"Touché."

At this, the server brings over our drinks and the fried spring rolls. I momentarily forget why we're in the city, as I'm so happy to dive into the food, until Emma asks, "So, Briggs, are you ready to meet the Rhodeses?"

I almost choke and have to swallow hard to push my food down.

"Sure. How bad can it be?"

"Bad isn't exactly the word I would use," she says.

"What word would you use?" he asks in a tone that makes me feel like he might be defending me against whatever harsh words she might say about my family.

"Unpleasant."

My stomach sinks.

"Emma, you really don't need to go. I know you know very well what these events are like, and you're right, they are unpleasant. I won't be mad if you change your mind."

"No way. Never would I miss this," she says, a sly smile slipping onto her face as she glances at Briggs.

"Why do I get the feeling there's more going on tonight than I'm aware of?" he asks, and Clay chuckles.

"There's not. But it's just like she said, unpleasant and boring. And given the fact that you're going to meet my family, I already feel bad for you."

"Goldie, I can take care of myself, and if you need me, I have your back."

"Goldie?" Emma asks, but I ignore her.

"Me too. I can take care of myself."

He pins me with a look that leaves no room for argument or discussion. "I didn't say you couldn't. But now you've got me in your corner too."

In my corner, behind the brick wall I'm already building to protect us both.

23

BRIGGS

I thought I knew rich people, but looking around the penthouse we just stepped into, with its black and white marble floors and walls, extravagant artwork, and floor-to-ceiling windows, I realize I've sorely been mistaken.

"Ms. Rhodes, you are late," says a gentleman who I perceive to be a butler, given by his jacket tails. Only his tone is disapproving, as well as the scowl on his face.

The muscles in my shoulders instantly tense.

What the fuck is this guy's problem?

Goldie tilts her chin up a tad higher and returns the glare.

"No, Frederick. I can assure you I'm quite on time, not that it's any of your concern."

Internally, I fist pump. I know this Goldie, the

mouthy one, and if that's who I'm getting tonight, it will be a fun night.

The man folds his arms behind his back and puffs out his chest with clear annoyance. If we were anywhere else, I'd be giving him a piece of my mind about how the staff should be speaking to a member of the family, but I won't. Tonight.

Having seen enough already, I slip out of my top coat, which is damp from the rain outside, and toss it over his shoulder. He scoffs in a shocked surprise, but I ignore him as I help Goldie out of hers and fling it in his direction as well.

"Hang these up for us, Freddy."

Behind me, Emma giggles, and she does the same. She flings her coat at him, and he catches it, while Clay, on the other hand, gently places his coat on his shoulder and then pats him in a "there there" manner.

Without waiting for a response, I guide Goldie away with my hand on the small of her back. Emma and Clay follow.

"What was that?" I ask lowly so no one else can hear.

"It's nothing. He works for my father and has always been very liberal with his opinions when he should have none."

"Why does he still work here?"

She shrugs. "My father trusts him."

That makes no sense to me. I would never keep someone in my company if they were openly rude to any member of my family.

She glances over her shoulder and up at me. There's mirth in her eyes, but also something else. Something I'm not sure I like.

We each take a glass of champagne from the server standing at the entrance to the parlor room. At least a dozen people are already here, and every one of them turns to stare at the four of us as we walk in. Granted, I expected to be stared at, but this feels like something else, and red flags start waving.

Ignoring them, I lean down and whisper into her ear, "Hey."

She pauses and turns to face me, her beautiful light brown eyes locking with mine. One hand is on her glass, and the other is affectionately on my arm.

"I just want you to know, regardless of our deal, I'm really happy to be here with you tonight."

"Thank you," she replies, and then, as if it's the most natural thing in the world, she pushes up on her toes and kisses me. This kiss eases the pressure in my chest after that first interaction. My family is unique in how they speak to me, but no one would dare talk condescendingly to me like he did to her. Certainly not a staff member.

Emma lets out a tiny squeal, but outside of her and Clay, once Goldie pulls away, the people around us are now openly gawking, and I'm not sure why. I don't even feel like I can ask her without causing a scene or stirring up gossip. So we just carry on like it was no big deal.

"Well, well, well, it seems you and I do have a few more things to talk about," Emma says as she loops her arm through Goldie's, and they walk farther into the room.

"Come on, Briggs, let me show you around," Goldie tosses over her shoulder. Clay and I follow.

Room by room, we stop into the library, the billiard room, the board room, the wine cellar—now I see where she gets her love of wine from—a formal sitting room, a formal dining room, and even a solarium. This penthouse is truly a mansion in the sky, and we're about to head up to the roof. She assures me it's covered and we won't get wet when a man a few years older than us approaches her. He's frowning at her like he's been sent to deal with an errant child.

"Cora," he says in a clipped way that has me reaching to put my hand on her back.

"Winston," she returns, pulling up to her full height. In her heels, she's taller than him.

"I was wondering when you were going to show up."

What is wrong with these people? It is a party. People can come and go as they please.

"As you can see, we've been here for a bit."

His nostrils flare. "Then it's time."

"Winston, I'd like for you to meet my boyfriend, Briggs Warren. Briggs, this is my brother, Winston."

"It's nice to meet you," I say as I hold my hand out. He looks down at it, and his nostrils flare again. Reluctantly, he slips his hand into mine.

"Thank you for coming," he says instead of, "It's nice to meet you too."

"And you remember my friend Emma. This is her fiancé, Clay Johnson."

Winston nods at the two of them and then turns his sharp gaze back on Goldie. Without saying another word, he turns on his heel and strides away.

Her shoulders deflate, and I don't understand why. Instead, she follows.

I glance over at Emma, and she just shakes her head, silently telling me not to say anything. The three of us trail them as we're led back to the library. It occurs to me then that someone never approached us to say hello. As this is her family's home, which makes her a host by default, one would think that proper decorum alone would force their hands. And where are her parents?

In the library, she walks to the middle of the room,

where there is a lone chair and a cello. While I did see this the first time we passed through, I thought it odd. Who was I to question it as their daughter is world famous, and maybe it is there as a shrine to her, but apparently not?

"What are you doing?" I ask her as she takes a seat, picks up the cello, and moves the endpin into an anchor attached to the chair.

"What I always do." She looks at me sadly but resignedly.

At my brother's party, her dress was classy and sexy, and she dripped in wealth from her diamonds, but as I take her in now, this black dress has a flowing skirt, and she's wearing pearls. I thought it was an elegant thing, but I'm realizing now that she's in concert attire.

Is she just playing one song? Is she expected to play the whole night?

Taking a step back, I move out of the way so people can see her. Emma and Clay have come to stand next to me as a few of the guests gather around. Goldie drags the bow across the strings, and a deep timbre echoes throughout the room. It's the first time I've seen her play in person, and that sound reverberates through my soul. It's at this moment that I know I am forever changed. With that one long chord, she's rewritten my very being, stitched her way into my DNA, and as I watch her play song after song, I feel each of my individual muscles tightening, my entire body tensing, and my anger climbing.

One song becomes two, and then three, and then four, and so on.

"Does she always perform like this at their parties?" I whisper to Emma.

"Yes. It's not only expected of her. It's one of the few times a year when they actually acknowledge her."

"You've got to be kidding. Why?"

"Because they're assholes?"

I shoot her a disgusted look.

"She plays for the whole event?"

"Yes."

Now I understand what Freddy referred to by her being late.

"Briggs, we could fill a novel with all the things her family has said, done, and not done to her over the years. What kills me the most is that they hold their love for her over her. They don't freely give it; it's conditional, and I'm not sure she sees this is wrong. We've tried to tell her that this is messed up, but she wants to make them happy. Like any person, she wants to be loved by her family."

Leaning against the wall, I think about what Emma has said and take Goldie in. She's obviously stunning in her black dress and the way she so eloquently moves when she plays the cello, but between the songs when her brown eyes search to find mine, it's then that I see everything Emma was talking about. I see the hurt and the anger, the crushing sadness, and the resoluteness as she knows with her family she will never be anything more. I think many of these emotions are ones I've felt myself with my own family, so I let her see me too. There's a reason that I've felt drawn to her, even if I didn't want to admit it. It turns out this is one of the reasons. I understand her, and she understands me.

And my heart aches for her.

Breathing in, I try to tamp down the debilitating fury I feel racing through me, not only for the people in this room and how her family thinks so low of her, but for the people who've treated me less than I am, too, just because I choose to make cider rather than manage billions of dollars that belong to other people.

I pretend I'm back on our mountain and think about the cool, clean air, the smell of dirt, and the smell of freedom. I pretend I can still smell her too, as I know she smells like citrus and floral. And it's with this thought I wish I was allowed to walk over there, pull her out of the chair, and crush her in my arms while I bury my head in her neck.

I want to protect her from these people, not that she

needs it. I know she can take care of herself, and now I understand her extreme level of independence.

I've never been the type of guy who is touchy-feely, but lately, the need to have my hands on her and my arms around her has been overwhelming. I've never had these feelings before, not even with Adele, but with Goldie, they consume me.

I don't date.

I don't do relationships.

I haven't wanted to. Adele was the only exception, and for a while now, I've had zero interest in pursuing that type of commitment with anyone else. I wasn't looking; I was working on the orchard and chasing a dream, but with Goldie, there's something about her. One day, she wasn't there, and then the next, she was. Each time I see her, and every time I'm around her, it makes this need I have for her worse and amazing at the same time. I'm in awe of her. She's strong, funny, kind, wildly independent, but most of all, she's easy to love.

And I do.

Love her.

And the overwhelming love that I have for this amazing woman screams at me to get her out of this fucking toxic place.

Right now.

Pushing off the wall, I take a step toward Goldie, but

Emma grabs my arm.

"Briggs," she pleads, silently begging me not to cause a scene, but Clay gently takes her hand off me and pulls her into him. He knows. His eyes lock with mine, and I know he would do the same thing.

As the song ends, she lowers the bow, then raises her eyes to find mine. Usually, a murmur picks up between songs, but this time, it's dead silent as people watch, and I now stand right in front of her.

"Cora. Let's go," I say to her, holding out my hand.

She glances at it and then at me. I'm certain my anger is visible as it radiates from every pore.

"But the party isn't over yet," she says, looking around at the people watching us.

"It is for us."

Her eyes come back to mine, and there's a desperate panic in them. She's not sure what to do, but I do. If this scene were in a movie, I'd tell anyone who gets in our way, nobody puts Goldie in the corner. I grab the cello from her and gently return it to the stand sitting in the corner.

"Briggs. No," she whispers sternly.

Leaning down so my face is directly in front of her, I swallow hard to keep from snarling with how angry I am.

"Cora, you are a star that shines so bright. You absolutely should be admired. But you are not the hired help. Ever," I tell her quietly, and her eyes turn glassy.

"I know my place in this family, and it's in this chair."

"Tonight, your place is next to me. Not because I think you're some kind of trophy to put on display but because you chose me to be here with you. I'm the luckiest fucking guy in this room, and no one is going to tell me differently."

She stares at me as I stare at her, and then I stand to my full height and again hold my hand out for her.

After one breath in and then one long breath out, she takes my hand and stands.

People part and move out of our way, as together, the four of us move for the door. I glance once at Emma, but her eyes are locked on Goldie. She's softly smiling like she's so proud, and it's a good fucking thing, not that I care. When it comes to Goldie and me, we are the only two people who matter.

We're just about to the foyer, when Winston grabs her arm. "Where do you think you're going? You're not done playing," he says to her like he has a right to be pissed off.

"Take your hand off her immediately."

Recognizing that I'm vibrating with anger and two seconds from ripping his hand off his own body, he drops her arm.

"Cora, there's still another two hours. You need to go back in there and play," he says.

"Are you fucking kidding me?" I ask him. "I don't know who you people think you are, but you should be ashamed of yourselves. Cora is a member of this family, not your evening's entertainment, and she's a grown woman, not a child. You will refrain from speaking to her in such a way."

"This doesn't concern you, so I suggest you back off, or I'll have you removed," he says to me.

I'm taller than him, but like I've witnessed my entire life from other rich, stuck-up pricks, he doesn't see the threat even when it's staring him in the face. And I am. Mentally, I've caused him physical harm.

"Winston," she calls out to get his attention. "I am tired, and I am done. If this is what I need to do for you, Dad, and Mom to love me, then I guess this is goodbye." She glances at Emma, and a silent conversation passes between them. Then she turns back to him. "Love isn't supposed to be conditional. It's supposed to be unlimited, full, genuine, and without expectations."

When she turns, we all follow her lead, and it's at this moment that the senator and his wife walk in.

"Cora!" the woman calls out in delight. "I'm so happy you're here. Are you leaving?" she asks. Meanwhile, her husband gives Winston a once-over and frowns.

"We are. We have an early morning, but we just thought we'd stop in and make an appearance."

"I'm sorry we couldn't get here sooner. Usually, they have you working, so I don't get to chat with you, but I'd love to catch up sometime. Maybe we'll make a trip to Horizons Valley." She winks at us. Out of the corner of my eye, I see Winston's cheek twitch in shock. Whether it's at the friendship he apparently didn't know about, or the fact that they know she lives in Horizons Valley, who knows.

"I would love that. If you'll excuse us, it really was lovely to see you again."

We turn for the door and see Freddy scowling while already holding our coats. He doesn't say anything, but Winston calls out to her again.

"Cora."

With her chin tipped high and her shoulders pulled back, she glances at him one last time. "Goodbye, Winston."

The ding of the elevator.

The ringing in my ears.

The smell of her perfume as she stands next to me, holding my hand.

And the adrenaline running through, it's all I can comprehend until we step outside into the cold rain. Clay holds Emma back to keep her under the awning, but I pull us so we're off to the side, alone, and then spin her so my mouth can slam down on hers.

The pressure of her hands as they wrap around my face, the warmth of her lips, the taste of the rain and of her tongue, everything about this woman fuses with me, and I need her unlike I've ever needed anything before.

"I'm not sorry," I mumble against her lips as I slip off my coat and wrap it around her. The moderately heavy rain has quickly soaked through our clothes. She shivers, and I swear she has never looked more beautiful.

Wiping my hands over her face, I push the wet hair back and lay my forehead against hers. Her hands have fallen to my chest where she's tucked them between us to keep them warm. I think we both needed a moment to catch our breath and let the realization of how we just left her family sink in. I hope this is truly what she wants and she doesn't feel pressured by me. I never want to make her feel anything less than who she is.

But then, she tilts her head so she can see me, says, "I'm not either," and then returns my kiss with one of her own.

This kiss says, "Thank you for choosing me."

This kiss says, "I'm in this with you just as much as you are with me."

And this kiss says, "While I could stand here all night in the rain with you, I'd rather you take me home."

24

CORA

He said my name.

To me.

It's the first time I've heard it pass from his lips while he was looking at me, and my entire body shuddered with a visceral reaction, so much so that either I lost all common sense when I stood and followed him, or I finally found it.

Either way, I can't believe I walked out of one of my parents' parties. A party that they had yet to come over and say hello to me. I did see my mother once as she stood in the library doorway watching me perform, but when I made eye contact with her, she flipped hers in the direction of Emma and Briggs and frowned. That's all she needed to do to let me know I had disappointed her by bringing them.

Briggs was right. I mean, Avery and Emma have been right all along, but I am an adult, and this treatment is ridiculous. My friends and I should be welcomed in the home that I grew up in. That's how it is with other people's families, and if this is what I have to continue to do for them to show me any semblance of love, then I think it's best if I don't. I showed up for them tonight, and all three of them, Winston and both my parents, treated me badly.

The truth is, and I've tried not to admit it over the years, they've always treated me badly. I can't make the excuses for them anymore that it's because they're wealthy or don't understand me. They don't want to understand me, and I'll never change their minds. They've written me off indefinitely as someone not really worth their time or love, and I'm only called upon when it benefits them or makes them look good.

I'm almost thirty. It's time I decide who I allow to be in my life and who I don't. Avery, Emma, and Juliet are my family, and it's taken a lot of years for me to realize that family isn't always what you're born into. It's who you choose, and because of this, I feel free. I feel lighter than I have in years. The burden of always trying to impress them and wondering if today is the day I'm either going to make them happy or disappoint them has vanished.

And as for Briggs, I don't know yet, but I'm starting to think I would like him to be part of my family too.

"Are you cold?" he asks, startling me from my thoughts.

"No, I'm okay," I tell him, and I am.

At some point, after we walked out of the building, Clay and Emma left, and while our car service wasn't there to pick us up, the doorman flagged down a taxi cab. Briggs wrapped me in his coat to help keep me warm, but the smell was the most comforting. The smell is home, something the city no longer is for me.

Pulling my hand, he flattens it on his thigh, his very hard and muscular thigh, while his hand envelops mine and his thumb swipes back and forth. He won't look at me, but he doesn't need to for me to know he is fuming —like steam coming out of his ears fuming—but all I really seem to be able to focus on is that he said my name, how he kissed me in the rain, how he's touching me, and that he looks so good tonight I want to climb him like a tree.

The scent of his skin and his cologne is a heady combination. He didn't realize I wasn't shivering from the rain; I shivered with this uncontrollable desire to be wrapped up in his arms and to be with him.

It doesn't take long for us to pull up to my condo building. He helps me out of the car as I hold up the bottom of my wet skirt from getting tangled around my legs, then he places his hand on my lower back and guides us inside.

"Good night, Ms. Rhodes," the doorman says, acknowledging the two of us. Briggs nods at him in recognition, but he still doesn't say anything.

In the elevator, I expect him to move to one side while I move to the other, but instead, he keeps his hand firmly on my lower back, and my side is pressed into his. In the reflection of the doors in front of us, I watch as his chest rises and falls with each breath he takes.

"Are you hungry?" I ask, but I watch as his lips press into a flat line, and I feel his fingers drag across my skin as his hand gathers the fabric of his coat as he squeezes it.

Does he want my clothes off me as much as I want his off him?

"Tired?" I ask, just trying to keep the tension somewhat manageable. Right now, it could be cut with a knife.

He turns his head so his eyes find mine. They are so dark and heated, and then they narrow. Slowly, so slowly, they rake down the length of me and land on my feet. My toes curl, and every muscle between my hips tightens as there's no mistaking his thoughts.

The ding to the elevator startles me, and I suck in a breath.

His hand gently nudges me to move, and I lead him to my door. Briggs stands behind me as I dig through my clutch for my keys. One of his warm hands slips under the bottom edge of his jacket and surrounds my waist, while the other reaches up to brush my hair off my neck. I pause my search as my head falls back against his shoulder. His size overwhelms me, and even in these heels, he looms.

"Goldie," he mumbles underneath my ear, his hot breath eliciting goose bumps to race over me, and that alone has my back arching as I press into him, and I feel how hard he is. His hand slides up my stomach where he palms my breast, kneading possessively through the fabric, and his lips suck hard into my skin.

A moan escapes me.

Outside of the apocalypse occurring, nothing will keep me from being with this man tonight. I would walk across hot sand and crawl over glass just to get to him.

Pulling the keys from my hand, he unlocks the door and ushers us inside. Once the door shuts, he backs me into it, caging me in with one forearm pressed over my head and the other, his hand flattened against the wall next to my head.

"Goldie." His voice again grumbles and makes every

muscle in my stomach quiver. "Why do you let them treat you that way?" His eyes search mine. He wants an answer, but I'm certain he won't understand.

"It's always been like this."

"Your brother better hope I never see him again," he says, tilting my chin up just enough so his mouth hovers over mine. We're sharing air, and I want nothing more than to breathe him in so he fills every pore and every cell.

"Oh yeah? What would you do if you did?" I ask in a challenge.

In one second, he lets off a grumbling so deep it vibrates his chest, and I feel it in mine, and then in the second, his mouth slams down on mine.

Blistering heat overtakes my mouth as his tongue pushes past my lips and makes itself at home. He doesn't quite taste like I remember. He tastes better. Champagne lingers from tonight; it's sweet and tangy, and so delicious I know I will crave more of him once this is over.

Shimmying out of his coat and mine, they drop to the floor and pool around our feet. I push his suit jacket off his shoulders, and the heat from his skin has drenched his shirt.

"I've wanted you since the very first second I saw

you. Dancing around in your yard, naked, teasing me with how perfect you are."

"Oh yeah?"

"Yes." His mouth leaves mine and trails over to my neck while his hands sneak behind me and pull on my zipper. It easily slides down, and the dress loosens enough to join the coats on the floor.

"These breasts," he says, as he places open-mouthed kisses on the top of the swells while squeezing them still wrapped in a strapless bra. "This perfect stomach," he mumbles as he bends down and bites the skin at my waist. "I can't wait to have you laid out before me so I can taste every inch of you," he says as he returns to his full height and locks his eyes with mine.

This man. This perfect man. My heart aches at the thought of what we're about to do and how it will change me. Briggs has worked his way in, and whereas in the past being with guys was for fun, this is already different. I know I'm not just going to be having sex with Briggs. For me, it's going to be so much more.

"Should we talk about this first?" I whisper, suddenly feeling nervous.

He pulls back to look at me more clearly. His lips are swollen, and his eyes are so dark with longing that everything in me tingles in anticipation.

"Do we need to?" he asks.

Tearing my eyes off him and looking over his shoulder, I push away my vulnerability. "I have a bad feeling you're going to break my heart, Briggs Warren."

He runs one hand down my arm and interlocks our fingers while the other gently grasps my chin where he forces me to look at him.

"Goldie, I'm not going to break your heart. That's the fear talking from the lack of love from your asshole family. I get it. This is a little scary. It's scary for me too, but it's also exciting. Give me some time, and you'll see, no breaking. Instead, I just might win it over."

"Is that what you want, to win over my heart?"

Speaking of heart, it pounds ferociously in my chest as I wait for his answer.

"Yeah, it is."

Relief courses through me, as that's what I want too. Mine and his, exchanged.

He runs his fingers over my head and tucks some of my hair behind my ear. He's so gentle and looks at me with such reverence that my worries slip away.

"Do you need to talk about anything else?" he asks, being the gentleman that I know he is.

"Not at the moment," I tell him as I lick my lips, watching his eyes flare.

And that was all he needed.

He runs the back of his fingers down my cheek, then

they gently slip into my hair, wrap around my head, and he pulls my mouth to his.

This kiss is much slower than the one a few moments ago. That pause shifted our gears. We're not in a hurry. We can take our time because we have nowhere to be and no one to answer to. We're doing exactly what we want, with who we want, and just the thought of his weight on top of mine leaves me breathless.

Over and over, our tongues tangle, and our hands explore. His as they unhooked my bra and drifted between my legs to find me very wet for him. Mine as they unbuttoned his shirt, pulled his belt free, and traced that line which acts as an arrow straight into the front of his pants.

He moaned as my hand wrapped around him, and I gasped as his mouth latched onto my breasts, his tongue swirled around my nipple, and his fingers pushed inside.

Who knew it could feel like this?

Why is it that when the heart is involved, everything feels like more?

Colors, sounds, the drifting of his fingers over my skin, his mouth, the sensations, all of it is amplified, and there is no going back after tonight. I'm choosing to believe him and trust him. He said he wanted to win my heart over, but he doesn't realize he already has.

Standing there, I'm left in just my heels. He groans like it pains him to see me this way, and my stomach clenches in the best way when he says, "Take me to your room, Goldie."

Without hesitation, I say, "Right this way."

25

BRIGGS

ast night, a chapter of my life closed, and another began.

I should have seen it coming. Over the past several months, this thing between Goldie and me has been building and building, and looking back, it's evident that she and I were going to be inevitable.

By the time we arrived at her room and all our clothes were completely gone, the need to be inside her was so powerful, every part of me ached.

Goldie is unlike any woman I have ever been with. Did I love Adele? Yes. At that point in my life, she was just what I needed. But as the years went on, I grew, discovered more of myself, and as much as me changing courses wasn't what she wanted, it was the best for me.

At some point, a man knows what his future will look like, and it wasn't with her. Goldie, on the other hand, I don't see a future without her.

Do we still have things to discuss and discover about each other? Of course, but after last night, there's no going back.

Her skin, the way it fluttered against my fingers. Her thighs, the way they quivered as I buried my head between her legs, her gasps and sounds that I elicited from hitting that spot so deep within her, it'll never be enough. The warmth that surrounded me as I slid inside, her hips as she lifted them to get closer and for me to go harder, faster, her arms wrapped around me as I tucked my face into her neck, every bit of it, every second was fucking perfect.

She doesn't realize it yet, or maybe she does, but after this . . . she's mine.

"This condo looks completely different from your home," I say as she's setting up a fancy coffee maker. She's standing at the kitchen counter in a T-shirt she's pulled on from somewhere, and I know without even putting my hands on her that she has nothing on underneath. It's sexy as hell.

"It's the lack of plants. I took them all with me, so this place feels devoid of life."

She glances at me and then does a double take. I've slipped on my boxer briefs and nothing else. I don't think she wants me wandering through the condo naked, but I'm not opposed to it, given the way she's looking at me. Seems I'm not the only one affected this morning.

"No, it's not that. It's white with sleek gray. Don't get me wrong, I love the windows and the layout, but it just feels cold. Well, colder than I would expect for you."

She looks around the condo and takes in the different architectural details. The outside wall is brick but whitewashed. The windows are bracketed by heavy dark gray drapes. The kitchen cabinets are white, the countertop is gray and white marble, the floor is gray tile.

"I see what you mean. I guess I just know what it looked like before the house. I brought with me most of the things that I loved. Like that painting in my living room, the plants, a few things that pop of color."

"Tell me about the painting," I say to her as the machine whirls to life.

She glances over her shoulder to where the painting once hung.

"I love that painting," she whispers.

"I know. I've seen you look fondly at it. Where did you buy it?" I ask as I take a seat at the breakfast bar.

"At a small art gallery in Brooklyn."

There has to be more to this story. No one loves a painting that much without it having some sentimental meaning to it. And while it looks like her now that I know her, it also doesn't.

"Why?"

"Because I know the artist."

Last night, the driver left a few items of food for us to eat. Goldie moves about the kitchen to toast some bagels and pulls a premade lox and fruit board out of the refrigerator.

"Don't get me wrong, I think it's beautiful, but I don't know, it doesn't look like something I would expect you to buy?"

She turns back to look at me. "What would you expect me to buy?"

I wave my hand around the room at the other decorations. Although she has primarily gray tones here, the pops of color she claims to have in the mountain house come from the couch, the plants, and now the dining room wallpaper. But looking around the condo here, the pictures in the dining room are modern black sketches, and she has a bronze chandelier hanging over the table. She uses accents like black and bronze. It's very contemporary while still remaining chic, and then there's the painting. I don't see it in this room at all.

"Yeah, I guess it doesn't necessarily match the motif here, but it doesn't not either." She looks at the vacant place on the wall. "Did I ever tell you how I came to love plants?"

"No."

She takes the board to the kitchen table and sets it down. "I had a nanny, and to say she was eccentric is an understatement. I don't think my mother ever realized this either, or she never would have kept her."

"How did she get the job?"

She looks at the wall again, then at me, and smiles. "My mother's assistant hired her for me. While she never gave me the time of day, as she was there to appease my mother, I guess it wasn't lost on her that I needed more than the crumbs of what I was given. This nanny, while we only spent one summer together, she changed my life."

Goldie keeps talking as she moves back to the kitchen and pours us two cups of coffee. On the bar, she's already laid out creamer and sugar. I move them to the table.

"She was kind to me, and even though our time together was short, I loved her. She hugged me, gave me piggyback rides, introduced me to farmers' markets, to plants, picnics in the park, and color. She was in college and studying to be an artist, and she always had paint under her nails. I've followed her career over the years, and it just happened that as I was moving into my condo, she was having her own show. I was so proud of her. I went and bought *The Garden*. That's what it's titled."

The timer dings on the toaster oven. She plates the bagels while I grab the coffee, and the two of us move to the table.

"Did you talk to her while you were there?" I ask as I dress my bagel and listen to her talk.

"No. She stood with her own family as people came up and spoke to her. Her husband and two daughters were there. I didn't want to make the moment about me, and as I watched the awe on those girls' faces, I knew at one time that was what I looked like too. I couldn't help but think how lucky they are."

My already wounded heart for Cora's childhood bleeds a little more as I listen to her talk about a woman who was more motherly to her over ten weeks than her own mother has been her whole life. But at least she had that. At least she saw another side.

"So this nanny loved plants too?"

"Yes." She blushes. "She bought me my first plant, and from there, I never stopped. I know people don't understand, but plants mean something to me."

"And you tried to give me one, and I turned it away."

"Yeah, there was that. Such a horrible neighbor you are," she teases, picking up her coffee and taking a sip.

"Well, maybe I'll have to buy one of her paintings too."

She gently places the cup down, and her eyes lock onto mine. Her hair is in a messy pile on top of her head, and she has zero makeup on, making her look younger. Yet she's never been more beautiful.

"You would do that?"

"Of course. I'm thinking I need to buy you a new plant, too, as an apology. I don't think there's much I wouldn't do for you."

"Briggs," she says as she slides off her seat and rounds the corner of the table. I lean back as she straddles my lap and hugs me.

Of course I wrap my arms around her and bury my head in her neck. If there was a way to live with this girl stuck to me, I'd do it.

"That's all it takes, huh? I just need to whisper sweet nothings to you about a plant, and this will get you climbing onto my lap?"

She laughs as she pulls back to look at me. By doing so, her very naked ass rocks against me, and my dick twitches with excitement. Her smile stretches even more, and she does it again.

"Careful, or our breakfast plans will change real quick."

Leaning forward, she whispers against my lips, "Okay."

My hands instantly slide underneath her shirt. Her skin is warm, and I already know she'll be even warmer when I push inside.

"Your stubble is a little sharper today," she says, running her hand across my jaw.

"Does that bother you?"

Her eyes flare with mischief as she says, "No way."

Memories of last night and the rawness of her skin have me taking her bottom lip between my teeth and sucking. I drag my tongue across it. There's a hint of coffee, enough to wrap my hand around her head, where I tilt her perfectly and disappear into the flavor of her mouth.

A grumble runs through my chest at the taste of her, and it doesn't take long before we're both glancing down at the tip of my dick as it pokes out of the elastic waistband on my underwear.

"I think your underwear is in his way."

I smirk, lifting my hips and both of us at the same time, so I can yank them down to free myself. Her hand wraps around me, then twists, and she moves it up and down. It feels so good having her touch me, but I need her to stop. I've never been opposed to a hand job, but currently, I want so much more.

"Are you ready for me?" I ask, slipping my hand between her legs.

"Always," she whispers, and my heart thumps almost painfully in my chest, as I find that she is.

I have fallen for this girl so hard.

Pushing up on her toes, she positions me, then sinks down. The sensation is out of this world, and my head drops to her shoulder as I exhale shakily.

"You feel so good," I tell her, and I mean it.

I'm not quite certain how we got to this place, where intimacy is so easy and so consuming, but you'll never hear me complain.

Slowly, she begins rocking back and forth as she adjusts to my size. My hands on her hips help guide her, and her head falls backward as she enjoys the feeling of us joining together over and over.

"So good," she agrees, and my mind shuts off.

Instinct takes over as she rides my lap and pleasures us both. I pull off her shirt to feel her skin against mine, and the only word that comes to mind is perfect.

Her hands are in my hair, her lips devour mine, and as I feel the flutter telling me she's close, I send my hand lower to help push her over the edge.

She tightens.

My spine tingles.

And as her muscles lock tight and a gasp slips through her lips, I follow her over the edge, only in more ways than one.

26

CORA

Yesterday afternoon, Briggs and I finally decided it was time to call the pilot and head home. As much as I wanted to stay in the bubble of the condo, we both needed to get back. I need to water my plants and start working on a few of the ideas Emma and I discussed at dinner, and Briggs needs to get back to relieve Cole of watching Duke and the orchard.

After the flight, the dinner we scrounged up and ate when we got home, and the hours we spent in my bed, I'm sore in places I didn't know I could be sore and wonderfully tired today. Tired and blissfully happy.

I've fallen for Briggs Warren, and it feels amazing.

He was right, I don't need to be scared about what happens next, just excited about the possibilities.

Briggs left just after the sun came up. He complained about me needing room-darkening shades, and he kissed me on the forehead. Then he slipped away while I drifted back to sleep. It was the best sleep I've ever had in my life. His side of the bed was warm. It smelled like him, like us, and it was easy to roll into his space and drift off.

I've just spent the past two hours working on accompanying instrumentals when I hear, "CORA!" float through my open windows.

At first, I'm alarmed because he's used my name, and then I start laughing because I remember today is the day his special present arrives in the mail. Needing to see his face, I jump into my boots and race from my house to his. He's still standing on the front porch, only now Cole and Jane have rushed over to see what he's yelling about too, and both are laughing.

Slowing to a leisurely pace, he locks his gaze on me as I stroll up the front steps and take in the scene before me. Instead of ordering a standard prank glitter bomb, Juliet and I found a guy online who custom makes them and the packaging. This one came in a FedEx box. By that, I mean it is the whole box, and the entire floor of the box is attached to a spring. There's a label that instructs which end to open, and when you do, your color choice of glitter comes flying out, and I just happened to pick hot pink.

Glitter is everywhere, and I squeal with delight.

Briggs is covered in hot pink glitter. It's all over the porch, a little inside the front foyer of the house as the door was open, and there are flecks all in Duke's fur. Also, Briggs's face can't decide if it wants to turn red or laugh, so I pull my phone from my back pocket and start taking a video.

"Just need a little proof here," I tell him as I see Jane and Cole wiping their eyes.

"This is a fucking horrible prank," he growls, swiping his hands down his arms and failing to get the ones stuck to his skin off.

"Don't you swear at me. I don't like it. Besides, you sooo had this coming." I grin. "Best. Prank. Ever!" I yell, and this makes Cole and Jane laugh even harder.

"Alright. You win," he grumbles.

I hold my hand up to my ear. "I'm sorry, I didn't quite hear you. Can you say that again?"

"I said, you win!"

"You both heard him, right?" I look at Jane, and she's nodding excitedly.

"You certainly won this one. I'll go get the broom," she says, shimmying around the mess and heading into the house.

And it's in that second, while I'm not watching Briggs, that he lunges for me. His arms wrap around me, and I start screaming. He's shaking his head, throwing the glitter all over me, and poor Duke starts howling.

Cole films both of us now, but I don't even care. My heart is so full.

"You're going to make this up to me," he says in my ear.

"Oh, I am?" I ask, with my head tipped back so I can see him and my brows raised.

"Yes, you are. Let me take you to dinner."

"Like on a date?"

He scowls at me. "What's wrong with that?"

"Nothing." I smile brightly at him. "This is a terrible punishment, but if you insist."

"I do," he says, leaning down to press his lips against mine.

For our date, Briggs picks me up at five forty-five sharp. He made a reservation for six, and I teased him about him being older even though it's only by a year and almost pushing into early-bird hours. He pinned me with a scorching look and said the faster we eat, the faster he can get me home and get me naked. No complaints here.

"Avery says this place is really good," I tell him as we walk into the new little Italian restaurant on Main

Street. It's not that large; there are no booths, only tables, but they are covered with white linens and beautiful stemware. A beautiful bar runs the length of the room on the left side of the restaurant, and the wall opposite the bar is ivory and textured to give off a distressed feel. The accent color is burgundy, and there's gorgeous lighting. I instantly love it.

"Cole says he's seen Juliet here twice sitting at the bar," he says, shocking me as the hostess leads us to our table.

"What?" I grab his arm and glance toward the bar, where people are already lined up for the evening and sitting there.

"Yep. Apparently, she's been spotted here talking to the same guy."

Briggs pulls my chair out for me. "Talking to a guy! She hasn't said anything."

"Well, we've been gone, and we've been busy. But you know how small towns are." He shrugs and smirks at me. This must also be his warning that I should expect people to talk about us after this dinner. Heading out of town, it isn't as noticed or known, but here we are, front and center, dining together at a new trendy restaurant.

Flutters dance on my insides. I find I like the idea of people talking about Briggs and me together.

We glance at the hostess as she hands us our menus, tells us about the specials, and wanders off.

Briggs watches me, but my mind goes seventy miles an hour.

"I'm just stunned. Did he say if they looked friendly or *friendly*?"

He chuckles. "I don't even know what you mean, but if she's been here with him twice, then I'm sure they're friendly enough." He pops open his napkin and lays it across his lap. Tonight, he's wearing a nice pair of jeans with a fitted button-down. The shirt makes his arms look incredible, his beard is growing back in, and the way his dark eyelashes perfectly frame his eyes, I'm not sure I've ever seen a better-looking man.

"Maybe we should call her and ask." This news is just a bit too exciting for me. Has she found someone she wants to date? It's been a long time. Since her ex, I think.

"Or maybe if we're lucky, she'll come in while we're here," he teases.

The server comes over and introduces herself. She pauses and looks at both of us, and I can't help but hold up my napkin to my face and laugh. Both of us have pink glitter stuck to us. I tried to wash mine off, as I'm sure he did as well, and needless to say, it's going to take a few more times.

"It's her fault," he says.

And this makes me laugh even more.

She takes our drink order and then is gone.

"Pink might be my new favorite color for you." I grin at him.

"Duke thinks so too." He smiles back. At least he's being a good sport about it. "Since you've been declared the victor, are we done with the pranks now?"

"Never," I tell him, my eyes sparkling with happiness, and he just shakes his head.

"Cole and I are going to decorate this weekend for Halloween. Do you want to come over and carve pumpkins with us?"

"I've never carved a pumpkin before. Is it hard?"

He leans back in his chair and studies me. I'm certain he's feeling sorry for me, thinking about all the things I most likely missed out on as a kid. But it's fine.

"No, it's not hard. But be prepared to get your hands dirty."

"Do I strike you as the type of girl worried about dirty hands?"

"You did at first, but now not so much."

"What kind of girl do I strike you as now?"

He thinks about his answer as he looks at me. He blinks a few times, licks his lips once, making me want to climb over this table and kiss him, and then one side of his mouth tips up.

"Mine."

An unexpected heat rushes to the surface of my skin. I wasn't expecting him to say this. Yet I feel so happy about it; it's a strange feeling for me.

At this moment, the server returns with our drinks.

"Are you both ready to order?"

"Yes," I tell her while holding up the menu. "He'll have the gnocchi with the beef ragout, and I'll have the shrimp orecchiette with grape tomatoes and spinach in a white truffle alfredo sauce."

"Wonderful choices, ma'am," she says, collecting our menus. "I'll be right back with some bread."

"Thank you." I smile up at her and then to Briggs, who's watching me with an irked but amused expression. "What?"

"Did it not occur to you that I might like to order my own food?"

I scoff. "But why would you when I can just do it for you? I picked the two best-looking dishes, and this way, we can share."

"I'm allergic to shrimp."

My face blanches. "What?! I didn't know that!"

"Actually I'm not, but you get the point. It's weird that you order for me. You've done it twice now."

I shrug. "You got a problem with a woman taking control?"

He chuckles under his breath and leans closer to me. "Now, you know that's not true, don't you?" His deep voice makes me blush, and I'm not embarrassed by that at all. "And although I think it's kind of hot, when it comes to food, maybe you just run it by me first."

27

BRIGGS

It's been a long day.

While Cora and I were gone over the weekend, we had our first frost. This usually makes the apples sweeter, but it also somehow signals to the trees that winter is coming and it's time to be done. The apples have been falling at a rapid rate, and we've been all hands on deck to collect them and get them ready for storage. I'm sitting on my front porch with Duke, drinking a hard cider and listening to Cora play, when a large black Mercedes SUV slowly pulls up the road and turns for Goldie's house. I know this vehicle doesn't belong to any of her friends, so the only person left must be her brother.

Well, that didn't take long.

Instantly, I'm on alert, and although I'm surprised

he's here, I'm not at the same time. And then it hits me. Maybe other members of her family came too. While I'm sure she can handle herself, she's got me now so she doesn't have to. I set my drink down, grab a small plastic bag from just inside the door, and make my way over to her house. I pause on her porch, not wanting to intrude, but if he gets even the slightest bit out of hand, then I'm here.

"What are you doing here, Winston?" she asks him. I almost chuckle because I've heard this tone before, and she's not happy.

"I needed to come here and see what you've been up to."

"Why?"

He doesn't answer at first. Instead, I hear his footsteps as he moves around the room. Then he says, "Because it's time for this phase to end and for you to come home."

Oh, these people have some nerve.

And over my dead body.

"I am home."

"Cora." He says her name in a chastising way, and my hands clench at my sides. "Is this about the boyfriend? Because you know it will never last. He doesn't fit into our world."

"This has nothing to do with him. I happen to love

this town. I've been coming here for years, and I bought this house long before I ever knew him. Not that I need to explain myself to you."

This guy has no fucking clue who I am or what world I can belong to, and with that, I've heard enough. She doesn't need to defend me. I can defend myself.

"Honey, I'm home," I announce as I step through the door and make my way to stand next to her. Her eyes are strained, and she's glaring at Winston.

"I'm sorry, this is a private conversation," he sneers at me. "You need to leave."

"Why? Is talking shit about people only something you do behind their backs?"

The look he gives me would make a lesser man take a step back, but not me. I'm familiar with his brand of entitled asshole, and I wrap my arm over Goldie's shoulders.

She leans into me for a brief second and then steps away. She turns her back on both of us as we're in a stare down, one I don't plan on losing. "It's fine, Briggs, you can go. I've got this."

"I know you do, Goldie, but I think I'll stay anyway. I'm good at taking the trash out if I need to." I cross my arms over my chest.

Winston's jaw falls open. I'm guessing no one has ever called him trash before. He may not be of a low social standing, but he is waste in this house, and I'd very much like to discard him.

"I'll ask you again, what do you want, Winston?"

Cora moves to the coffee table where she starts collecting the sheet music she was working on. She stacks it in a nice pile while Winston lays in.

"Do you have any idea how much you embarrassed us this past weekend?"

She stands up straight, and my blood starts to boil.

"You're kidding, right? Do you have any idea how much you embarrassed me? I didn't do anything but show up, play a few songs, and leave. On the other hand, you all were horribly rude to my friends, to me, and I'm just over it."

"You can't just leave in the middle like that!" he snaps. "Our parents had to explain why you walked out on their party."

"That's not my problem. And yes, I can leave whenever I want! I am not the hired help. I am a member of the family. If I want to play or not play, that is my choice. If I want to stop and eat, I can. If I want to bring half a dozen of my friends, I will because that is supposed to be my home too. I am not beholden to any of you. However, if you would like to hire me, I'm certain my agent will negotiate with you for a very hefty price."

Unable to help myself, I ball my hands into fists and ask, "What is wrong with you people?"

He looks at me and then back at her.

"Cora," he says as if she's exasperating. "Yes, you can eat and bring friends, whatever, but you're supposed to play. You always play."

"Right. And why is that?" she asks him.

Only this time, he doesn't have an answer. Silence falls over the room. A pin could drop as they're in a face-off, and my heart aches for her.

"I don't want to play for any of you anymore," she says as she picks up her cello and moves it back to its stand.

"You're not making any sense." Winston rubs the back of his neck. I really should introduce him to Jaxon. I'm certain that both of them would get along brilliantly.

"I'm making perfect sense. I'm done."

He stares at her like she's someone he doesn't know.

"Well, then, I guess next year you won't need to come."

"Right." Her eyes turn glassy. I know what she heard there. *You aren't needed anymore, so you aren't invited.*

It's almost unbearable standing here and listening to the two of them. I know I have no place in this conversation, and she can handle herself, but man, would I like to insert a few very choice words.

Breaking eye contact, Winston sighs deeply and looks around her house. She's done so much to this place from when she bought it, she has to be proud. I know I am.

"This house is small," he says, not caring at all how anything might make her feel.

"What do I need a big house for? It's just me."

And that's when his gaze finds mine again.

"You and him." He looks me over from head to toe, and I know what I look like at the moment, a farmer. I've washed my hands but haven't showered or changed my clothes. I'm dirty, my shoes are filthy, and I don't even care. I know who I am.

"And?" I ask.

"Don't think I didn't look into you. We knew all about you before you showed up to my parents' place."

This doesn't surprise me. I'm familiar with his type. They're definitely keeping an eye on her, and from the look she's giving, she's realized it, and it's pissed her off.

"And?" I ask again.

His face transforms as if he's just had the best idea ever, and he looks back at Goldie.

"I don't know why I didn't think about it sooner."

"Think about what?" she asks warily.

"It's perfect. It'll explain why you're choosing to live here."

"What will?"

"You'll marry him." He points at me. "His family is known in the South, his brother and his father have a ruthless streak that fits in appropriately, and this helps cover up the stain of you leaving your family."

I chuckle. "Do I get a say in this?" Although I don't hate the idea, which is surprising to me for a different reason. I would be marrying her for love, not image.

He ignores me and starts pacing the room, and Goldie never glances my way.

"Of course the wedding will be in New York, and he'll have to take on a more involved role with his family's company, but we can spin this perfectly. Where the North meets the South and falls in love."

"No," Goldie says.

"Yes," Winston replies. "You will marry him."

"Over my dead body. Why don't you listen to me? I've told you this before, I will never *ever* marry someone you pick for me. Ever. It doesn't matter who they are."

A loud ringing waves through my ears as I comprehend what they just said. Him telling her to marry me, and her saying she'd never marry someone he picked.

Ever.

I know he's done this before, she's told me, but hearing it is entirely different.

Hearing her say no to a question I haven't asked is also different.

Not that I was thinking about asking her this question, but how I feel after last weekend, I wouldn't have ruled it out down the road.

But she did.

So dismissively and definitively.

Almost like she wouldn't marry me even if I was the last man on earth.

Well, then.

Fuck my life.

The air in my lungs slowly leaves my chest. I think about that night in her condo when she expressed concerns about me breaking her heart. It turns out, I should have been worried for me, not for her. How I feel right now, this feels like she just broke my heart, and I'm not sure what to do with myself.

Glancing back and forth between the two of them, they're arguing in a way that's similar to a dance. They've perfected this over the years. She knows what he's going to say, and he knows how to push her buttons. They've forgotten I'm here, and I realize I don't have to be.

I was here for her, and well, she made it perfectly clear what she ultimately thinks about me. About us. Do I think she likes me? Yes. Fond of me? Yes. Loves me? No.

This realization has smacked me in the face. I had no idea all of this was one-sided, and it feels terrible.

What am I even doing here? She was right. She doesn't need me.

Turning, I leave the house, and I don't think either one even noticed. That's fine. I don't want to be here anymore anyway.

Pulling the plastic bag from my back pocket, I shake it and wait. It takes maybe two or three minutes, but here comes Rocky and Bullwinkle. I toss a handful on top of Winston's car that I know will take them a while to eat, then walk down the driveway back to my house. Do they have plenty of fresh apples to munch on? Yes, but after my first year here, I quickly discovered they loved them dried. After five years, all it takes is for me to shake the bag, and they come running.

Shoving the bag in my pocket, I make my way back to my house. My eyes latch on to the rocking chairs on my porch, and I can just barely still see my mother sitting in hers. I wish she was here. I wish she was waiting for me when I walk back through that door. Not because I think she can fix my bruised heart, but because then I wouldn't feel so alone.

Alone.

I've never really thought about it. I didn't consider myself alone, but now that I'm here, the stillness and the silence are deafening. Cora likes to be alone. Instead of seeing it as a trait of her being an independent, strong woman, I should have seen it as a red flag. Because truly, what twentysomething woman buys a mountain house by herself and basically lives off the grid?

Does she go into town and do things? Yes, but she spends most of her days there alone. She never asks for help, she doesn't want my help when it's offered, and if I hadn't been so blinded by long legs and a spunky atti-tude, I would have seen the truth of the situation. She said it to Winston, but it just never occurred to me.

She has chosen this life.

And it isn't conducive to adding someone else like me in it.

Good for her, I guess.

But not good for me.

This stops now before I end up in too deep. It already hurts, but at least I know the truth.

Losing my mother took a lot out of me. I don't need the stress of worrying about losing Goldie too. Not that I think she's dying, but it's possible one day she'll just up and go and leave the mountain, and where will that leave me? Reality sucks, but she is a superstar, and maybe this is a phase. She has endless funds to do what-ever she wants and go wherever she wants, and she has another home in New York.

Why would she want to stay here long term? It certainly won't be because of me.

The front door slams behind me as I make my way inside. I head for the shower and completely ignore my responsibilities like feeding Duke. He can wait a few more minutes as I need a moment to gather myself.

Clothes go off.

Hot water goes on.

I stand with my face under the spray and just breathe in and out.

I fell in love with her, of this I have no doubt.

I told her I wanted her to be mine.

Why did I never think to ask her if she wanted me in return?

My heart aches, and my nose and my eyes sting. Could there be tears? Maybe. But as long as I don't see or feel them, I can't be sure they ever happened.

Just like us.

I'm not sure we ever really happened either. It's like I made it all up in my head. But now I know better, and this ends today.

28

CORA

I can't believe that Winston had the nerve to come here and humiliate me in front of Briggs. I'm horrified over the way he acted and talked to Briggs, and I'm horrified that Briggs listened to him talk to me the way he does. I had already decided that I was done being their marionette, where they pulled my strings any way they wanted, but after today, I see no point in speaking to any of them ever again.

I am not a child.

And I am done.

After this feeling of obligation I've had toward them all these years, Winston may as well have been the scissors today who cut the strings. What he did was not okay, and the moment he left, I shoved my feet into my boots and ran through the dark straight to Briggs's house. I owe him a million apologies.

Knocking on the door, I flop down in the closest seat and try to contain the adrenaline racing through me. The air is cool, but my heart races, my palms sweat, and more than anything, I want to make sure he knows I am not like them, and I will no longer answer when they call for me.

But then again, I think he already knows this. We talked about so much over the weekend and on the flight home. I've opened up to him more than I have anyone else ever.

I'm nervous, I'm excited, and for the first time in what feels like forever, I feel truly free.

Heavy steps get louder the closer he gets to the door, and if I didn't feel like I owed him many apologies first, I'd jump straight into his arms. He gave me the push I needed in New York. So many times, I've thought about getting up out of that chair and walking out, and once I finally did, it was so much easier than I thought it would be.

He's also shown me that I can be me, and there's nothing wrong with me. Avery and Emma have been telling me this for years, but to allow myself to love someone and have them love me in return, flaws and all, I feel like I could fly to the moon.

And I do, I love him.

After what feels like forever, he opens the door, and Duke wanders out first.

"Hi, buddy," I tell him as he places his head on my leg for me to pet him. His fur is soft, his tail is wagging, and I squeeze him with a hug. I have so many emotions running through me, new ones too, that it's hard to contain them, and I need this hug.

"You're sitting in my mother's chair," Briggs says to me. His voice sounds strange, and when I glance up at him, the smile on my face falls right off. His grumpy face has returned, and as his words register, I slide out of the rocking chair.

"Oh, I'm sorry. I didn't know," I tell him, reaching over and grabbing the back of it to get it to stop moving.

He doesn't say anything. He just looks at me, and I'm reminded of the night we met all over again.

"Thank you for coming over. Can you believe he did that? And said those things! I promise you I didn't know Winston was dropping in—"

"Did he leave?" he asks, cutting me off, even though I'm sure he already knows the answer to this. There's no sneaking a car up and down the mountain.

"Yes, and I'm so sorry. I came right over because I need you to know that I think he's awful, and I am thoroughly embarrassed by what you saw. I know you know this, but I promise I am not like them. I don't think the way they do, I don't act the way they do, and well, I'm really hoping you know these things."

He's been pretty clear about how he feels about his brother and Adele. Both of them act like Winston and choose to submerge themselves and conform to that world. I'd like to think that Briggs and I are kindred spirits in that we aren't like them, but as he continues to stare at me, my nerves kick into overdrive.

I step toward him and raise my hand to place it on his arm, but he takes a step back.

My hand drops.

What is happening here?

I don't remember him leaving my house, but he's had enough time to shower and put on a pair of sweatpants and a T-shirt. He looks so good, I want to plaster myself to the front of him, but right this second, warning bells are going off.

His brows pull down, and his lips pinch into a straight line. He's really not happy with me. Something in my house has triggered this, and I have no idea what it was or how to fix it. I take in his posture, his face, and how the aura pouring off him right now really is reminiscent of when I first arrived, and my heart starts slamming into my chest. This guy standing in front of me is not the guy I've gotten to know over the past three months. Right now, he's the first-night guy.

The one who judged me and didn't like me.

I stare at him, and he stares at me.

Only I feel like he's getting taller, and I'm somehow shrinking.

What did I do that was wrong?

I blow through the memories of our dinner last night, how we left things this morning, and even the words said in my house tonight. I can't find anything.

"Do you want to come back over? I can cook us something to eat," I offer, thinking food is supposed to be the way to a man's heart, and this might work, but it doesn't.

"No. I'm fine here. Thanks anyway," he says curtly.

This is not good. I'm pretty sure I'm about to live out my fears when it comes to him.

"Okay, well then maybe tomorrow. Do you have plans?"

I'm putting myself out there for what I already know will be a rejection, but I have to see him say the words and hear it for them to be real.

"I do."

The air in my lungs freezes, and my mouth dries. My nose burns, but I push it down and do my best to shut off my splintering heart.

"Oh, what are they?" I push for him to give me something.

I don't think this is a bad question to ask. Isn't that what normal people do with their person? At least I thought he was becoming my person. Last night, he did say I was his. But if that's changed and he's not, then I don't really know what was happening over the past couple of days. Or really what's been happening over the past few weeks.

Or maybe I do.

We made a deal, and then, at the moment, I was convenient for him.

Or maybe he had some type of hero complex in New York and mistook those emotions for something else.

He looks off to the side and out over the yard. His hands dangle by his sides, and although he's not outwardly doing anything, the muscles in his jaw clench, and he looks so tense he may as well be a statue.

And with that, I have my answer. He doesn't have any plans. He just doesn't want them to be with me.

That was quick.

Just like a match. The fire was lit, and then it quickly burned through the wood before it snuffed out.

"Never mind," I mumble, tipping my chin up. Because if I've learned one thing in my lifetime, it's that you never show them your weakness. You never let them know it hurts. People use pain. It gives them a power to hold over you and use to exploit as a weakness. My family did it for years until I learned it would never matter. They mocked my tears, and no matter how much I begged for time, attention, and love, I never got it.

Until recently, from Briggs.

I wipe my hands across my hips to the front of my thighs and force myself to breathe in.

I thought that even though he saw how my family treated me, he didn't care. At least he didn't seem like he did. But here we are, after one awful conversation with Winston, and he's somehow changed his mind. Did I embarrass him like I apparently embarrass them? If so, I didn't mean to. Maybe I shouldn't have argued with him, maybe he didn't like that side of me, but he's never had any problems when I argued with him before. I'm not going to stop being who I am for anyone, even him. I mean, did he expect me to just stand there and take it?

Duke brushes against me again, but my chest is so heavy that I can't bend over to pet him.

"Listen, I had a great time with you over the weekend, but we both know that taking things further will just complicate what we've got going on up here on the mountain. I'm not going anywhere, and I believe you're not going anywhere. We've become friends, and we need to remember that."

Friends.

I'm being friend-zoned.

I went from being so incredibly happy this morning to now being this.

"Did I do something wrong?" I ask him. I have to know.

"It's not like that." He shakes his head.

"Like what?"

"Cora." He uses my first name, and I have to pinch my lips together to keep them from trembling. "I really did have fun with you, but we've fulfilled our obligations to each other. I've declared you the winner of the prank war, and I think it's time for us to settle back into our lives before things were disrupted."

The lump is so large in my throat that I can't swallow.

He just told me I disrupted his life.

Seems to be a common trend between my family and now him. I don't make their lives better, I disrupt it.

"Sure, no problem," I tell him, looking at the ground and then at the rocking chair, even though I know I will never be his friend. I have all the friends that I need. Stupid me for thinking he might be something more. "Thanks again for coming over earlier to check on me."

I wanted to apologize for how Winston treated him and how he was included in one of his grand master plans, but what's the point? He doesn't care.

In fact, I don't really know why he showed up in the first place.

I didn't need him there. I can take care of myself, and he knows this.

He nods, accepting my gratitude, then calls for Duke to go back in the house.

I guess we're done.

Holding my head high, I turn and walk down the steps of his house. My chest aches, my heart feels like it's been doused in liquid nitrogen and then hit with a hammer, and the tears I didn't shed earlier for Winston and my family continually hurting me finally break free and streak down my face.

It turns out I'm used to not being chosen by them unless it's to be a pawn in some plan they've devised, but I didn't expect this from him. Not that I knew what to expect, but I thought it might have been the beginning of something great.

I guess not.

This odd, hollow feeling takes over inside me when I have these moments. Moments when I know no matter what, I'm not going to be loved, and I feel like the space is big enough to swallow me whole. Sometimes I just wish it would.

What about me is so unlovable?

What am I doing wrong?

As I make my way back to my house, I hear him shut the door between us, and I stumble in the darkness. It feels so final, but then again, I guess it is. I barely make it to my couch before I fold in half to hug myself and openly cry.

29

BRIGGS

I didn't think drawing the line in the sand between us would hurt her the way that it did.

I've gotten pretty good at reading her facial expressions over the past few months, and the way her eyes seemed to grow just a little bit larger on her face, how she rolled her lips between her teeth and breathed in through her nose just enough that her chest expanded were all it took for me to realize my words did damage.

And then, to make matters worse, she basically asked me why.

No man wants to pour his heart out to a girl who has no intention of returning the feelings. I mean, I'm certain she has feelings for me, but when I distantly dream about a future, it includes a wife and kids. A family.

That isn't what she wants, at least not with me, and that's fine. She's entitled to her own future. Ours just don't align. Am I such a bad guy for wanting to stop everything before I'm in too deep? It hardly seems fair to me, or her, especially if she already knows I'm not the one for her.

I just wish she had shuttered her emotions instead of letting me see them. Maybe she didn't realize she was, but she did, and when I close my eyes, I see hers. And what I saw was hurt, betrayal, and something I can't quite put my finger on.

She asked me in New York if we needed to talk about us, and maybe I should have pushed her a little more as to why she wanted to. I didn't think at the time we needed to have any conversations, certainly not the "where do you see yourself in five years" one, but clearly, I was wrong. I told her I wanted to win over her heart, but I never asked her if that was what she wanted. I just assumed she was on board, and she never led me to believe otherwise.

I also assumed she wanted to win mine as well, which she did, and boy, am I glad I never told her.

"So much for having a guys' night out. You're terrible company," Cole says.

"What do you mean?" I turn to face him.

We've come into town to Route 11. There are other places we can go, but we like Graham. He opened this brewery a little over a year ago. He brews a tasty IPA, and he keeps two of my ciders on tap.

"You've said four words since we've been here. 'I'll have an IPA.' You didn't even say hi to Graham. You just gave him a head nod," Cole chastises me.

I look around the place, and it's quite busy for a Friday night. Then again, we're still in season for fall, and tourists are heavy in town. It's almost November, though, so this will die down quickly.

Just as I'm about to swivel back on my seat, in walks Clay and Ash. It didn't occur to me that we might run into them, but here they are. Clay's face lights up when he sees me, and the two of them make their way toward us. Guests of the brewery have spotted them, and a few phones have come out, but other than that, there's no fan activity. It's nice that these two can walk into a bar in town and not be bothered.

"It's the man, the myth, the legend," Clay says to me as he claps me on the shoulder, smiles at Cole, and takes the seat next to me at the bar. Ash posts up next to him.

"Hey," I tell him as Graham pops over, says hello, and takes their order.

"You should have seen your boy here on Saturday

night." He grins as he talks around me to Cole. "Emma and I are still talking about your showdown at the Rhodeses' place. You did what the girls have been wanting to do for years."

"Avery and I wish we had been there to see it, too. Her jaw fell open when Emma called and told us."

I have mixed emotions about their reactions. Part of me feels proud that they're excited for her, that she finally stood up to them, but the other part of me feels angry that they've known her for all these years and didn't help her sooner. I know she's stubborn and independent when it comes to her life, but these people are her people, and they should have put a stop to it sooner. Goldie's family is emotionally abusive.

Needing to change the subject, I turn to Clay. "Didn't expect to see you out tonight. Figured you'd be at home soaking up being back in town."

"Oh, trust me, I'd love to be there, but Emma and Cora are fussing over the baby shower decorations, and I thought it was just best to flee. Ash here took pity on me."

"It's fine. Avery's friend Rosie is in town and staying with us, and I'm certain the two of them didn't even notice I left," Ash says.

This surprises me. One, because I didn't know Avery's shower was this weekend, and two, I didn't know

Goldie wasn't at home. "Cora's at your house?" I ask Clay.

"Yep. She has been for the last two hours."

"Huh," I say more to myself than him. I look down at the bar and think about how many times I've heard a noise over the past couple of days, pulled back the curtains, and looked out the front window to see if she was driving by. It wasn't her. She hasn't left her house since Tuesday, and only once did I see an Amazon truck and a FedEx truck roll up the road. She must have left today when I was in the shower.

"Are you glad to be back?" Cole asks Clay.

Graham drops their drinks and wanders off.

"So glad. I had a great time in New York, but I was ready. I think Emma was too. I know she loves it there and wants to split time, but I'm hoping down the road we'll be here a little more than there. Central Park is great in the fall, but nothing beats the mountains here. I missed it. Moose certainly is glad to be back, too. He raced around the house like it was a speedway track for a solid five minutes."

"Avery was on pins and needles too. She was basically counting down the minutes until she could drive over and be with her friend," Ash says, sipping his beer and angling more so he's facing us.

He looks at Ash. "You could have warned us about

the baked goods coming. It's the most we've ever received in one haul. Banana bread, apple cobbler, and double chocolate chip muffins."

Ash chuckles. "She just wanted to make sure y'all had some food."

Cora once told me that Avery is the baker of the three of them, and apparently, she meant that.

"How was Cora after last weekend?" Clay asks as he turns back to me.

Cole lets out a groan, and all three of us glance at him.

"I think she's fine," I tell them, ignoring the look Cole gives me.

"You think?" Clay's brows rise. Ash takes another sip, but he's watching me over the rim of his glass. It's funny because, at this moment, it's not Winston who feels like her brother. It's these two, and without anything else being said, I already know I'll be in the hot seat.

"Her brother showed up here on Tuesday," Cole chimes in, and I shoot him a look that says, "Will you please keep your fucking mouth shut."

"He w-what?" Clay asks, louder than usual for him. A few people glance our way, not that they're listening to us. They just heard the outburst.

"Yeah, I could hear him and Cora yelling at each other all the way from her house to the barn," Cole says.

"And you didn't think to step in?" Clay looks at me curiously.

"Oh, I did. But you know Cora, she didn't need me. She doesn't need anyone."

All three of them eye me warily. There wasn't a bite to my tone. In fact, it sounded more resigned than anything, but by the way they're looking at me, they're certain they know there's more to the story but aren't sure they want to ask. One by one, they each pick up the beer in front of them and take another sip.

At this moment, I wish I had stayed home tonight.

Eventually, Cole breaks the silence. "Briggs here also hasn't talked to Cora since Tuesday."

Cue the record scratch. I'm going to kill him when he shows up for work tomorrow. Sometimes, things need to stay just between us and not be shared with everyone we know. Especially when it comes to my personal life.

"Why?" Clay asks.

I shrug my shoulders. "No need to, I guess. We're just friends."

"Friends?" He lets out a low laugh. "I'm not sure that's what I would have called you last weekend. Don't forget, I was there, and the two of you, well, let's just say the way y'all were looking at each other went way beyond friends. I also seem to remember a very vivid scene in the rain."

My eyes drop to the IPA in front of me. That kiss in the rain was the best kiss of my life, and my heart aches thinking about how there won't be any more of those. "She made it clear that she didn't see a future with me."

More silence and then I look back over at Ash and Clay. They've known her the longest, and I find I'm envious of the extra time in her life that they've gotten to know her and spend with her.

"She said that to you? Out loud?" Ash asks, confused by what I've said.

"No, she said it to her brother. They were talking about me, and I was standing right there. He was going on and on about marriage, and she told him she would never marry me. I guess I just didn't see the point of continuing with us after that. I'm not one for friends with benefits. I'm too busy with my life to deal with that."

"Ouch," Clay says.

My soul seconds that sentiment.

Ash runs his hand over his chin as he thinks about this.

"But something about this doesn't add up," Clay says. "Emma and I saw the two of you together. Emma's known her for almost ten years, and she said she's never seen Cora with someone like she was with you."

"Maybe she just missed those moments."

"But that's what I tried to tell you at the grocery store. There are no moments. Sure, she's had dates here and there to events and things, but there's never been a someone, and you were clearly her someone last weekend from what I've heard too," Ash says. "I feel like you might have listened to the words coming out of her mouth, but you aren't really listening to all of the other things she's been saying to you."

I rub my hand over my face. I've tried very hard to listen to the words that come out of her mouth on purpose. I wanted her to know that I hear her. Always. "What does that mean?" I ask him, feeling more tired than I have in a long time.

"It means I wouldn't write her off just yet. If you want her, then maybe stick around and prove it to her. You know about her family. Other than the girls, no one has ever made her feel valued or loved. She lives alone like she does for a reason."

I hear him, I do, and maybe I do need to talk to her about this a little bit more. I'm just not ready. I jumped the gun knowing how I feel, but I haven't really allowed her time to figure out how she feels, what we are, and what we can be together. I'd like to think that when you know you know, like I do, but she's not me, and maybe I was so consumed with myself being hurt that I didn't stop to look at the full picture.

"I'll talk to her soon enough. I'm not going anywhere, and we do live next door to each other. Maybe after this weekend, after Avery's party. Did you find out what the baby is?" I ask, again desperately trying to change the subject.

At the mention of Avery and the baby, all talks of Goldie cease. Either they realize I need a break, or Ash is just ready to talk about something else, but seeing the smile that lights up his face, I would be lying if I said I wasn't a little bit envious.

30

CORA

I know I'm not being very sociable today, but I just can't bring myself to feel happy. I tried last night with Emma, I did, but she pushed one too many times and eventually I broke down and cried. I've cried every day this week.

She knows.

She knows me.

She knows how hard this rejection is hitting.

I opened up to Briggs and let him in, and it hurts so much more than I'm willing to admit to myself to know that I'm not enough once again. There's a reason people like me choose to be hyper independent. For many years, I didn't know this was me. I stumbled across a *Women's Health* magazine article discussing the topic and instantly recognized that I'm a classic cut-and-dry case.

Hyper independent people don't ask for help. They don't share personal information about themselves. They don't trust people. They have limited close relationships. They also avoid any situation where they have to depend on others. I am all of these things. Some might say this isn't true because I have the girls, but it wasn't all rainbows and sunshine in the beginning. Even still, I feel the need to write the bulk of our music. They understand me, and they love me for who I am, so it works. But it was hard at first.

I am hard.

Maybe he found me hard to deal with too.

I thought I was getting better, at least with him, but maybe I'm not.

Looking around at Avery's beautiful baby shower, my heart is full with how many people are here today at Emma's to celebrate her. We spent hours last night decorating Clay and Emma's house and pulling everything together. They don't know the baby's gender, so there's been no reveal, and today, we've gone with neutrals and yellows. Avery hasn't had it the easiest, but she deserves all the love in the world. There's me, Emma, Juliet, Rosie, and her sister-in-law Molly, Blair, Amelia, Jane, Mona, Avery's mother, Clay's mother, and Mrs. Wheeler.

Mrs. Wheeler insisted on making the cupcakes today, and Avery teared up at the sight. They look just like her favorite cupcakes from New York, only we like them better. Sorry Kelly's Kupcakes, you've been outdone.

Emma's house is also heavily decorated with sunflowers. They fit the theme of the party from the song, "My Little Sunshine," and all they do is make me ache for the dead ones I have on my counter at home.

Yes, they're still on my counter. From the moment I accepted them from Briggs, I knew I was ultimately going to dry them and take the seeds for next summer. It seemed sentimental at the time, almost like these particular flowers are the gift that keeps on giving, but now they've become a sad memory I'm not sure I'll ever be able to separate from him. It's too bad too, because I love sunflowers, and the fields here are so beautiful.

Friends.

Neighbors.

Disruption.

Past me would have fired back and given him a piece of my mind, but instead, the new me who's secretly in love with him just had my heart squeezed so hard it ripped in half. I couldn't form words in my head, much less speak them to him.

For my whole life, I've never felt like I fit in

anywhere. I tried at home, I tried in school, I've tried with my friends, and I really tried here.

I thought just maybe I'd found someone else who felt like me. Who understood.

I guess I was wrong.

Maybe I just need to pack up and go home. Home to New York, that is. Being here, close to him, I don't think I'll be able to do it. I wouldn't say I feel used by him, but I definitely feel embarrassed. I gave myself to him, letting him see me at my most vulnerable moments. I don't want to be reminded of any of it every time I open my windows and hear his laughter float across the mountain. A laugh that feels very directed at me even if it's not.

I'm standing by the window, looking out at the lake, when Juliet slides up next to me.

"You need to spill it," she says quietly. She looks pretty today. She's wearing a pale green dress, and there's a light to her that's not usually there.

My eyes grow large as I look at her, and then they narrow. "You need to spill it," I whisper.

She pulls back. "What do you mean?"

"What I mean is people are talking about you being seen multiple times at the Italian restaurant. What gives?"

"Really?" she asks, shocked, but then her cheeks

flush bright red. Busted.

"Of course! It's a small town. Word travels fast."

"The same can be said for you. You were spotted out with Briggs looking cozy." She smirks.

"It's not like that." I feel myself frowning.

"What do you mean it's not like that? It's been like that for weeks. We've all talked about it."

"Glad to know I can be a topic of conversation for all of you, but it's not. He doesn't want it. He doesn't want me."

A lump rises up in my throat. Talking about him makes me want to cry, and I really don't want to. I know I'll get past this soon enough where it won't hurt so much, but not today.

"That's crazy. I've seen the way he looks at you. Did something happen? What exactly did he say?"

She isn't going to let this go, so I may as well give her the highlights and get it over with. Maybe if I pull off the Band-Aid enough times, it won't be as sticky and hurt as much.

"Winston showed up here on Tuesday to chastise me over leaving my parents' party early. Briggs was there, and Winston embarrassed me thoroughly in front of him. Not shocking, Briggs tells me we're better off friends because we're neighbors right afterward."

"Eww," she says, as her face scrunches up.

"My sentiments exactly." My heart aches.

"There has to be more to it than that. Briggs doesn't strike me as the type of guy to let anything or anyone get in his way once he knows what he wants. Did you push him to be more specific?"

"I did. I asked him what I did wrong, and he said nothing."

"I'm still not buying it." She frowns.

"It is what it is. I haven't seen him or talked to him in days. Your turn. Who are you meeting at the bar?"

"Michael." She smiles softly. "Bryce and I went to the Italian place to try it out after Avery suggested we eat there, and he came out of the back to greet the tables. We talked, he bought our dinner, and he invited me back in. So I went."

"He's the chef there?"

I'm shocked. I never saw her dating a chef. Not that there's anything wrong with chefs. Maybe it's that I just didn't picture her dating anyone. I never met her ex Dillon. Then again, I've never seen her with anyone.

"Chef and owner. He's really nice." The look on her face is dreamy.

"Wow, I didn't see this coming."

"Me either. He's also divorced and has custody of his daughter half the time. His ex-wife wanted to move here, so he followed."

"How old is his daughter?"

"His daughter, Bella, is ten."

Bella, the name of the restaurant.

"Are you going to see him again?"

"I am." She blushes.

"This is good. I'm happy for you. I might need to secretly drop into the restaurant a few times before I'm introduced to watch him and do my due diligence. Maybe have a background check run," I tease, and she laughs.

"You're still good to come over for Halloween and hand out candy, right? He's got Bella next weekend, so I think we're going to go trick-or-treating together."

"Yes, I'll be there to hand out candy. But only if you take a bunch of pictures of Bryce. I need one for my house." I've been thinking about adding a few new photos to my stairwell or swapping some photos out.

"That's so sweet. Of course I'll get you a photo."

Behind us, we hear Avery laughing. We both look over to see her standing in a small group, including Clay's mom. Ash moved in with them when he was thirteen, so while she doesn't have baby stories to tell, she has plenty of him and Clay in their teenage years. She loves talking about the two of them, and Avery loves every single story.

"Does he know who your brothers are? Your

friends?" I ask Juliet, hoping for her sake that this guy will be able to deal with the spotlight that will inevitably come her way after a new album is released or when a tour is kicked off.

"Not yet. Or at least I don't think so. It's possible someone said something to him, small town and all, but he hasn't uttered a word."

"Do you think he'll be able to handle it?"

"I do." She smiles, then her gaze switches to one of contemplation. "Have you ever had one of those moments when you're looking all over for something, say like your phone, but then it turns out it was right in front of you the whole time, like in your hand?"

"Yes, I've done this." But I'm not following her train of thought.

"I feel like that's what's happening with Briggs. We're missing something that is right in front of our faces. What he said doesn't make sense. Especially after the way Emma came home and talked about the two of you."

"I don't know. I tried to get him to talk to me, but he was completely shut down and closed off. He was the guy I first met when I moved into the house."

"Grumpy asshole?"

"Yeah, that one."

"Well, I wouldn't give up on him yet. Things always

have a way of surfacing. Whatever it was that flipped his switch off. Eventually, he'll get tired of sitting in the dark."

"Easier said than done. He broke my heart, and I don't want to relive that or hang on to the possibility if there's nothing truly there."

"Well, maybe it's because I'm happy at the moment, but I think you should see the possibility and not the problem. If he's worth it, he'll be back."

"I'd like to say, 'I hope so,' but we'll see."

I also have to ask myself, do I even want him back?

31

BRIGGS

With every day that gets further away from that awful night on my porch, my heart feels less wounded and more longing. I'm not really mad at her, and I don't even know if I'm hurt anymore, but I do know that I miss her. I'm not sure if absence makes my heart grow fonder or weaker, but I know within a day or two, we need to talk again. It'll have been a week, a week too long.

"Plans tonight?" Cole asks as we've just finished for the day and are sitting in the barn enjoying a glass of cider. It's almost November, and apple season is almost over. I'm ready for it. Plus, the cider currently in the tanks from the June drop of Heirloom apples is ready to be bottled, canned, and racked.

"Nah, I'm just glad things are about to slow down for us. I feel like this season has been really long."

"Long for you because you're dragging around like a lovesick fool."

"Maybe." I don't even have it in me to argue with him.

"Do you hear that?" Cole asks, angling his head toward the door.

"Yep," I tell him, making no move to do anything about it.

Distress creeps onto his face as the sound doesn't stop.

Just like last time, the echoing sound of her smoke alarm screaming into the early evening has my skin crawling. I have no idea what's going on over there, but she's repeatedly made it clear she doesn't need or want my help, so she can figure this out on her own.

But it's when we hear the sirens, and our eyes lock with the realization that they're getting closer, that panic overrides every other emotion I have. I take off as fast as I can and run past my house, over the road, and down her driveway.

Tendrils of black smoke have started to rise from the back of her house, and I damn near stop breathing as I see she isn't outside safe where she should be.

"Oh God."

My head whips in all directions, looking for her, but she's nowhere to be found. With my heart pounding and my stomach in my throat, I head for the house and burst through the front door. This time instead of seeing her fanning out the smoke, she's surrounded by it and waving the hose of a fire extinguisher as a white foam spews from it and lands on the fire, which is doing its best to take over the back cabinets in her kitchen.

Sprinting toward her, I snatch the extinguisher out of her hands and take over.

"Go outside. Now," I yell at her.

She looks at me with wild, panicked eyes, and I yell even louder. "NOW!"

For once in her life, she listens, and I squeeze the handle as hard as I can and sweep from one side to the other, trying to put out the base of the flames.

What the hell was she doing?

Why was she still in here trying to put it out?

Why didn't she just yell for me? I would have heard her, or Cole would have, and I could have helped her sooner.

Irrational and unthinkable thoughts barrel through my mind as I do my best to contain the fire. Fear like I've never known has my eyes watering, but then again, maybe it's smoke.

The fire department arrives within minutes, and I'm

being dragged outside. I don't even realize I'm coughing until one of them shoves an oxygen mask onto my face, and Goldie stands in front of me sobbing, wearing one of her own.

"Are you okay?" she's asking, so distraught that her words barely come out. Tears stream down her beautiful face, creating tracks where there's soot covering her, and it's the most terrible, gut-wrenching thing I've ever seen.

Breathing in, I pull hard on the air. In many ways, this feels like the first full breath I've taken since I saw her last Tuesday, and I need to be closer to her. I need to touch her, to know she's okay and mine.

"Come here," I tell her, pulling her into my arms. This need is so fierce, I'm not sure I could let go of her if I tried. She collapses into me and cries with her face buried in my shirt. Her chest convulses. The sound is so gut-wrenching my eyes flood with tears of my own. I've never thought about her crying before, but I know for certain after this, I never want to see her cry again.

My heart pounds hard, and my arms tighten.

She's safe. I keep telling myself this as the sound of water flies from the truck onto the back of the house. A fireman stands next to us and explains that it's not really needed, but it's better to be safe than sorry. The fire inside was contained and has been extinguished. I hear him, and I don't, as the adrenaline runs through my ears, blocking everything out. And that's when I see Cole standing beside him, looking devastated and panicked.

At this, something inside me snaps. I know he's got it from here. He can finish up with the fire department, and I can take care of my girl. Even if she isn't my girl.

For fuck's sake. I think I just lost five years of my life.

I shift the mask and tuck my head in next to hers. "Goldie, you're okay. I've got you."

She cries harder, and this makes me cry too. I don't care who's watching. I could have lost her, and she's so upset she's almost inconsolable. In many ways, this feels bigger than the house. I'm just not sure why. The house is fine. It'll just need a bit of repair. She is fine, and we will be fine. I will make us fine if it's the last thing I do.

"My painting," she whispers, and I calmly ask Cole to go inside and get it and take it home.

Of all the items in her house, this is the one item she wants. Not her music, not her cello, not her plants, but the painting. The painting that she keeps as a reminder of what it's like to be loved by someone.

My poor, lonely girl.

Maybe that's it, maybe she thinks I don't love her or can't love her, or maybe she doesn't know how to love me, I'm not sure . . . but soon, I will be rectifying this, and just maybe she'll realize that one day she can love me too.

A few minutes later, she pulls back and looks me in the eyes. There's fear and pain, but not the emotional. This is one hundred percent physical.

"My arm," she says as she holds it up. I gasp as my stomach turns over, and I try not to vomit. While I'm certain it could be a lot worse, more tears drip down my face seeing that she's hurt. If I hadn't been so stubborn and just came and checked on her when I heard the alarm, this might not have happened to her. The underside of her forearm is red, angry, and blistered in quite a few places. It one hundred percent feels like it's my fault.

"Goldie," I whisper. "What happened?" I ask while simultaneously looking around for one of the firemen. My eyes lock with Cole's. He nods and heads toward the truck.

"I was trying to make the apple fritters again, and I don't understand how I'm getting the oil too hot. It started smoking, and I thought I turned the burner heat off, but I didn't. The burner has two settings where there's a small burner or a large one, and I turned it where it didn't click off, so it was on the small setting. I turned around to start cleaning up, and before I realized it, the smoke had turned to fire, and some of the grease had popped and splattered out. It happened so fast. I went to get the fire blanket and remembered I hadn't replaced it from before, so I ran to grab another towel and soaked it in water. I went to lay it over the top, but more grease splattered, hitting my arm. I jerked, dragging the towel through the grease, and it spread the fire. I tried to put it out, but everything happened so fast, and the flames engulfed the whole stove."

She starts coughing again, and I shove the oxygen mask back over her face. I can't take this. My soul hurts so badly.

"I called 911 and then panicked about my painting, plants, my cello, and other things, but instead of trying to get them out, I thought I could put the fire out with the extinguisher."

She cries more, and all I can do is hold her to me.

"Ma'am." We're interrupted. Cole is back with a fireman standing next to him. Goldie pulls away from me as he slowly reaches for her arm. She turns it over for him, and his eyes flick to mine. "I'm going to call EMS. She needs to be seen."

"No. I'll take her in," I tell him.

"Sir—"

"I said I'll take her," I repeat, leaving no room for argument. We don't need to wait for an ambulance. This isn't life and death, and she's not leaving my side.

"I'll get your truck," Cole says, taking off, running back toward my house.

The ride to the emergency room is quiet. Neither one of us says much, and Goldie just stares out the window. Once we're there, they immediately take her back as the fire department had called it in. She didn't ask me to go with her, but then again, I didn't think she would.

It hurts to know she doesn't want me with her, and I honestly don't know if it's because she likes to do things on her own or because of how we left things.

Two and a half hours later, we're back at her house, standing in the living room and staring at the damage. The fire really was contained to the back wall of the kitchen and didn't crawl its way out to other parts of the room. Obviously, restoration will need to come in, and the kitchen will need to be redone, but the whole thing could have been much worse.

"I am never going to fry anything ever again," she says, looking more defeated than I've ever seen her. Even her hair has lost its shine.

"I think that's probably a wise decision," I tell her, trying to keep the mood light.

She turns to face me, and her eyes are so sad. I just want to pull her against me again, but she's put up a wall. I feel it, and I'm doing my best to respect it.

"Thank you for going with me." She shuffles from one foot to the other. She's dismissing me.

I take a step toward her. "You should probably stay with me until this smell is gone."

"It's okay. I'll be fine here," she mumbles as she looks around again. There are black streaks all over the other cabinets, and the ceiling is covered.

"Goldie." I pin her with a look that says please don't argue with me, but I should have known that wouldn't work on my girl.

My beautiful, stubborn, resilient girl.

"Briggs, I'm not trying to be rude, but I'm ready to be alone," she pleads. She's not trying to be rude. She just wants to get rid of me.

"Then be alone at my house. Take whichever room you want, and I'll leave you be."

"Thanks, but no thanks." She cradles her arm to her chest, and I instantly track the movement.

"Why are you doing this right now?" I ask softly. She can't mean it. Who would want to be alone after something like this?

"What do you mean? I had a rough night, as you well know, and I just want to go upstairs, attempt to get clean, and get in my bed. Briggs, I'm exhausted," she says, her eyes filling with tears.

"Fine. Then I'll stay here," I tell her as I walk toward

the couch and start wiping it off. I'm pissed that she just won't let me help her, and I'm doing my best not to show it, but I'm like a bull in a china shop. There's no tiptoeing around my emotions.

"No. You are not staying here." This time, she is firm, and where I thought I might be able to persuade her, I can see now that's not happening.

I turn to face her, and our eyes lock. "Why not?"

"Because I don't want you to," she says like it's the easiest decision she's ever had to make.

I swallow as my heart goes numb. It's preparing for the impact that it knows is coming.

"I don't understand. Goldie, I want to be near you. Tonight was rough for me too. I'm not asking much. I just want to share space with you."

"Briggs, we're not friends." Her voice cracks. "I appreciate you helping me, but I'll take it from here."

"Not friends? That's news to me."

"Is it? You made it very clear that's what you want, but it's not what I want. I don't want to be your friend."

"What?" I look at her like she's lost her mind, only she doesn't answer me. She glares at me with glassy eyes like I'm suddenly enemy number one.

No explanation. No excuse. Nothing.

I can't believe she doesn't even want to be my friend? Boy, I read the room wrong on that one too, because what the hell has she been playing at all these months? What were we doing last weekend?

"You are the most frustrating, confusing woman on the planet."

"Me?" She points at her chest.

"Yes!" I throw my head back and stare at the ceiling. My attempt to be calm flies right out the window. "Well, isn't this just the fucking cherry on top of the cake."

"Don't swear at me!"

"I'm not swearing at you. I'm swearing at me!" I point at myself.

How did I let myself get so tangled with her? As if I didn't think she could hurt me anymore, suddenly she has. I get not wanting someone to be their spouse. Marriage isn't for everyone, but to say she doesn't even want to be my friend? I just can't.

Taking a deep breath, I rub my hand over my face to hide my heartache and compose myself. The fatigue I feel is bone-deep, which means hers is too. I remind myself tonight isn't about me. It's about her, and hopefully, her emotions are just running high.

"Don't worry, Cora, I heard you the first time. The message was received loud and clear. But will you at least consider going to one of your friends' houses until this smell is lessened? It would really make me feel better."

I don't want to fight with her; I want to fight for her, but nothing good is going to come out of tonight.

"I'll be fine here."

I let out a deep sigh. Realizing there's no convincing her otherwise, I start making my way toward the door. You can't help someone who doesn't want to be helped.

At least not tonight.

I'll have to try again tomorrow.

"What do you mean you heard me the first time?"

I turn and face her. "I heard you. I stood right there when you told your brother you'd never marry me." I point at the spot.

"That's not what I said."

"Yes, it is. You said you would never marry someone he picked for you, and he had literally just picked me. He made this whole big scene about it, and you said no. And that's fine, but maybe you should have told me first. I would have done a lot of things differently."

Her eyes are large, and she's shaking her head like she doesn't understand. "I don't know what to say and what do you mean differently? I didn't realize we were at the 'I do' phase of our very short affair."

"That is all it was to you, right? An affair?" I had to ask even though I probably shouldn't have.

"It wasn't, but correct me if I'm wrong, we"—she waves her uninjured hand back and forth between us—

"just happened. No declarations had been made. I didn't even know if we were going to be a 'we.' You never said anything to me, much less getting married."

"I guess we'll never know now, will we?"

That's the hurt talking, so it's time for me to go.

She straightens her spine and stares at me. "I guess we won't."

Not needing to hear or say any more, I take my lovesick heart and make my way to the front door. I've just stepped onto the porch when she says, "And just so you know, I know exactly when you left that day. If you had stuck around like you'd offered, then you would have heard me not only tell my brother that I would never marry someone he chose for me but also, that if I did decide to marry, it would be because I chose them. Me."

With that, she slams the door in my face.

32

CORA

*M*y arm hurts.

But even more than that, my heart hurts.

I've always claimed that I never understood all those sappy, brokenhearted love songs, but now I do. This feeling is debilitating and makes it hard to breathe. Why do people intentionally do this to themselves? Falling in love is awful.

After Briggs left, I made my way upstairs to my room and shut the door. With the windows open and a candle burning, the smell wasn't too noticeable, and after a while, I forgot it was even there. I carefully took a bath, climbed into my bed, and cried.

I feel so stupid.

I know better than to use water on a grease fire, but

when I saw the flames, I panicked, and the sink was right there. So many flames and it was so hot. Hotter than anything I've ever felt before.

And then there's my poor arm.

The hospital told me I had second-degree burns. They also told me the burn may worsen over the next couple of days. They peeled the skin off the top of the blisters, and I have to go back daily to have it reassessed and the dressings changed. They already warned me it would scar. Just what I need, a daily reminder about my mistakes and failures.

Of course I didn't tell Briggs any of this. He doesn't need to know. The whole night was embarrassing enough.

And I did want to go home with him and climb into his bed, but what would be the point? The type of friend he wants me to be, I stand firm, is the type who isn't going to be sleeping in his bed.

I can't.

All of this is just terrible.

And my arm hurts.

Sometime around ten, I finally make my way downstairs. I've been dreading what my house will look like in the light of day, and I'm afraid of the project that will come my way. I called for restoration cleanup, so someone will be here at lunchtime, but after that, it's insurance adjusters, contractors, permits—all of it feels daunting and not like anything I want to deal with. Maybe I'll go back to New York now and let someone else deal with this.

I'm staring at the coffee maker, trying to decide whether I want to wade through the mess left behind from the extinguisher foam and the people in my house, when Jane comes bustling through the door with two coffees and a large bag. Her eyes instantly find the charred kitchen, and her jaw drops.

"Oh, your poor kitchen," she says, blinking at the damage.

"It's fine. Well, it's not fine, but it could have been worse. I can replace the kitchen," I tell her as I head to the dining room to open the windows. It seems most of them were opened at some point last night, but I still need them all opened to ventilate the house. The air is cold this morning, but I don't mind. After the heat last night and how bad my poor arm feels, I welcome it.

"That's right, you can replace the kitchen, but we can't replace you," she says as she drops her stuff and turns to me. Tears fill her eyes, and the next thing I know, she's rushing my way and hugging me.

And because I'm such a hot mess myself, I start crying too. Affection is not something I'm generally familiar with, so to receive it when I desperately need it, she'll never know what this means to me.

Jane is the first to pull back. Her eyes are filled with worry as they scan my face, and her fingers tuck some loose hair behind my ear. "I'm just beside myself today. Cole called this morning and told me what happened, and then between Briggs this week and thinking I could have lost you, my old body can't handle it."

"What do you mean, Briggs? What happened to him this week?" I ask. He seemed fine last night.

"I . . ." She thinks about how to answer the question and moves back to her bag. She pulls out a smaller bag I recognize and places it next to the coffees on the coffee table. She's brought me cider donuts. "Well, when you get to be my age, it's easy to see things that maybe people don't want you to see."

"What did you see?" I ask, following her to the kitchen table.

"He's not been himself," she says as she dumps out a whole bunch of cleaning supplies.

"How so?"

She doesn't answer right away. Instead, she takes a bucket, pours in some vinegar, and then water from a gallon jug she brought.

"You're gonna push this subject, aren't you?" she asks as she eyes me and my bandage-wrapped arm.

My response is to stare at her, hoping she'll go on and tell me.

"Cora, Briggs has a broken heart."

Instantly, I'm furious. Despite what is going on between the two of us, Briggs is a great guy. I can't imagine someone hurting him. If it was someone in his family, I might have to tuck my tail between my legs and call Winston to take care of it. "Who broke it?"

She reaches in the bag for a hand towel and looks at me. "Well, you did, sweetie."

"No, I didn't," I tell her and then watch as she dips the towel into the solution and moves to the wall to start wiping it down. "Jane, you don't need to clean. I've already called a company to come and do this."

"I can't help it. I have to do something. Tell me, what happened last week? Tuesday maybe?" she asks, not looking at me but making broad vertical swipes. I can see the residue as it smudges.

"Tuesday?"

"Yes. I showed up to work on Wednesday, and he didn't utter a word to me. He's always told me hello, too, so I just left him alone, but he didn't speak at all. To anyone. For days. What he did do was work. Hard. And there are only two reasons a man works like the way he's been working. One, he's angry, or two, he's hurt."

"Maybe he was angry? I didn't hurt him. He told me he just wanted to be friends."

But then my mind flips to the conversation we had last night where he mentioned hearing me say I wouldn't marry him. How bizarre is that? I feel like all of this is uncharted waters, and maybe I was insensitive when I said that.

"But why did he say that?" she asks. "For the past couple of weeks, Briggs has been the happiest I've ever seen him. And don't get me started on the pranks, which I think are hilarious. I've known him since he was a boy, and no one has ever riled him up like you do."

"He said that after he overheard a conversation between my brother and me. But what I said wasn't directed toward him. It was a general statement that I didn't think was relevant to us at all."

"The biggest communication problem people have is they do not listen to understand. They listen to reply. I heard that once, and it kind of stuck with me. He should have taken the time to understand why you said what you did, and maybe you should try to understand why he replied the way he did."

I think about last night and how he was so worried about me. His reaction to the situation, his tears, his worry, it wasn't one of a friend, but of something more.

"Men are stupid," she says, pulling me from my

thoughts. "Sometimes we have to think for ourselves and for them, but Cora, darling, you need to have a real conversation with him, one where you listen to understand each other and not reply. I think the outcome will be good for both of you."

"Right, I think I'll go do that now." I don't want to be away from him. I want to be with him, so I sure hope she knows what she's talking about.

She smiles at me, and it isn't a good luck smile. It's a go-get-your-man smile.

Slipping into my boots, I make my way outside. The driveway and the grass are damaged from the fire truck, but that's okay. These things too can be fixed. Slowly, I make my way over the familiar path from my house to his. I'm not even sure if he's at home. He could be up on the mountain, but I at least have to try.

Knocking on his door, I'm nervous. Too many times I've stood here hoping for a different outcome than the one I received. My heart races, my chest tightens, and my nose stings. Like always, the heavy tread of his footsteps alerts me that he's coming. My stomach dips, and when the door swings open, I'm so happy to see him that my eyes blur with tears.

"What's wrong?" he stammers, stepping out of the doorway and scanning me from head to toe. His hands raise to touch me, but then they drop.

Briggs wears sweatpants and a long-sleeved T-shirt. His hair is wet like he just got out of the shower, and he smells so good standing next to me. I don't know if it's because my sense of smell is heightened or if my nose is relieved to smell something else. Either way, he smells like home.

"Nothing, I'm fine," I tell him, moving so he has room to stand directly in front of me.

He lets out a deep breath and runs his hand over his head and his face. I know last night was taxing for him too. I can't imagine how much of a wreck I would be if the situation was reversed and this happened to him.

"Actually, no, I'm not. Can we talk?"

"I hate it when people use that phrase," he replies, moving to the side so Duke can make his way out. Duke is wearing his sweater, and this makes my already damp eyes let a few tears escape.

"Oh." I take a step back and look at the ground. "Never mind then."

"I'm not saying no, just that I don't like the phrase. Do you want to come in?"

"No, out here's fine. But I'll sit down." I glance at the rocking chair next to me and remember him not liking me in this one before.

"You can sit in the chair. I was an asshole that day, I'm sorry."

"It's fine." But I still don't sit there. Instead, I turn and sit on his porch steps and wipe my eyes. Duke flops down next to me. I run my fingers through his fur and watch as Briggs leaves the door open and follows. He sits next to me on the step but leans on the opposite railing.

"How's your arm today?" he asks gently.

"It hurts, but if I don't move it, then it feels a little better."

He frowns. "Did you take the pain medicine? After you went upstairs, I remembered it was in my truck and put it on your counter."

"You came inside after I went to bed?"

"Yes, sorry. I was worried, and I wanted you to have it." He looks at the ground like he's contemplating telling me more and then does. "I know you wanted me to leave, but I stayed anyway. I opened your windows and slept on your couch. I wanted to be there in case you needed me."

My jaw drops. I had no idea he was in my house, but now that I do, I somehow feel better about last night. My heart squeezes at this beautiful man sitting next to me. I should tell him thank you; I should say a lot. Instead, I ask him the question that's been haunting me for days.

"Why do you only want to be my friend?"

"Why don't you want to marry me?" he asks.

And then we both laugh.

"I feel like . . . this argument is . . . ridiculous. I don't even know another way to put it. I never said I didn't want to marry you. I said I would never marry someone Winston picked out for me. You made that up over a situation that hasn't even occurred yet. There I was, still reeling by how great I thought we were together, and I came over that night wanting to tell you and hoping you might feel something for me too, but that's not what happened. And now this." I hold up my arm.

"You felt something for me?" he asks, almost timidly, which feels so out of character for him. Briggs is the type of guy who is confident and sure about everything. It feels weird to know that I can make him feel insecure like this.

"Of course I did. You know I did. I never would have gone there with you if I didn't." And I wouldn't have. He isn't a one-nighter, a nobody. He's my neighbor, my friend, and someone I wanted to love. "I felt so much for you that I even mentioned that I was worried you would break my heart, and you did just that. This past week has been awful for me, and all I've done is replay everything to try to figure out what I did wrong."

"Cora." He reaches for my hand. "You didn't do anything wrong. This is all on me. I'm sorry. I got overwhelmed. I didn't just feel something for you. I felt everything."

"You did?"

"Yes." He looks up toward the sky, takes a deep breath, and his eyes find mine again. "I am in love with you. And not the sweet first love kind of love. This love I have for you is consuming and raw. I feel exposed and vulnerable, and I don't like it. I know we aren't anywhere near the place of marriage, but the moment he said it, I could see it, and when I heard your reaction, I thought you couldn't or wouldn't love me back. It hurt."

"But I do love you back. So much," I tell him as more tears free themselves in relief and drip down my face.

With this confession, Briggs's expression shifts to one of elation and devastation. He scoots next to me and cups my cheek. His thumb is gentle as it wipes away the wetness.

"Please don't cry."

"I can't help it."

"These tears rip my fucking heart out, and I can't take it. I want you happy all the time."

I lean my head into his hand. "I want you to be happy, too."

"I am, but with you . . . I want to stand outside in every storm and kiss you in the rain. I want boxes of Cheez-Its all over my house and in my truck. I want us to play pranks on each other for years to come. I want to watch you perform on a stage. I want to help you with your projects. I want to build your dream garden and fill our home with unnecessary plants. I want you laughing and smiling and teasing me incessantly. I want to bring you joy, and I want to be yours as much as I want you to be mine."

"I am yours."

He exhales. "It's about fucking time."

"Your mouth." I shake my head at him, but I'm grinning so big my face aches.

He scowls. "I can't help it. You bring it out of me."

"Ha! I doubt that."

"Can I kiss you now?" he asks like he needs this kiss more than he needs air.

"Most definitely."

Leaning over, Briggs gently places his lips on mine. They're warm and familiar, and I feel a sense of peace trickle through my veins. I know he's afraid of hurting me, but I need to be closer, so I slide onto his lap and thread my fingers through his hair.

"I missed you," he whispers as he sucks my bottom lip between his. "I couldn't stay away from you even when you asked."

"I'm glad you didn't. I really did want to be with you. I just didn't know how."

"No more," he says.

"No more," I agree.

When I tip his head, our lips fall open, and we sink into the deliciousness that is us. He kisses me like he needs to make up for lost time, and I let him because I know how amazing he is when he takes the lead. His tongue wraps around mine, his lips permanently imprint themselves, and somewhere deep down, I know he is going to be the last man I ever kiss.

"I love you," he says, and if my heart had wings, I know it would fly.

"I love you, too," I tell him, and he groans in response and smiles against my lips. It's funny how hearing these little words can mean so much.

Breaking away, I lay my head on his shoulder. He wraps his arms around me and holds me in the best hug I've ever received. This is what I need, and my eyes drift shut as I breathe him in and let the enormity of what this declaration means sink in.

Briggs loves me.

Me.

For who I am.

I don't think I've ever been happier.

"So does this mean you'll marry me?" he asks, his face buried in my neck.

I laugh. "Too soon, Briggs. Too soon."

He pulls back to look at me, and I get lost in his eyes. Eyes that say I'm the only one he'll ever see.

"Well, you should know I'm not going to stop asking." He smirks.

I run my hand over the stubble on his jaw and down to his heart. "Then you should know, when you least expect it, I just might say yes."

33

BRIGGS

It's been a month since the fire incident.

A lot has changed in that month, but not a lot at the same time. We've both been more open about how we feel, and I'm continually surprised by how far we've come since the very beginning. Me thinking all commitments to a woman would be like Adele and a terrible thing, to her removing the wall she's kept herself behind. Goldie's had to learn to let me help her, and I've had to accept that it's okay to let her do things on her own. But the biggest change was that Goldie agreed to stay with me while her house was being repaired. We fit together far better than either of us expected.

I've continued to ask her to marry me at random

times, and of course she just laughs. I'm not sure if she thinks I'm serious or not, but I am. I would marry her tomorrow. Soon enough, I'll convince her, I'm sure of it.

We're sitting on the couch in the living room, discussing what we're going to take to Clay's for Thanksgiving, when I decide to ask her a different question.

"I do love your painting. It's going to look great when you finally decide where you want to hang it."

Her feet are propped on my lap as she's stretched out across the couch looking for recipes on her phone, and I'm watching her to see when my words register, and the moment they do, her eyes flick up to mine.

"Wait. What? Why would I hang it here? It'll go back with me once the kitchen is done." She glances toward the painting, which is propped up against the wall, and then back to me.

"You should hang it because I think you should move in with me."

She stares at me like she doesn't understand, but I do. I want her here with me, permanently. She makes my life better, and every day, I'm thankful that she moved in across the street.

"But we haven't been dating that long," she counters, then sits up so we're more eye to eye. My arm is stretched out across the back of the couch, and my fingers find her neck and shoulder. She's warm and soft, and I love touching her.

"Really?" One brow pops up. "We could argue about when we started dating, not officially of course, but are you going to change your mind about me? About us?"

"Well, no," she says, drawing out the word and scooting on her knees a little closer. The gold flecks in her eyes become visible. She's so beautiful that sometimes it hurts to look at her. Like right now. She's in sweatpants, one of my long-sleeved T-shirts, and fuzzy socks. Her hair is piled on her head, and she's makeup-free. She's comfortable, relaxed, and authentically herself. I could never ask for anything more.

Well, except for her to be naked.

"Does separating us by a road make that much of a difference?" I ask, and she chews on her bottom lip. My dick twitches at the sight, as it knows exactly what those lips can do.

"I guess not. I've just never lived with anyone before."

"Me either. Well, except for when my mother was here."

"You and Adele never lived together?"

"No, thank God. I never even thought about it. It should have been my first clue that we weren't meant to be. I wasn't interested in spending as much time as possible with her. On the other hand, I never want to be away from you."

She's quiet as she thinks about what I've said, and then she frowns.

"Talk to me." I reach up and cup her cheek, loving how her skin feels.

Her eyes find mine. "I don't know why I thought you lived together in Charlotte. But whatever." She shakes her head just a little, and my hand drops to her lap. "I guess I just feel strange. No one has ever wanted me like you do, and I'm trying to process this."

I can't help the smile that creeps onto my face, and she rolls her eyes. Of course I want her badly, all the time, but I know that's not what she's talking about.

"I think I'm still adjusting getting used to you loving me. Sometimes you say things like this, and I'm surprised. Not in a bad way. I just wasn't expecting it."

"Good thing I'm not going anywhere," I tell her as my hand spreads over her thigh, and my thumb swipes back and forth.

"So what do you say? Want to move in with me?" I ask softer this time and I realize I'm nervous for her answer. It's one thing for her to laugh when I propose, it's another for her to say no to this.

"What will I do with my house?" Her hand slides up over my arm and wraps around my shoulders.

"How do you feel about selling it?"

She pulls back, and two little lines drop between her eyes. "Why? Do you know someone who wants to buy it?"

"I think for the right price, your house would be Cole and Amelia's dream house."

"Really?" Her brows pop up in a way that tells me she doesn't hate this idea.

"Yeah, he used to go over and wander the property when it was still vacant. He never said anything, but I knew. There was some heartbreak on his face when the sign came down, notifying us that it had been sold."

"Why didn't they buy it?"

"All of this happened right when he and Amelia were getting married. I imagine it was a money thing."

"And you think they can afford it now?"

I shrug my shoulders.

"I think we could work something out with them if that's what you want to do. It's your house. Your decision."

She thinks about this. Her eyes sparkle, and a smile tips her perfect lips.

"It is fun to know your neighbor," she says while looking at me mischievously and flirty at the same time.

I chuckle at her brazenness.

"Damn straight, it's fun," I tell her as I flip her onto

her back and hover over her. My hips settle between hers. She's warm, she's perfect, and she doesn't have to do anything other than breathe to turn me on.

"So what do you say?" I ask her again while looking into her beautiful eyes. Hell, I'll ask her a thousand times if I have to. I want her. Forever. "Move in with me."

"Okay," she whispers, and my heart soars.

Closing the distance, I seal this deal we've made with a kiss.

A long, slow kiss that I'll never get tired of.

My weight settles on her, and her feet wrap around my legs. One of my hands stays propped next to her head, but my other slides under her T-shirt, or should I say mine, to tug it off. She's not wearing a bra, and the sight of her topless on my couch has me instantly hard. I drag my teeth to one of her nipples, and her hands thread through my hair. As I bite down, she arches her back and lets out a sound that shoots straight to my groin.

I take my time as I move from one breast to the other, enjoying the taste of her skin and how she feels as she rocks her hips against mine. Slow, lazy afternoon make-out sessions on *our* couch, with the fire burning and no place we need to be, might quickly become one of my favorite things. That is until I'm suddenly being shoved off and onto the floor.

"There! Did you hear it?" Goldie jumps up from the couch and moves toward the plants we brought up from her house and where I hid the chirper. Having it in the house has made changing the battery easy. The pressure of me lying on it or her pushing against it must have triggered the remote.

"Hear what?" I ask nonchalantly, like she's going crazy, while enjoying the view. Pieces of her hair have fallen loose, and the skin on her chest is red from my beard scratching it, but her boobs are as perfect as they were the night we met.

"Oh my God, I know you heard it. You had to have." She's waving her arms wide. "There's a cricket following me, and it just won't die! It was in my house for weeks, and now it's here. I can't take it anymore."

I push the button again, and the cricket chirp goes off again.

She whips around and looks at another plant. "There!" She moves toward it and looks around, only coming up with nothing.

I don't know how they do it where it sounds like it's coming from different places around the room, but it does.

"I might have heard something," I say to her, only this time she spins to face my direction.

Smart girl.

"You." Her tone is deep, her eyes have narrowed, and I can't help the grin that splits my face. A deep blush creeps up her chest and into her neck. I swear, one by one, her fingers slowly curl into fists, and then she leaps at me. "I'm going to kill you!"

EPILOGUE
CORA

"I have to say, I really am shocked they actually went through with a Christmas Eve wedding," I tell Briggs as we walk into the most Christmassy-themed ballroom I've ever seen. The five-star hotel in downtown Charlotte has been transformed with red, gold, and green colors. There are decorated Christmas trees, black walkway lanterns, snowflakes hanging, a sleigh to take photos in, and the entire room glows with candles.

"I'm not. Don't you know my brother eats small children for breakfast," Briggs says, threading his fingers through mine. I stifle my laugh so as not to draw attention our way.

Today hasn't been as terrible as I thought it would be. No one wants to be at their ex's wedding, and no one wants to be the date of the ex when they were together for such a long time. But with the positive way people have greeted us and how disinterested Briggs has been over the two of them, my nerves were quickly settled.

The ceremony was at a small quaint church just outside of town, and for convenience, they bused all three hundred guests to and from. There was no bridal party, just the two of them, and they requested that everyone wear black. Jaxon's tux is black with a gold and red boutonniere, and Adele's bouquet was exquisite with poinsettias and white roses. While they genuinely look happy, I found Briggs studying them a few times. It's like he still can't believe they're together, but then, at the same time, he can.

"It is really pretty in here, though. Adele did a good job."

"If by that you mean the wedding planners did a good job, I'm sure landing this event will rank high in their portfolio. Adele is not the type of person to pull all this together. Her mother, now, she's a different story. She always had an eye for these types of things."

"Adele is the type of daughter I'm certain my mother wishes she had."

Briggs looks down at me and frowns. "Goldie, you are perfect just the way you are. Fuck her."

Oh, this man and his mouth. I laugh even though I

shouldn't.

"Still, she had to have had some of this vision. It is her wedding after all."

I glance in Adele's direction. She and Jaxon are standing in the middle of the room on the dance floor, receiving people. In all white, she is literally the center of attention, and she's soaking it up. As she should, I guess, since it is their wedding day.

"Maybe she has been dreaming about this day for years. Regardless of who the groom is."

"Do you think they'll be happy together?" I ask him, looking at him to see his reaction.

He tilts his head as he thinks about this. "I don't know, but most likely yes. Despite it all, I do want them both to be happy."

Leaning into him, I hug his arm closest to me. "I know you do."

We both turn to look at them. At the moment, they are by themselves and smiling at each other. Their conversation looks genuine, and no matter how they got together, there's no denying she's glowing today.

"I do know that I never would have been happy with her or this life. It's not for me, and every time we do something like this, all I crave is to be back home on the mountain. Home with you." I look up at him, and all I see is love shining back at me.

"I know what you mean, but don't get too homesick. Tomorrow, we have that long flight to Positano."

While I am currently not talking to my family and setting boundaries, ones which they don't approve of and I'm not surprised by, Briggs and I decided we do like the tradition of taking a vacation the week between Christmas and New Year's. I know there will be years we stay home, but then again maybe not.

"I am looking forward to this vacation with you. We'll stay in our room, we'll go out to eat, and then head back to our room." He smirks, wiggling his brows.

Dropping his hand, I turn to face him and wrap my arms over his shoulders. His large hands run down my bare back and settle on my hips.

"I don't think so. We're roadtripping the coast, exploring old cathedrals, hiking, and stopping at every roadside stand we see."

He frowns. "I think your idea of a vacation and mine might be slightly different. Perhaps I shouldn't have let you plan everything, and we should have talked about this more."

"It's going to be great. The tour company said that since there are only twenty-five of us, we'll be able to do more than some of the other tours. There are these ancient Roman ruins—"

"Wait, what? You hired a tour company?" he asks,

cutting me off. His expression is one of horror and anger, and I can't even control myself. I start laughing.

"What the hell, Goldie?" He pinches my sides. "I thought you were serious. I mean, I wouldn't put it past you. This totally sounds like something you would do, but to me, it sounds like a nightmare."

"It does not sound like something I would do. Loner here, remember?" I point at myself.

"It does sound like something you would do to torture me!"

I grin because he's so right. Torturing, harassing, and playing pranks on him—all of these are so fun to do to him.

"Well maybe."

He shakes his head and bends down to kiss the corner of my mouth without messing up my lipstick. I exhale at the sensation of his soft lips and the stubble surrounding them. Briggs is my favorite person in the whole world, and every time he shows me an unexpected moment of love, my heart grows a little larger.

"At this time, we would like to welcome Mr. and Mrs. Warren to the dance floor," the lead singer of the band announces.

Turning, we watch as Jaxon takes Adele by the hand, and he sweeps her into his arms. Their guests love the dramatic gesture, and Briggs lets out an exhausted sigh as he steps behind me. He's so warm, and his unique smell of pine and rich man surrounds me.

The room is quiet, except for the band playing, but that doesn't stop Briggs. He bends down so his mouth is pressed next to my ear and whispers, "I know I told you this earlier, but you look beautiful tonight. I always love you in black."

"Thank you," I tell him as chills race down my arms and I flatten my backside to his front.

"Reminds me of a night I'm so fond of, the night we met."

I silently laugh and softly slap the arm he has wrapped around my middle. I look back up at him and roll my eyes. "You never stop talking about that night."

"I can't help it. There I was, minding my own business, when I heard a woman screaming. She was all damsel in distress. I grab my gun, race over to save the day, and lo and behold, standing there in my neighbor's yard, my only neighbor, is a naked woman. Naked in the sense that she was so incredibly beautiful, my world shifted. Perfect breasts just begging me to stare at them." I groan at his obnoxiousness and shake my head. "Wild hair, tiny underwear, and all packaged in a short black satin robe. Fantasy come true."

"You had fantasies that included your neighbor?"

"Apparently. I didn't know it until I saw you, but after that, most definitely." He smiles.

Turns out, I might have had a few fantasies about my neighbor too.

Eventually, the dance ends. Adele dances with her father. My heart goes out to Jaxon who doesn't get to dance with his mother, then they invite all family members to join them. We know eyes will be on us, but that's okay. We're both used to it.

The band starts playing another song, and we walk out onto the dance floor. Briggs pulls me into his arms. Arms that feel like home and love. Seems he's feeling sentimental too, as he bends down and whispers he loves me.

With hearts in my eyes, I can't help but adoringly look up at him and smile.

"How do you feel about one-upping them tonight?" he asks, that mischief I love so much in him making its presence known.

"What do you mean?" I ask suspiciously.

"What I mean is are you in or are you out?" His hand that is clasped around mine pulls in and lays over his heart, and his other on my lower back slips even lower.

I don't even hesitate to answer him because he knows as much as I do that when it comes to him and us, it will always be the same.

"You know I'm in."

The smile that takes over his face is so genuine and so happy that I shouldn't be surprised when he leans in close to my ear and asks me, "Will you marry me?"

Jerking back, he keeps his hand firmly on my back so we're anchored together, but his smile now is a mixture of mischievous and nervousness.

"What?"

"You heard me," he says, as his thumb swipes back and forth, dragging the satin-like material across my skin.

"This again?" I smile at him, thinking he's teasing just like all the other times.

"Goldie, I'm serious. Marry me."

I watch him as he watches me. His eyes roam over my face like I'm so beloved and cherished by him that it causes a lump to rise in my throat.

"But . . . we haven't been together that long."

"So?"

"What do you mean *so*? Shouldn't we be together for like a year or something first?" I ask him.

"What do you not know about me that you think you need a year to learn?"

"I don't know, that's the whole point. Umm, are you up to date on your taxes?"

He throws his head back and laughs. It draws attention to us, but he doesn't care.

"Taxes?"

"Well, yeah. Those are important."

"Definitely important for the eldest son of the owner of the largest private equity firm in the state."

"You know what I mean."

"Come on, Goldie, what else?" His nerves have vanished, and the confidence he always wears shines through. I love it when he feels larger than life. I love it because he's mine.

"You've never been to one of my concerts. You may decide you don't like what I do."

Briggs's face drops, and he gives me one of those looks. You know, the kind that says, "Really?" as well as, "I'm going to put you over my knee for that statement."

Yes, please.

"Well, you never know." I shrug.

"You're wrong. I do know. I know that you are the person for me. There will never be anyone but you. Are there things we still need to learn about each other? Yes. But I think that's exciting, and I hope to be lucky enough to learn things about you for the rest of my life."

"That was really sweet."

"I'm a sweet guy." He grins.

"So what, you propose and then we run off to Italy and get married?"

"If you're asking, then my answer is yes."

"Briggs."

"Goldie."

"Why do you call me that?"

"Well, the obvious is that you're blonde, but you light up my life. You're bright like the sun, and no matter what you say, do, or where you go, I'm drawn to you."

He's called me this since the very beginning. Maybe I should believe him when he says his life changed the moment he met me.

"But you didn't get on one knee. What kind of proposal is that?"

"Is that an important detail to you?"

"Of course it is. Every girl wants their man down on his knee."

And don't you know, in front of everyone, Briggs takes a step back and drops to one knee. I gasp, my hand flying to cover my mouth. Of all the times he's asked, he's never gotten down on one knee.

Bending over, I silently ask him, "This isn't about your brother, is it?"

He smiles up at me like I hung the moon. "No, Cora. This is all about you. You and me. Will you marry me?"

He reaches into his pocket, pulls out a loose

diamond ring, and holds it up to me. It's a single soli-taire diamond, and it's so beautiful my breath catches.

"Briggs," I whisper.

The band has stopped playing, and now everyone stares at us.

"Goldie?" He pops one brow and then gives me the most devastatingly handsome smile.

How could I ever say anything else?

"Yes. Yes, I will marry you."

I bend at the waist, grab his face, and kiss him. The whole room cheers.

Standing, he slips the ring on my finger, kisses my left hand, and then pulls me straight off the ground and into his arms. Home, my soul sings.

"Finally," he says, his lips teasing mine.

"I can't believe you just had this ring in your pocket!" I hold my hand up behind his head and stare at it.

"I've been carrying that ring around since the third time I asked you. I knew eventually you would say yes, and I had to be ready."

"You really are an incredible man."

"I'm just so happy we're doing the damn thing."

I pull back and look at him. "Italy?"

"Most definitely." His smile stretches from ear to ear, and I'm so happy my eyes blur while at the same time I laugh.

"How much do we think that will piss everyone off?" I ask him.

"Ask me if I care," he says, closing the distance between us and properly kissing me.

This kiss is sweet and naughty at the same time. This kiss is so Briggs, and I love it. But not as much as I love him.

"You care. Five minutes ago, you asked me if I was in the mood to one-up them tonight. So maybe it's a little about him?" I tease.

"Maybe." He shrugs, still smiling as he sets me down.

Both of us turn to look at Jaxon and Adele. Her mouth is open, and her face is beet red with annoyance. On the other hand, one corner of his mouth quirks up, and he just shakes his head. He knows what we've done and why we've done it, and he still gives us a smile. A real one. Maybe their relationship isn't a lost cause after all.

And maybe our prank wars don't have to end. We might have just found a new target, and knowing us, he better watch out.

THE END

ACKNOWLEDGMENTS

To my husband and my two amazing sons, thank you for continuing to allow me to follow my dreams. Your support and love is what keeps me going and makes me so proud. Seeing your enthusiasm each time I type 'The End' lets me know it's all worth it. I will forever love you more than you know.

Kelli, thank you for always being my person. We did it! Again! I promise to not talk your ear off anymore about raccoons, home improvements, and pranks to play on your neighbors. You push me, encourage me, and listen to me more than anyone else and I am blessed to know you. Each one of these releases feels like it's for both of us, and I wouldn't have it any other way. Time to celebrate!

Karla, thank you for being my friend. This book deadline was overwhelming and you endured all my complaining, for that I am so grateful. Thank you for the long hours, the plotting, planning, and overall cheer-leading.

Megan C, thank you for always being willing to alpha read my stories when they are in their worst shape, and for providing feedback that makes them better, especially when I need a rapid fire turn around. I appreciate your time, your honesty and your love for my words, and I hope you know how grateful I am for you.

Jenny and Julia, thank you for your eyes and your editing expertise. I've always said grammar is not my friend, and you understand that about me. This story is crisp and polished and I can't thank you enough.

To Naj from Qamber Designs and Julie from Heart to Cover: I love what the two of you have created for this story. The original cover fits so perfectly with the romance world, and the alternative cover is so beautiful it draws the eye of so many different kinds of readers. Thank you for always bringing my visions to life.

To the book bloggers: Thank you! Every year, my love for the book community deepens. I am indebted to each of you who continue to support, show love for my stories, leave reviews, and make me beautiful graphics and reels. Thank you. It's because of you that my dreams continue to come true.

And finally . . . to the readers: While I love writing the stories, it is you who keeps me going. I am always in awe by how much you love my characters and my words.

Every review, every inbox message, and every comment means so much to me. You keep writing them and I'll keep writing you new stories. Thank you! Thank you! Thank you!. . . Kathryn xoxo

ABOUT THE AUTHOR

Kathryn Andrews loves stories that end with a happily ever after. She started writing at age seven and never stopped. Kathryn is an Amazon Bestseller for her much loved Starving for Southern series, Chasing Clouds and is a contemporary romance, women's fiction, and Southern fiction writer.

Kathryn graduated from the University of South Florida with degrees in biology and chemistry, and she currently lives in Tampa, Florida. She spends her days as a sales director for a medical device company and her nights lost in her love of fictional characters.

When Kathryn is not crafting beautiful worlds that incorporate some of her most favorite real-life places, she can be found with her husband and two boys while drinking iced coffee and enjoying the sun.

Website: www.kandrewsauthor.com
Facebook: Author Kathryn Andrews
Instagram: @kandrewsauthor
TikTok: @kandrewsauthor

ALSO BY KATHRYN ANDREWS

Standalone Titles

Chasing Clouds

Hats off to Love

Where the Light Shines

Starving for Southern series

The Sweetness of Life

Last Slice of Pie

Lessons in Lemonade

Horizons Valley Series

Blue Horizons

White Horizons

Gold Horizons

The Hale Brothers Series

Drops of Rain

Starless Nights

Unforgettable Sun